~ A **Disnep** PRINCE NOVEL ~

Prince
of Glass
& Midnight

~ A DISNEP PRINCE NOVEL ~

Prince
of Glass
& Midnight

LINSEY MILLER

DISNEP PRESS

Los Angeles • New York

For information address Disney Press, 1200 Grand Central Avenue,
Glendale, California 91201.
Printed in the United States of America

First Hardcover Edition, October 2024
10 9 8 7 6 5 4 3 2 1
FAC-004510-24200

Library of Congress Control Number: 2023947267
ISBN 978-1-368-08548-9
Designed by Scott Piehl

Visit disneybooks.com

SUSTAINABLE FORESTRY INITIATIVE

Certified Sourcing

www.forests.org
SFI-01681

Logo Applies to Text Stock Only

To everyone wishing for a second chance.

—L. M.

Prologue

Ella,

You were right—it doesn't get better, only different. Father is still quiet. Everyone treads on eggshells around me. I hate it. I keep expecting Mother to wake me up or come check on my lessons, and every time she isn't there, it's like she died all over again. I dream of her, too. Do you still dream of your mother?

I should have known you would be right. You always are.

For my birthday three years ago, Mother took me to her favorite ash tree and gave me the bracelet she always wore. It was made of the thinnest, most fragile glass scales I have ever seen, and shouldn't have survived as long as it did without breaking. She wanted me to look after it until I found someone to love and gifted

I

it to them on our wedding day. Back then, I liked that she trusted me with it and that it glittered even on cloudy days. I never took it off.

After she died, I couldn't stand it.

So many people shook my hand at the funeral. I hated the way it slipped up and down my wrist, weighing me down. Each movement was a reminder of her being gone, and it made me sick. I didn't know I could hate something so much.

Thank you for convincing me to leave the funeral. Mother would have preferred walking around Fresne with us. She always talked about the sun-warmed paths of grass and thrum of birds nesting in the trees. She would have liked the crown of irises and summer snowflakes you left atop the helm of the statue guarding the cemetery gate. It's a good tradition, leaving gifts for the dead with the statue. After you left, I sat before their feet for what felt like ages. The seed-pearl necklace that was dangling from their spear snapped in the wind, and something in me snapped, too, I think. Everything became too much.

The rustling flowers. The pearls glinting

Prologue

in the grass like frost. The click and clack of
glass forget-me-nots on the soldier's wrist. The
red threads of a scarf woven in a bird's nest
in the statue's elbow. The rattle of a tarnished
cuff on their spear. The baskets of spoiling food
at their feet.

I climbed up the statue of the soldier,
slipped Mother's bracelet from my wrist
to theirs, and left it for the world to take
back.

She wanted me to give it to the person
I marry, but I don't want to lose anyone else. I
don't want anyone I could lose.

I don't know when I shall be able to return
to Fresne. Father hasn't said anything about it
yet, but I don't think he will be willing or able
to return there for quite a while.

I'm sorry this letter is sadder than usual. I
don't have any funny stories or jokes, but I did
find this pattern for knotting lace you might
like. It's popular in court right now. Everyone
looks like they're covered in spiderwebs.

In friendship,
August

◦——→

Prince of Glass & Midnight

FRESNE, SUMMER

August,

I admit to fearing you wouldn't write. I wouldn't blame you. I barely wanted to move after my mother died, but I'm glad you're still writing. My father says we cannot live our lives afraid to love, and I think in a few months when things are less foggy—I always felt like sadness was a thick fog that looked too dreary to ever go away but eventually did—you will agree with me.

I did dream of my mother after. At first, I would wake up devastated all over again, but after a while, I was happy I remembered what she looked like. The dreams are still sad, but they're not the same sort of sad. Now, it feels almost like getting to speak with her again.

I do remember your mother's bracelet. I'm sorry you couldn't bear it anymore. She would understand. Do you remember the shawl my mother made me? You were the one who wrapped it around the soldier's shoulders for me. It's gone now, but I see pieces of it in nests all around town. Mother would have loved the idea of its becoming a home for creatures in need. Every flash of blue in the trees makes me happy now.

As for giving it to your future beloved, the glass

may withstand the years, and you could reclaim it. The tradition of leaving items is meant to make people feel better. No one would question your taking back your mother's bracelet. Fresne is too kind for that.

That's why I like the memorial: you can visit or avoid it depending on how you're feeling. The soldier watches over the cemetery like a guardian of the memories we can't quite bear.

Could my father and I visit you? Perhaps our parents can help each other, since my father is a widower as well. Father's considering renovating, especially Mother's old study. I don't venture in there.

You don't need to ply me with jokes and funny stories to keep my friendship. If I get desperate, I shall try to teach the mice tricks or take up knitting. I made you mittens years ago, and I barely knew how then. Maybe I can practice on the mice.

Thank you so much for the pattern. It's called tatting, if you must know, and I've never seen a pattern like this. I'll make you something far better than the mittens this time.

With love,
Ella

CHARMANT, AUTUMN

My Dearest Friend,

Are you telling me that I've been suffering through comportment when I could have been learning something called tatting? You know how to do all the most interesting things.

I kept the mittens, you know, and still wear them when it's cold. You made them, and so they are my favorite mittens. If you insist on making me something else, then perhaps a hat to match?

Unfortunately, I don't think Father would agree to your visiting. He's become even more reclusive recently, and he takes my studies very seriously. I can't say I mind much. The history lessons keep me occupied.

Tell me more about these mice, please. Did they learn any tricks yet? Could you sew them costumes and teach them to stand as if on a stage? You could pay them in cheese and have them go on dashing adventures to stop the Dread King Catticus. It's been ages since a troupe visited Fresne. Your father would be thrilled were the mice to take up theater instead of cheese thievery.

Forgive me for this, though—even if your father says we cannot fear love, whenever he speaks of remarrying, it is not for love. It is to provide you another mother.

Sincerely,
August

$\triangleright\!\longrightarrow$

Fresne, autumn

August,

Father got me a dog! A hound! His ears are bigger than he is, and he will never grow into his paws! By the time this letter reaches you, I shall be teaching him how to hunt and eat old mittens.

I've had to pause training the mice. Bruno, the dog, is a bit of a handful and scares them. He's not a mouser—to the contrary, I caught him playing with one of the larger, braver mice—but he does love to give chase. Alas, they will have to overthrow the Dread King Catticus later.

If that is how you feel about my father's stance on love, I doubt anything I say could sway you. He did change after my mother's death, that much is true, but

I imagine anyone would. Most of his traits remain the same.

Do you know, for all his love of music and dancing, my father doesn't care for plays? He took Mother to an opera once, but they enjoyed the orchestra more than the story. The old carpenter's apprentice has married a musician, and they're coming to live in Fresne next year. Father is thrilled.

The only person in town even remotely interested in plays is the baker, but you can't tell anyone that. He's a romantic at heart, I think, and he scoffs when they pass through but watches the entire show. The last one was about the late queen. I only saw the first half, but I quite liked it. Did you know she had a fairy godmother and made a wish? The play was about wishes and why fairies are so strict about who gets one, but it was interesting. The play said that magic only goes wrong when fairies lose track of it. The magic leaches and starts acting on its own. I asked the baker what leeches had to do with it and was so embarrassed. He didn't laugh, though, which was nice. He said I shouldn't take any of the play seriously, because plays, he said, are entertaining lies.

Have you ever come across the royal family in Charmant? Is that why your parents named you after the prince? It must be awkward to live somewhere with so many others who share your name.

I cannot wait to debut and visit the city. Fresne is perfect, but it does get old after a while. Father's traveling now (not in the city, but I still begged him to take me), meeting someone for something. He was very tight-lipped about it.

I think that's why he got me Bruno. He hates it when I'm alone. You know, you are the only person I could mention mouse plays to and get a real response, but I think Bruno might take your throne.

> With love (despite your mockery),
> Ella

$\triangleright\!\longrightarrow$

CHARMANT, WINTER

Ella,

Don't you mean that you've had to "paws" with the mice?

Regardless, I would gladly abdicate for Bruno. He sounds delightful, and if he likes you, he has good taste. I suppose I can share best friend status with a dog.

I have not met the royal family personally, but they covered them and the queen's wish in my history class.

And I shall thank you to remember that I am one of a kind despite sharing my name with fifty-odd other children. There is only one of me.

As for my comments about your father, I am sorry. It was uncalled for. My father's recent change has simply made me look at your father's fixation on you after your mother's death with more focus than necessary.

And, most importantly, I have made a note to never, under any circumstances, invite him to an opera.

In friendship,

August

$\vartheta\longrightarrow$

FRESNE, SPRING

August,

As much as I have enjoyed the mouse plays you've sent with your last few letters, I must put a stop to it and deliver some upsetting news—you do not have a future as a playwright. Honestly, August, how did you find the time to write them, or did you put off your real studies to send me a three-act comedy of manners about mice and rats meeting for the first time? Your last letter was just the play!

Also, most importantly, I don't think the mice really cared for them. They like adventure—daring sword fights, runaway cheese wheels, and devious heists.

Father has returned, by the way. He brought me several gifts from his time away, including a music book from a lady he met. Lady Tremaine seems nice, and she must love music. I have already surpassed the lessons in the book, but it was a very kind thought. Father's been writing her recently. I'm glad he's finally talking to someone.

With exasperation,
Ella

Prince of Glass & Midnight

CHARMANT, SPRING

Ella,

I wouldn't have thought your father would court anyone again. That said, it's nice to hear this. I hope they're exactly what the other needs. Your father deserves some happiness.

To be fair to the mysterious Lady Tremaine, your musical skills are a touch advanced compared to others'. If songbirds could hold candles, they couldn't hold one to your voice.

Father is sending me away for the next few years to study at university. We can still write, but the letters will take longer in transit.

As an apology, I've included some ivory silk and shuttles. Consider them an early birthday present, since I shall be at university when it passes.

In absentia,
August

Prologue

FRESNE, SUMMER

August,

Forgive the lapse in my letters, but I have news—they're getting married, and I am to have two new sisters!

I can forgive Father for springing this on me suddenly given that he's gifted me siblings. We haven't met yet—Lady Tremaine left them with their governess when she came to meet me—but I am sure they'll be lovely. Lady Tremaine says she cannot wait for the three of us to debut together. She wants to make it a year to remember. Her daughters are nearly a year younger than me, but I don't mind waiting.

Father will return with her to meet them alone, and then all five of us shall meet.

I don't think you will be able to attend the wedding, but you are invited. It is in Fresne. Lady Tremaine said the town was quaint. I hope her daughters—my sisters!— like it. Lady Tremaine is very proper, like your mother was. She knows *exactly* what she wants.

I think Father's happy to not be making all the decisions alone anymore. She has already ordered new dresses for me, and Father's promised to supply my sisters with a new wardrobe more fitting of Fresne's weather as soon as they arrive. Apparently, they have nothing suitable. Lady Tremaine says my face is so pretty that a plain blue dress will suit me best. She ordered the loveliest fabric for it.

Thank you for the silk and shuttles! I have decided to use them to make a collar for my dress for the wedding and a shawl for Lady Tremaine. She said I'm far too accomplished for a girl my age. I think she'll like the shawl.

With love,
Ella

Charmant, autumn

Ella,

Studying has cut terribly into my sleeping and, worse, time when I usually would be writing to you. The wedding is wonderful news, and I wish I could attend. It will have passed by the time this letter reaches you. Please tell me how it goes. It will be far more interesting than my approaching geometry examination. Who

Prologue

knew university professors were far stricter than personal tutors?

I wrote my father telling him about it and asking him to send a gift to yours.

Too accomplished? I would never dare put a limit on you of all people. I am sure she will appreciate the shawl, and I know it will be lovely.

Blue is a good color for you. Your eyes always reminded me of a Fresne sky in spring.

In absentia,

August

$\diamond\longrightarrow$

FRESNE, WINTER

August,

The wedding was lovely. Lady Tremaine did not wear the shawl I made her, though she was very complimentary of it. She had a veil from her last wedding she preferred for sentimental reasons.

My new sisters are quite the handful. They are not used to country life, and I hope they will find their footing in Fresne soon. Father is happy, I think, and that is what matters in the end. Lady Tremaine has taken over my studies and day-to-day life. She is determined to mold her daughters into the perfect ladies.

I am not allowed to work on embroidery or music with my sisters. She is afraid that my advanced study in these arts will discourage them. It's mostly understandable. Once everything is settled, she has promised to find the perfect teachers for me to study under alone. I'm looking forward to being able to progress. I asked her to find someone to teach me lace making, too. Lady Tremaine seems quite competitive. I am certain she will settle for only the best tutors.

Otherwise, life is not much different, save for the sounds of my sisters in the house. It's odd to live with more people my age, but I think I shall adjust fine. Father makes sure we have tea, only us, every other day when he is here. It's nice to have him to myself for a time. He is taking pains to spend time with his new daughters as well. Hopefully, they will be settled in enough to spend time with me soon.

My sisters are pounding on my door! I shall send you news of my new advanced studies soon!

With love,

Ella

CHARMANT, WINTER

Ella,

Thank you for your last letter about how married life is treating your father, and your gift of dried flowers. You needn't have sent me your bouquet if you wanted to keep it, but I do like having something of yours. University is quite dreary.

The school term is going how it always does—relentlessly slow. I barely have any time to sleep. You wouldn't believe how many books, whole books, I have to read each week.

I shall send a letter next week with a keepsake from university for you. I know you have never been this far north. Unfortunately, everything is covered in snow right now.

In friendship,

August

Fresne, spring

August,

Please tell me this letter is water stained due to the weather and travel and not from your attempting to send me snow.

The pressed leaves from your last two letters were more than enough, but I cannot explain to my sisters why I am laughing at a stained, slightly rotten blank page. I told them I had discovered invisible ink, but they were less than impressed.

Do it again and I shall send you live crickets.

With love,

Ella

Charmant, summer

Ella,

Two months, one letter, and zero peace since you sent those crickets, and still I am finding more daily. How did you do it? I've never been so happy to see such small creatures. Did you send everyone at university a package of them? I've had to round them up to keep them from dying in the mountain chill.

It's so much easier to sleep now. It's like I'm back in Fresne.

Encased in a prison of crickets,

August

$\partial\!\longrightarrow$

FRESNE, SUMMER

August,

My father is dead. It was sudden. I cannot write. There are no words. Do not come. I cannot stand to see anyone yet.

Ella

$\partial\!\longrightarrow$

CHARMANT, SUMMER

Ella,

I'm so sorry. Your father was one of the best people I ever met. I hope Lady Tremaine and your sisters are taking care of you.

If they're not, my father would be thrilled
to help.

Consider me at your command for whatever
you need whenever you need it.

August

CHARMANT, AUTUMN

Ella,

You need not respond if you cannot find it
within yourself to. I simply wanted to offer in
case asking was too exhausting.

Would you like for me to send anything to
Fresne? Take something to the soldier guarding
your parents? Write to you of my favorite
memories of your father?

My schooling is not more important than
you, and your father was as good as family. I
would gladly take a leave of absence.

In friendship,
August

Prologue

Fresne, spring

August,

  I know you would, and that is why I cannot ask. In truth, there isn't much you could do for me if you were here. It's nice to know that you're out there still living, and my father would very much have liked to know that, too. He had been planning on talking to you about your studies, you know. Did he write to you?

  This is the second time Lady Tremaine has been made a widow, and she is distraught. I am helping out as best as I can since I know the house, Fresne, and my father's business better than she. It's oddly comforting to be busy. It keeps my mind off him.

  I do not want stories or anything like that. Please keep writing, but I might be too occupied with the home to respond as I once did. I don't really want to see anyone, but I do miss talking to other people. You're my reminder of normalcy.

With love,
Ella

Prince of Glass & Midnight

CHARMANT, SUMMER

Ella,

Your father did write to me once. I have saved the letter and tried to preserve it so that the ink does not fade.

I have included in this letter my notes on a history lecture I received that included the development of various dyes and how they affected the kingdom. (If we were to be pedantic about it, did you know that anyone who isn't related to the royal family isn't allowed to wear velvet?) I hope you'll find it interesting.

Unfortunately, there isn't much I can say about what I have been learning. It will all be very useful, but it is drier than week-old bread. Unless you would like to read about my newly developed loathing of antiquated tax law in Charmant, I'm afraid that this letter will be short.

You were always the more prolific writer of the two of us, not including the mouse plays, so I suppose that's normal.

In friendship,

August

⟶

Charmant, summer

Ella,

Perhaps, given your recent work helping with the household, my notes on the upcoming changes to taxes and the recent rise in counterfeit money (which, to be fair, is the result of one very ambitious but recently caught merchant and his apprentice) would be interesting to you. The court is considering changing the standard.

The king has suggested creating a coin with the image of the late queen on it, but all I can think about is how uncomfortable that might be for the prince. The king asked him beforehand, I hope.

Unrelated, my father committed me to a trip to several of the neighboring kingdoms this summer, and I shall not be able to go to Fresne. He didn't ask me first. You said you did not want to see me, but is that still true? If you want, I can refuse and visit Fresne.

In friendship,

August

Fresne, winter

August,

I'm so sorry. I am unimaginably busy. My sisters are with their governess now, and I fear they don't know enough to be of much use. It's better they continue with their studies.

My work does mean that I am learning how to effectively run a household with much more experience than most ever get by my age. Lady Tremaine says I do not need more tutoring in academic pursuits.

I know it has been nearly a year since Father died and that I should be leaving the mourning period, but we both know that grief hardly plays by societal rules. I still don't want to see anyone yet.

Nor do I think now is a good time to introduce you to Lady Tremaine and her daughters. They're all quite stressed by the past year.

With love,
Ella

CHARMANT, SPRING

Ella,

I hope my last few letters reached you. I am certain you're simply too busy to respond, but I do hope you're not overworking yourself. To that end, please enjoy the enclosed patterns I found. I have no idea what they're patterns for; the seller found them in their inheritance and had no use for them. I thought the mystery might be fun.

In friendship,
August

CHARMANT, AUTUMN

Ella,

Thank you for the note confirming you received my letters. I must admit to wishing it were longer. I hope you aren't too busy. How are your sisters? Have they helped with your duties around the estate? Is sisterhood all you dreamed of?

In friendship,
August

$\triangleright\!\longrightarrow$

Charmant, winter

Ella,

*I inquired as to whether or not my letters
were being delivered, and they are. I do not
want to encroach upon your privacy, but should
I write to Lady Tremaine? I cannot think of a
reason for silence other than sickness or fury.*

In desperation,

August

$\triangleright\!\longrightarrow$

Charmant, summer

*Ella, please write me back even if just
to admonish me for writing so often. Are you
well?*

$\triangleright\!\longrightarrow$

Charmant, autumn

~~*Ella, do you hate me? Because I'm beginning
to hate you.*~~

Prologue

⊳———→

CHARMANT, AUTUMN

Ella,

When you said to keep writing you, I assumed you would write back more than once in two years. I feel as though I am writing a ghost who has no wish to haunt me but does nonetheless. Have you forgotten me completely?

I doubt there's any point in sending this, but consider me done. It has been years~nine hundred and eighty~two days, to be exact~since I last heard from you. I wouldn't have minded if you told me you no longer wanted to write. I wouldn't have minded if you told me I had done something to offend you. I wouldn't have minded anything if you just told me instead of vanishing.

It's not fair, it's not nice, and it's not something you do to a friend. Though I suppose we aren't friends anymore, are we?

I shall save you from having to suffer the

injustice of my correspondence—there will be no more.

If ever you need to write me, don't. Enjoy your new family.

Sincerely,
August

CHARMANT, SPRING

Ella,

I'm sorry. I didn't mean that. I don't understand why you won't say anything at all. I only know you're alive because I haven't seen a death announcement in the Fresne post. You can always write to me, and I shall always answer.

In atonement,
August

Prologue

FRESNE, SUMMER

Sirrah,

Being obliged by my late husband's memory to respond in kindness, though your letter caused me great concern, I must admit to some confusion as to your inquiry. My dear stepdaughter, Ella, whose health you are asking after, is perfectly well.

For what it is worth, I have never heard the girl mention you, even in passing, and I find it in me to offer blunt advice, though it is intended to be kind and to save you from wasted time.

The girl does not write to you because she does not wish to, and that should be answer enough. She does not think of you nearly so often as you think of her.

Should you write to us again, I shall assume there is some deviancy or obsession afoot and insist upon contacting a sheriff.

The Honorable Lady Tremaine,
at House Saint Aubin
Fresne

~ I ~

A Very Nice Prince

THERE WAS nothing quite like the bustling streets of the royal city at dawn. The spring sun scoured the frost from the cobblestones, leaving a swirling haze in the wake of passersby. A warm breeze perfumed with the heady scent of freshly baked bread smeared with butter rippled through the colorful flags decorating the palace's towers, and the musical greetings of a dozen different languages slowly overtook the songbirds lingering in the ramparts. Rain or shine, the streets were always alive, a potent reminder of everyone who depended on Prince August to maintain the peace and prosperity of his father's reign. There was nothing he wouldn't do for Charmant.

"Lord Robail's daughter has given him a grandchild. How wonderful," said his father, staring at August over the top of the letter. "Imagine that—a grandchild."

August's love of Charmant was the only thing

keeping him from leaping from the window of his father's study and vanishing into the crowd.

"You have always had a lively imagination, Father," August said. "I'll send his daughter our congratulations, then."

His father harrumphed and tossed the letter aside. "Imagination doesn't keep me company."

"That's what friends are for, isn't it, Martin?" asked August.

Martin, his best friend and partner for all court-related investigations, didn't look up from the timetable he was making for their upcoming day and muttered, "Of course, Your Highness."

It was difficult to be the human personification of a cloudy day in a room filled with promising sunlight, but Martin Tremblay managed it. He had mastered it while they were working opposite each other at school. Martin had thought August too carefree and impossible to take seriously, and August had considered the dreary older boy too sad for someone with so much. As sardonic as he was tall, Martin didn't believe in silver linings. He tempered August's more idealistic tendencies.

"See, Father? You need a Martin," August said, and he gestured to the small pile of letters spread out across their table. "Are there any letters of actual import?"

August and his father always met like this on the first morning of the week, in a small room awash in peachy early light. From a little after sunrise till sunset, the nobility gathered and citizens brought their concerns directly to the court. August called their little meetings *meetfasts* since he had to eat whatever he could find while working if he didn't want his growling stomach to interrupt the proceedings, and Father steadfastly ignored the name. The Grand Duke would join them once it was time.

"I have one here from General DuBois." Father shook a thin, already unfolded letter. "His daughter is remarkably pretty, you know. Quite accomplished, too."

August pried the raisins from his pastry and ate them one by one. "Is that relevant to the letter?"

Father didn't answer outright, and that was answer enough.

"Father," August said softly, "I will get married— I'm looking forward to finding someone I want to marry—but please stop interfering. Let me meet someone. It's not as though I'm taking over from you anytime soon. Children shouldn't be born to keep people company."

He wished his father would give him the time and space he needed. Marriage didn't conjure images of roses or sunrises or whatever romantic things people talked about. It made him remember his father's utter destruction in the wake of his mother's death.

At the same time, he wanted—so badly that it hurt—to love and be loved and not feel the sinking dread that washed over him when he thought of marriage. He didn't want to be afraid, but he didn't know how to stop. The contradiction made meeting someone all the more daunting.

Father scowled. "Don't give me that look. If you're going to meet someone, meet someone!"

August swallowed his response. His mother had always said it cost nothing to be nice, and successful ruling required frugality.

"You will have to consider marriage one day, August."

"I consider it every time you ask," said August, popping another raisin in his mouth, "but I have yet to meet someone I feel strongly enough about to court."

"It seems that every eligible maiden falls short of your standards," said Father with a huff.

August scoffed. "I've hardly met *every* eligible maiden."

He hadn't met anyone he got along with like . . . well, it didn't matter. He had no misconceptions about their relationship, or lack thereof, and he specifically didn't think of *her* when meeting new people.

"No, I don't suppose you have," muttered Father. "Twenty million subjects—"

"Twenty-three million," corrected August without thinking. If Father didn't want to be corrected, then he shouldn't have given August such a thorough education.

"—and you can't find a single one to marry. It's absurd."

The reason he hadn't married was simple— he hadn't found anyone he trusted with Charmant. Whomever he married would have a say in the future of the kingdom, and if something happened to him, they might have the only say. It was all tangled up in what his mother had asked of him when she had gifted him her glass bracelet all those years ago, and he couldn't mention it to Father, because the man still went quiet whenever the late queen was mentioned. The bracelet had been a lesson in responsibility, something for him to take care of and give to his future spouse years later. August might have left the bracelet at the cemetery with her, but he hadn't forgotten her words.

This was given to me as a reminder of the wish I made. Magic, like our roles as royalty, is powerful, and we alone are responsible for how we use that power.

And one day, it would be his responsibility to look after the kingdom, though that sentiment had been far less understandable for a seven-year-old. Her implications were clear now.

If only he remembered more of his childhood with her, then he might know how to go about finding a partner.

"Father," August said, leaning across the table and taking the older man's face in his hands, "are there any important letters we need to discuss before court?"

Father scrunched up his face. "Fine. Be that way, but one of these days, August, you're going to be old and gray and wondering where the time went and wishing you had listened to your old man."

"On the contrary, I do *listen* to everything you say." August let his face go and sat back in his chair, eating the last few bites of his pastry. "Whether or not it stays in my mind is an entirely different matter."

His father sighed. "Let's see. I had something here I knew you would want to look at." He shuffled through the correspondence addressed to the court and pulled free a thick fold of papers covered in cross writing. He had already broken the white wax seal featuring an ash tree. "It's from Fresne."

Shock gripped August's lungs and ripped his breath away. He had been waiting for a letter from Fresne for years. He had never been able to smother the hope still smoldering within him, and the part of him in which that hope had smoked and sputtered raged back to life.

"From Fresne?" August asked, trying to sound nonchalant.

Martin, who usually ignored them entirely in favor of his own work, glanced up at that and set his papers and pen aside. August refused to glance his way.

Father eyed him. "From the mayor of Fresne."

Well then, that was completely different, and there was no reason for him to tie himself up in knots over it. August's roiling stomach didn't settle, though.

"What does the letter say?" August asked.

Even if he didn't want to think about *her*, there were plenty of people he remembered and cared for from his childhood summers in Fresne. It was a town within his kingdom. He had a responsibility to it.

"I skimmed over the contents when it arrived," Father said, flattening out the first piece of paper. "There's something odd afoot, that's for certain. I had thought it was sent in jest at first, but the urgency and details are far too real. Mayor Blanche Fauconnier insists that people in Fresne are losing their memories."

"Losing their memories?" August asked, pushing everything aside and leaning across the table to study the letter. A sick, burning dread bubbled up in the back of his throat. "How many?"

"Five, when this letter was written," said Father. "According to Fauconnier, it started—so far as they can tell—a few years ago with one person. She's written a time line in here somewhere, she says. Two people have lost their memories this year, though, and people are worried that whatever is happening is occurring more frequently."

"I'll go," said August, bracing for Father's refusal.

"Absolutely not!" Father threw up his hands. "You've been gone all year."

"Assisting the royal court on behalf of the crown," said August, and he couldn't help laughing. What parent didn't like that their child was responsible? August liked his work—accounting for the kingdom, hearing out those who visited court, and serving the realm in whatever way was needed. August and Martin had spent most of the year investigating a rather tricky case of tax fraud and trying to find enough evidence to change some of the older and out-of-date inheritance laws. He knew he was lucky to have been born into his position during a time of relative peace and prosperity, and he intended to keep Charmant safe and sound. "Fresne was my home for half of the year growing up. Mother is in Fresne. If they need help, I shall be the one to offer it."

Father flinched at the mention of Mother, and August knew he had won. Perhaps it was underhanded, but he couldn't bear it if someone else were sent in his place.

"Forgive me," said Martin, frowning, "but wouldn't a physician be a more appropriate choice to send?"

"Something in the food or water, perhaps?" August wondered aloud.

"Smart boy," said Father, ignoring August's contribution and wagging his finger at Martin. "They had multiple physicians visit, and none was able to help."

"Something magical in origin, perhaps?" Martin asked.

August nodded, and his father cut him off.

"Tremblay, you can handle this by yourself, can't you?" Father asked. "You and August have been solving problems like this for years. Surely you could do it alone."

"Thank you, Your Majesty," said Martin, slowly. He looked at August, who frantically shook his head. "I'm afraid that I would be insufficient. August knows Fresne and several of the people there, and he is more familiar with magic than I am."

That last part wasn't true at all, but August appreciated the lie. Martin had been in all the same classes with him at university, including the ones on how to identify magic. Their jobs demanded the ability to spot magic—humans stealing wands or coming up with absurd schemes to try to steal magic happened far too often. They made up perhaps a third of the jobs he and Martin took.

"One day to do the initial questioning, and then

you return and Tremblay takes over," said Father. "Let him handle the investigation."

August let out a short laugh. "A day? Two weeks. It's summer. There's little for me to do at court, and I'll be within a day's travel in case I need to return."

"No," his father said, impersonating his tone. "Three days."

"One week," said August. "You'll have me the rest of the summer, and I want to do this right—I shall do an initial investigation, and then I shall return and report back to court with a plan for how to move forward."

"Five days and not an hour more. You'll take Tremblay with you—keep an eye on him and make sure he doesn't try to stay, Tremblay—report back in five days, and then get a proper homecoming. Make your rounds at all the suppers. Make your calls to friends and play nice. Make yourself presentable for the season."

The unsaid *so that you can meet a nice person to marry* hung between them. August wrinkled his nose. He didn't want to leave Fresne in unfamiliar hands. Though he had to keep his identity as the crown prince a secret, just as he had when he was a child, he could still help them.

Then, there was Ella.

"Of course, I'll take Martin, and it will be five days," said August, holding out his hand. "But this is a serious matter and it needs serious attention. If something happens or I think I need to return, I shall, because that is my duty."

"You're a good boy," Father muttered, and shook his hand. "Infuriating but good."

August smiled. "Would I be less infuriating if I were bad? I would be happy to oblige."

"Hush." Father turned over the first page of the letter. "Don't get your hopes up. This is odd, the sort of thing that people will say was a story and not real years from now. The malady happened without apparent warning or reason and affected only specific memories."

Memory loss wasn't unheard of. Injuries and illness caused it often enough, but those were usually traceable. Martin had forgotten three years once after falling from a horse. The memories had come back slowly. The lack of apparent cause was more reason to suspect magic.

"What does 'specific memories' mean?" August asked.

Father turned the paper sideways. "A person,

apparently. The first to lose his memory completely forgot one of his coworkers, and the second, his wife. Here. There's a list."

He handed August one of the pages, and August hesitated. Slowly, he skimmed the names of those who had forgotten, and relaxed. Ella wasn't listed.

He didn't recognize all the names, but two stood out: Monet was the family name of the carpenter's apprentice he had met once as a boy, and Monsieur Allard was a cobbler who had always been nice to August regardless of how hard he was on his shoes. Blaise Jullien sounded familiar, but he couldn't quite recall meeting them.

"They're only forgetting a single other person?" he asked.

"Sounds like," Father mumbled.

At first glance, August could find no similarities among the five people who had lost their memories *or* among those who had been forgotten. At second glance, he was still stumped.

Martin unfolded his sinewy body from his chair and pushed aside the curtain of black hair that fell in front of his face. "Let me see."

"Here," August said, and handed him the first part of the letter. "About five years ago, a footman lost his memories of a lady's maid he worked with. He forgot her completely, as though they had never met and he had never heard of her. Then, a little over a year later, the local cobbler, that's Monsieur Allard, woke up with no memory of his wife. They've been married for ages, since long before I met them. An older woman forgot her neighbor completely eight months later. Five months after that, a retired guard—that's where I know the name from; Blaise used to work here, in the city—forgot one of their oldest friends. The latest person to lose their memories is a musician. Her son reported that she had forgotten his father."

Father sighed and said, "Terrible thing, forgetting a spouse."

"Terrible, Your Majesty," agreed Martin, frowning. "How long after the previous instance was that?"

August handed Martin the papers. "Four months, give or take some days."

"It's accelerating," said Martin.

"So far, the only people who have lost their memories have been people who live in Fresne. Not all of them were born there, but perhaps you have to be there a while for the memory loss to happen," said August as Martin read. "There's not enough data to form a real guess. Fresne is a small town surrounded by several estates, so there are people moving through it constantly."

Martin held up one of the pages. "The mayor says they asked around for anyone passing through who's experienced the same thing, but they've found no cases. That's promising."

Father cleared his throat. "And why I'm letting you go, August."

There was an awful lot of information, but very little of it seemed useful. That was the issue with most mysteries—there was so much information that whoever was looking at it couldn't discern the relevant evidence from the chaff.

"This will be difficult, even for us," said Martin.

"Don't discount us before we even start," said August. "We have better resources than anyone else."

"You're also not alone," Father said. "I shall write to your mother's fairy godmother to ask if she can help. No one is a better expert on magic than a fairy. And, for all their isolation, they usually return my letters."

His mother's fairy godmother was something of an ambassador to Charmant. Fairies had an amicable relationship with nearly every kingdom, offering advice on magic, since it was rare and almost always theirs. They seldom interfered with human politics and appeared only when a person had lost all hope. They delighted in restoring it with a wish. If this was magic, she would know for sure.

Martin folded the letter back up and muttered, "We can leave first thing tomorrow morning."

Someone knocked on the door, and August heard the Grand Duke's familiar footsteps coming down the hall. It was time for court.

Father snapped his fingers and stood, poking Martin in the chest with his finger. "Very well. But if you don't have him back here, I'm rolling you in honey and leaving you for the bears."

His father left without so much as another backward glance, and August eased into his chair. Martin was as tense as a tightly coiled spring next to him, face set with fear.

"The more outrageous the threat, the more likely he is to not remember he asked you to do anything at all," said August, rolling his eyes. "He's only upset because he knows I'm right and that I should be the one to go. I recognize some of the names in this letter. I won't abandon them. Looking after the kingdom is my job."

Martin hummed. "And you're sure your resoluteness has nothing to do with the girl you used to write when we were at school? Those letters you got were from Fresne."

"No, she's not mentioned in any of this," said August. "She might have moved away for all I know."

Her utter lack of contact still smarted despite the years, and August couldn't stand Martin's pitying silence.

"Think about it like this," said August, and he gathered up all the papers. "Regardless of my ulterior motives, this is something that needs to be done, and it needs to be done with kindness. These are memories. They're personal. Whoever goes to help must be gentle. We'll do right by them."

"I understand," said Martin.

"I know, and I trust you more than anyone, which is part of why I want you with me," said August.

Martin might have seemed like a pessimist of the highest order, but he truly cared about anyone and everyone. Every moment he wasn't working for the court, he was back in his family holdings taking care of the people and land.

August clapped and let out a deep breath. "Now, we can do this. We can figure this out."

"Must you be so hopeful?" Martin asked.

"If people see a noble frowning, they worry,

whether there is cause or not. Members of the court showing up and looking defeated will make them think there's no solution. I don't want to contribute to the fear. I'm sure they're experiencing enough already." August slapped him on the back. "Regardless, it's a week in the countryside."

But August was sure if he thought too long about Fresne, of his childhood friend who had left a hole in his heart, and the prospect of seeing *her*, he might not smile ever again.

～ 2 ～
No One Is Alone

*T*HE FRESNE sky was still the exact same shade of bright blue as Ella's eyes, but it lacked the shock he imagined her glare would contain.

"After that speech about smiling yesterday, you have the gall to frown?" Martin asked. "What's wrong?"

August rubbed his face and forced himself to relax. "I haven't been back since my mother—"

"No," said Martin, scowl deepening. "You look anxious, not sad. You don't allow yourself to look sad anymore, but nerves I recognize."

People usually felt too awkward to continue speaking when August brought up his mother and his grief, and it was the easiest way to avoid topics he didn't want to discuss, like Ella.

"Can you let me have this moment of weakness?" August asked.

"Considering that your father will feed me to a

bear if I don't return you in five days, no." Martin checked the silver pocket watch he kept fastened to his waistcoat and snapped it shut with a sigh. The glare made the time unreadable. "It's brighter here than in the city."

They had been traveling since well before dawn and had spent the last few hours on foot.

"Isn't it lovely?" August asked, trying to enjoy what he could before the reality of why they were in Fresne required his attention. If he focused on only the grim facts and his own anxiety about seeing Ella, then they would consume him. "Fresne is over these hills, though most of the fields we've been walking past belong to people from town."

"It's too hot to be lovely," muttered Martin, and he pulled a broad-brimmed hat from his bag. "You're already turning pink."

"Because I'm flush with life," August said, but he accepted the hat when Martin offered it.

The pair of them were on the outskirts of town, at the final hill blocking Fresne from view, and he gestured for them to keep walking. "Mayor Blanche Fauconnier will be at the inn, most likely. I did know her, and unless she sold it, it's her family's business."

They crested the hill, and the town came into

view. Fresne was quaint, the sort of sun-soaked market town where everyone knew each other and gossiping was the most common hobby. Most of the buildings were plain but neat wood with thatched roofs, and most of the people who didn't work on the nearby estates ran shops with living quarters on the second floor. Fresh flowers decorated the doorways, scenting the air. The familiar canopy of the ash tree at the center of town rustled in the breeze.

The sight of it all stopped August in his tracks. The day of his mother's funeral was a blur, but his other memories weren't. The clench of grief was sharper here—the image of his mother gliding down the street before them, one hand on his father's arm and the other twirling freshly picked wildflowers, was clear as day in his mind—and he tilted his head back to keep from crying. It wasn't only that he had lost his mother; his childhood had died with her. He and Ella had become aware of death in a way few children ever were.

"No one has seen you," Martin said softly, his tone far gentler than it usually was. "You can turn back, and I'll investigate alone if being here is too much."

"No, I can't," said August, taking a deep breath. "But thank you."

"Don't mention it."

August chuckled and dropped his head. "You're the only person in the world who means 'don't mention it' sincerely."

They made their way into town. Fresne was as beautiful as August remembered, but the farther they walked, the more uneasy he grew. The stalls were set up in the market square, littered with interesting trinkets and perfect produce, but there wasn't anyone perusing. No elderly couples gossiped from shaded chairs, and not a single soul waved from the doorway of a shop. The streets were bare. Every shutter was drawn. Fresne, for the very first time for him, felt bereft.

"Well, this is different," said August, peering down an empty side street. There weren't even shoe prints in the dirt. "And unsettling."

"Was it not usually like this?" asked Martin.

"Take a guess," August muttered, and looked down the street where the seamstress lived. Ella had almost always been there when he visited. "The shops don't even look open."

Ella wasn't there now, though. No one was.

"Who are you looking for?" Martin asked.

"Anyone, honestly." August straightened and

nodded to the three-story building ahead. "That's the inn."

"And what's down that path?" Martin looked down his nose and over August's shoulder to the seamstress's. August was tall, like his mother, but Martin was towering. Most people told him what he wanted to know out of misplaced fear.

"I don't know. Nothing and no one, apparently," said August.

Ella had been the one to stop writing, and Lady Tremaine had been very clear. They had grown apart. He shouldn't be looking for her.

"Adroit August strikes again," muttered Martin, and August rolled his eyes.

"You're running out of synonyms, aren't you?"

"I've no notion of what you mean," said Martin, sniffing.

"Good," said August, opening the door to the inn. "I'll pretend I don't know what you meant, and we'll both be undistracted."

The first floor of the inn was a large, dimly lit room of warm wood. Dining tables and chairs covered most of the floor, leaving enough room between them and the counter for folks to carry luggage unimpeded. The scents of fresh bread and leek soup lingered in the air, and elegant roses decorated every table. August made his way to the counter, smiling at the little display shelf of sundries travelers might need. There was no one around, but the place felt livelier and better cared for than it used to.

"Mayor Fauconnier?" he called out. "Blanche?"

A stout woman maybe a decade older than August, with curly red hair and a splatter of freckles across her nose, hustled down the stairs on the far side of the room. She was smaller than August remembered. Or perhaps everyone had appeared tall to him when he was a child.

"Hello," August said, smiling. "How are you?"

She came to a stop across from him, hands resting on the counter, and nodded in greeting. "I can't complain."

The familiar response made him chuckle. Her father had said the same whenever asked, and she had started saying it after he died. August had heard it nearly every morning when walking through the Fresne streets with Ella as they got breakfast from the bakery.

"Now, we've got plenty of rooms available, and you can have your pick of them," she said, giving him a tight smile and pulling a logbook out from behind the counter. She relaxed when she gripped the book, as if running the inn were a comfort rather than a sentimental chore of sudden inheritance. The idea filled August with a joyful grief. He had missed so many changes. "I'll need names and dates for your stay."

"Two beds, please, Blanche, but we—"

"Sorry," she said, and looked him up and down. "Have we met?"

August winced, and he had never been so happy that Martin wasn't inclined to laughter.

"We have met." Blanche narrowed her eyes at him, fingers tapping against the counter.

"I used to be shorter when my family came here for the summer," August said, and smiled again, holding out his hand. "August."

"August?" She knocked his hand aside and pulled him into a tight hug from over the counter. "Look at you! Oh, you take after your mother, don't you?"

The sentiment landed more sweet than bitter after so long without her.

"I do," he said, smiling even more widely. "You look well, too, Mayor Fauconnier. Mayor—when did that happen?"

"No one else wanted the job, and I didn't mind

taking on the work." She laughed. "What are you doing here? Last anyone heard, you were at university."

"I was at university for what felt like centuries," he said, keenly aware of how little people here knew about him. His parents had always presented themselves as nobles who needed to escape the city during the summer. Most noble children were sent away to study at university, and those who didn't inherit could stay on for further education or training. He gestured to Martin. "We're here on behalf of the royal court to conduct an initial investigation into the memory loss. In five days, we'll return and report our findings."

That sobered her up quickly.

"Well, you certainly have grown up," she said, and nodded at Martin. "Come. Sit. You were always a nice boy, August, but why you?"

August smiled instead of taking offense. Most people who called him nice really meant he was naive. He had heard it often enough, given his cheery disposition, and he had learned long ago not to fight the point. Most people saw kindness and optimism as the opposites of cleverness and realism, but August didn't. Eventually, people would realize he was nice *and* capable.

"August volunteered for the job," Martin said.

"We work for the royal court investigating crimes and oddities outside the purview of the guards."

They sat down at one of the empty tables. Blanche was all business, pulling a small notebook from her coat pocket and setting it on the table. Martin laid his own notes next to it.

"We're less intimidating than soldiers and easier to talk to," said August. "Risk assessment, bookkeeping, and clandestine inquiry is what we called it at school."

"Good on you," she said, and patted August's shoulder. "You were always a dab hand at numbers, and I'm sure the others will be happy to see you again."

"Thank you." August felt himself flush at the compliment. "I am sorry I'm back under these circumstances, but I didn't want them to send someone who had never been to Fresne when I was perfectly capable of helping."

"The circumstances are hardly your fault," Blanche said, and sighed. "It was a good choice, though. Everyone's on edge worrying about who's next and what will happen if no one gets their memories back, and so people are clamming up. Hopefully, with you they'll be more open."

"I hope so," said August, offering up his most

consoling smile. "I shall make no promises, but I would like to get this solved quickly for everyone."

"Then let's get to it," she said. Her mouth was set in a grim scowl. "What do you need to know?"

"So how does it happen?" August asked.

Blanche sighed. "One day, they have their memories, and the next, they're gone. It's like someone reaches into their mind and plucks out every single memory of a person. There's no warning or signal, but it was obvious with a few. Monsieur Allard, Blaise, and Madame Monet were almost certain we caught the day they forgot. With the other two, we're not sure."

Monsieur Allard was the cobbler, and August had fond memories of the older man teaching him all sorts of fun ways to lace his boots so that they looked like rabbit ears or flowers. Blaise had been a local legend—a villager who was serving as a guard in the royal city with their best friend—when August was in Fresne. Madame Monet he had not heard of until the letter yesterday.

"The other two are Henry Heroux and Lucie Renaud, right?" August asked. "Neither of their names were familiar to me."

"They wouldn't be," said Blanche. "Henry's only

a few years older than you and moved here with his parents about seven years ago. Lucie is mostly self-sufficient and rarely comes into town. She's not being cooperative and refuses to believe she forgot anyone. Thankfully, the neighbor she forgot has never seemed fond of her, so there's not been much disruption to her life."

August sat back in his chair, thinking it over. "Is it always only one person that's forgotten?"

"So far as we can tell, yes," said Blanche, and she tapped her book. Reading upside down, August could tell she was looking at the notes on Madame Monet. "We haven't found anything definite that connects all of them."

"Leave that to us," August said, and glanced at the notes Martin and he had brought. "So, five people have completely forgotten their memories of a person, and despite the work of multiple physicians, they have been unable to recover the lost memories?"

"That's it in a nutshell," Blanche said.

It was worrisome that they recovered no memories. Complete memory loss like that was rare, and when he'd researched it last night, he'd found no record of its being focused on one person. It made

August afraid in a way he hadn't been before.

"Has anyone described what they *do* remember?" Martin asked, and his frown deepened at Blanche's shrug.

"It's like I said, the memories of the person have been plucked. Madame Monet remembers eating breakfast the day her husband left, but he's not there in her memory. Only her son is."

"Curious," mumbled Martin. "That is incredibly and oddly precise."

"If you say so," said Blanche. "People have plenty of opinions and theories but no real answers."

"That's perfectly fine," August said. He already had a dozen things he wanted to investigate once they left here. "Now, the only question remaining is what happens after the memory loss. Are people able to form new memories with the person they had forgotten, or do they forget them all over again?"

Blanche laughed. "Why, yes, they can form new memories. Henry Heroux is actually the one bright spot of this whole sordid mess. He had forgotten his coworker Danielle. They've since met again. He still cannot remember any of their interactions from before they were reintroduced, but they're making plenty of new memories. The two got married last year."

"That's sweet," August said, grinning. The good news had probably been a boon for the pair and for Fresne.

"We don't have proof it will hold," said Martin, tapping a finger against his mouth. "What if he forgets her all over again? Best prepare for that."

August inhaled and patted Blanche's hand, her knuckles white from how hard she was gripping her notes.

"Martin likes to prepare for the worst, and while it can be disheartening, it does mean almost nothing takes us by surprise," August said. "Now, we don't want to interrupt everyone's lives, but we do need to speak with the people who lost their memories and maybe those whom they forgot."

"Madame Monet is usually home right now, and Monsieur Allard's almost certainly working," she said, and stood. "I'll send word for the others to meet you at the inn tonight. Before you head off, let me show you to your room and get you settled."

Blanche gestured for them to follow her upstairs. After a few years of traveling, August and Martin had learned to travel light. Each of them had only a single pack, which earned an odd look from Blanche, and she led them up to the third floor. There weren't that many rooms up here, and she took them to the door farthest from the stairs. If more people rented rooms, August and Martin would be undisturbed. Blanche handed August the key.

"Now," she said, pushing the door open, "you've got two beds and a room for bathing. Ring the bell when you need hot water, and it will be brought up to you. Meals aren't set. We've always got a little something going, but if you want anything specific, let me know."

The room was a large corner space with plenty of natural light and a desk beneath one of the windows. Two small beds were pushed up against opposite walls, and a little curtain separated the living space from the bathing area. Martin set his bag on the bed nearer the door, and August dropped his into the chair at the desk. While Martin took most of their notes as they worked, August preferred going over them later. This would be ideal for that.

"Will this do?" Blanche asked.

"It's perfect," said August, liking how she smiled. At least someone in Fresne was happy to see him. "Thank you."

"Ring if you need anything," she said, and pointed to the bell on the desk. "I'll go track down everyone and tell them you're here. Madame Monet lives in the old carpenter's house—you remember where that is—and Monsieur Allard's where he always has been."

She left, and August leaned over the desk, forehead against the thick window glass. The glass was pretty but distorted his view outside. A wavy figure walked down the main street.

"Do you remember where the carpenter's house is?" Martin asked once the sound of Blanche's footsteps grew distant.

August snorted. "Not even a little bit. I'll ask someone when we leave."

"Not a lot to go on," Martin said softly. "We're going to have to pry into people's lives and determine if someone caused this deliberately. You didn't ask her about that."

August paced the length of the room. "I didn't want to upset her or make her defensive before we've even started."

The quiet stillness of the town beyond the inn's windows made his skin crawl. There was a small jug of water in the bathing area, and he splashed his face. There was no time to waste. Fresne shouldn't have been like this.

The familiar snap of Martin checking his watch echoed in the room. "Ready?"

August ran a hand through his hair and nodded. "Let's go."

The sooner they spoke to everyone, the sooner they hopefully solved this.

August took the lead going down the stairs. Martin followed a few steps behind him, the click of his pocket watch chain against his buttons like a timer. They didn't have any time to lose, and August wasn't sure if he could track down Blanche again to ask about the carpenter's house. He stepped onto the first floor and rounded the corner into the main room.

And slammed into someone else.

August fell back and cracked his elbows against the floor. Whomever he had struck let out an *oof*.

"Oh, drat!" they cried.

"I'm so sorry," August said, pushing himself up and rubbing his smarting arms. Silver specks spotted his vision. "Are you all right?"

"I think so," they said. "For now."

August looked over to them, and words failed.

Ella—so similar and so different—knelt on the floor. Gone were the round, dimpled cheeks she had had last he saw her, and her curls had darkened to a honey blond. Her simple dress was patched with small floral designs. The sight of her filled him with such overwhelming longing for their friendship, but when he tried to say her name he couldn't. Chest tight, he cleared his throat. She didn't look up from the crushed hat in her hands.

"Is that the only casualty?" he asked.

"I don't think it's a mortal wound," she said, and let out an awkward chuckle.

More than his elbows stung now that he knew she didn't recognize his voice.

She shrugged and looked up, and August offered a hand to help her stand. The brush of her bare fingers around his palm felt far more tender than an embrace, and she slipped her hand from his the moment she was standing. She stared up at him, scrutinizing his face. Her nose was scrunched up like it used to be when she was thinking as a child. August smiled at the familiar sight. Though a part of him twisted under her scrutiny.

"You're . . ." she muttered. Something like recognition flashed through her blue eyes. "August?"

She threw her arms around his neck, and relief forced aside his petty anger.

"It's so good to see you," Ella said into his

shoulder, and then she pulled back suddenly and clasped her hands in front of herself. She blushed.

Was it good to see him? Her years of silence would have suggested otherwise. August stared at her, uncertain as to what to say or do and keenly aware of the awkwardness settling between them.

"It's very good to see you, too."

"What are you doing here?" she asked.

Behind him, Martin cleared his throat.

Right—propriety. August should start there.

"Martin, may I introduce you to Ella?" August asked, and gestured between them. "Ella, this is Martin Tremblay."

Ella curtsied slightly. "It's nice to meet you, sir."

"And you, mademoiselle," Martin replied.

She smiled quickly at Martin and glanced at August. Again, she asked, "What are you doing here?"

"We were sent by the royal court to investigate the memory loss," said August. "You've heard about it, I assume?"

"Heard about it?" she said, blinking. "Of course I have. You're who the court sent in response to Blanche's request?"

"It's why I went away to school," he said. "We're trained to be helpful, from balancing budgets to finding embezzlers and con artists who are trying to manipulate magic to their own wills."

August had wanted a skill set and a history that would make Charmant proud to call him their king one day, and so he had set out to solve the issues no one else did, no matter how small or insignificant the problems seemed. It wasn't about the learning, though he had learned quite a lot in the last few years. It was about actually doing something.

Even if that something was increasing funds to a certain province and trusting that they knew what they were doing when they said they could fix things if they had the resources. Those stories weren't all that interesting, though.

"That last one has only happened twice," said Martin. "It's mostly embezzling."

"It's happened twice, which is two times too many," August said, hoping Ella would ask about it. Most people did. "Most of our work involves investigation and problem-solving concerning rarer things, like magic. There's never been a specific group to handle it, so we've taken it on until one is officially formed."

Which would be soon, if August had his way, but changing things like that was slow going.

"Oh, that's why. That makes sense. Why else

would you come, after all," she said, as though she had expected something else. She shook her head, squared her shoulders, and smiled slightly. "That's good, though I didn't know this is the sort of thing you do now."

How would she know what he did now? August flexed his hands, trying to think of a kinder way to respond. Her smile was already forced. She seemed equal parts thrilled and disappointed that he had returned.

"We only got here, so we've yet to speak to anyone involved," he said, ignoring the way Martin tried to catch his eye. "How are you doing?"

"Well! Busy," she said, and held up the hat. She bounced onto her toes, like a bird about to take flight. "I was running errands—had to give Blanche a note from Lady Tremaine, and then I'm off to Madame Monet's—and I don't want to keep you from your work."

It made August uneasy. She had never been so . . . contrite?

She shifted as if to leave, and August reached out after her.

"Wait!" It came out sharper than he expected, and he stuffed his hand into his pocket. "We were actually hoping to speak to Madame Monet. A friendly face, even just for the introduction, might help put Madame Monet and the others at ease." She hesitated, and before she could decline, he added, "Also, to be honest, I don't remember my way around town and didn't want to correct Blanche when she assumed I did."

Martin looked like he might smother August in his sleep, but Ella didn't notice.

Her nose wrinkled, and then she nodded. "I have to be home before supper, though. I cannot be late."

Surely they could speak with each other like acquaintances long enough for him to find out why she had stopped writing.

"Of course," said August, gesturing to the door of the inn. "I'll escort you home after."

Her expression changed in a blink, the hesitant awkwardness turning cold. She looked at him with her frost-blue eyes, but it was like she didn't actually see him.

"That won't be necessary," she said, voice flat and emotionless. "I shall introduce you to Madame Monet, but there's no need for you to join me after that."

Perhaps Martin was right—August was too optimistic.

~ 3 ~
A Very Nice Maid

AUGUST WAS still unsure what to say as
they walked to the Monet home.

"I know I prefer silence," whispered Martin
behind August, "but not this kind."

He hadn't expected a friendly reception, but it
was like a layer of ice had grown between them.

August nodded. He took Ella in again, gaze drawn
to her collar. Vines of pink roses twined around it,
embroidered with ribbons instead of thread. He knew
it was Ella's work from the attention to detail; she
had even added extra pistil stitches for the thorns. He
couldn't believe he remembered what those were called.
How tricky memory was, and how daunting that they
had to figure out how memories in Fresne were going
missing.

"Do you know Madame Monet well?" August
asked Ella, lengthening his stride to catch up with her.

"Fairly well. She teaches all the music lessons

in town, though her son took over when she lost her memories." Ella wasn't as impassive as before, but she didn't smile when she looked at him. "She's just up here."

"What instrument are you studying?" asked August. She had always been a lovely singer. "Piano? Harp?"

Ella didn't seem to hear him and pointed to a small building in the middle of the street, speeding up to knock on the door. It opened before she could.

"Ah! I thought you would be by soon." Madame Monet was a small woman with large brown eyes, rich brown skin, and a handful of white strands in her curly black hair. She smiled at Ella and peered around her. "Forgive me, Ella. I didn't realize you were bringing me company."

"These are August and Martin, the two sent by the royal court to figure out why you lost your memories of Monsieur Monet," said Ella, gesturing at them each in turn. "Do you have time to talk to them?"

"Come in, come in," said Madame Monet. "Mind any dirt, sirs. It's bad for the instruments."

"Thank you, Madame," August said, tapping his boots together in the doorway. "We'll try not to take up too much of your time."

"If you can help us, then you can take all of my time and then some," she said, and huffed. "My son's insisted I rest despite my remembering perfectly well that I hate being idle."

"It's sweet," said August.

"That it is," Ella said, "and it is also my cue to leave."

Madame Monet scoffed. "I haven't even given you the sheets yet, dear. Come. Sit. I'm nearly done organizing for tomorrow's lessons."

"Music sheets?" Martin asked.

"Oh, yes," said Madame Monet, nodding. "I usually plan all my lessons and send the music sheets ahead of time so that my students have plenty of time to practice, but I've been a bit distracted of late. I don't want Lady Tremaine to take it out on you, though, so let me grab the girls' music."

"The girls' music?" August asked. He wasn't oblivious—Ella had avoided answering his question about which instrument she played, so maybe Madame Monet would be more forthcoming.

"Drizella and Anastasia Tremaine," said Madame Monet. "Those two have been my students, and dear Ella has suffered through my teaching them for years."

A Very Nice Maid

Ella, staring pointedly away from August, softly said, "I would hardly describe it as suffering."

"Are you taking lessons as well?" asked Martin, stepping up beside them.

"Oh, no," said Ella. "Lady Tremaine doesn't think I need them."

Madame Monet went quiet, lips pursed, and studied Ella.

"Come," she said, much more gently. "There's no need to rush off."

She led them upstairs. Music notes were carved into the walls in swirling designs and lined the doorframes. She touched one at the top of the stairs.

"This is a lullaby I sang to Oliver when he was a baby. I know now that my husband, Quentin, carved it." She smiled sadly. "It's the strangest thing. I remember all the love, there just isn't a person involved in it anymore."

She led them to a small table upstairs. Martin held a chair out for her, and August moved to do the same for Ella. However, she reached for the chair as he did. His hand settled over hers, and she pulled away. August sat down without looking at her again.

"Do you remember when you lost your

73

memories?" asked August, hoping no one else had noticed the chair debacle.

She nodded. "Three days after my birthday. It only took a few hours for Oliver to notice. I didn't believe him at first."

Martin pulled out his notebook and started writing. August always learned best by listening.

"Oliver tutors several young children in music and mathematics. He leaves before me some mornings and studies before working, so I was alone for most of the morning," she said, and swallowed. "I got ready for the day like I always do, or at least I thought that was what I always did. It was simply another ordinary day to me."

"Please be as detailed as possible," said August gently. "Even the smallest detail might help."

She nodded. "I woke up a few hours after dawn, washed, and dressed in what I'm wearing now. My mother made the dress, and Ella did some of the alterations. I put on my necklace—a birthday present from Quentin before he traveled up north to complete a commission—and played a bit before my first lessons. Nothing fancy." She gestured to a violin case and music stand near the window. "I went to my first student of the day. Nothing seemed wrong. I passed too many people to name on the road but didn't really talk to anyone. I returned home a little after noon. Oliver returned later and was confused to not find me writing my usual letter. I had no idea what letter he was talking about or who I was supposed to be writing. I don't think I shall ever forget the way Oliver looked at me. As if he might weep. I dream about that look now."

She sniffed and squeezed her eyes shut.

"Here," August said, and handed her a handkerchief. "Take your time."

Martin rose, expression grim. "I'll make tea."

He moved to the small hob in the corner and busied himself with a kettle and packet of tea from his pocket. Ella watched him go.

"He was taught that warm drinks make everyone feel better," said August. Martin had never been sure how to comfort someone and clung to having something to do with his hands.

"Smart teacher," muttered Madame Monet. "According to Oliver, I've been writing my husband every day, and he's been doing the same. We agreed to write that much since he was planning on being gone for three months. He's traveling home, now, though it will take him a few more weeks. I have no memories of being married. People mention Quentin, and it draws up nothing in my mind. It's like he never existed."

"Did you and Oliver discuss what happened the last time you saw your husband before he left?"

She nodded. "We did. Oliver says Quentin cooked dinner, and I can remember the meal. But since he doesn't exist in my memories, I think Oliver cooked it."

"But he hates cooking," said Ella.

"I know!" Madame Monet laughed, though it was forced. "It's odd. I don't actually remember Oliver cooking. I assumed he did, because who else would do it? If it had just been Quentin and I, would I even remember the meal at all?"

That was an interesting question—in forgetting one person, could people have forgotten entire events because there was no reason for those events to happen if the forgotten person wasn't there? If Oliver hadn't noticed she wasn't writing letters, how long might she have gone with no one noticing she had forgotten Quentin?

August asked a few more clarifying questions about the days leading up to her memory loss and the day of, and Martin began making a time line of events in their notes. Madame Monet hadn't noticed anything unusual before she forgot her husband and insisted everything was normal save for the anxiety over who would forget next. There had been no warning at all.

"Is this the necklace Monsieur Monet gave you?" asked Ella, and she pointed toward the golden chain around Madame Monet's neck. Half a locket hung from it, a small portrait of a man inside.

"Is that him?" asked August.

"It is! It's quite useful since he's gone," she said, face lighting up. "He had Nathalie make it for my birthday and has the matching piece with my portrait in it, apparently. I didn't look at the portrait that morning, thankfully, or else I might have been very confused."

"Do you remember receiving other gifts from him?" August asked.

She shook her head. "Either I believe that I've always had that item, or I believe someone else gave it to me."

"And nothing has triggered any of the lost memories to return?" asked August.

"No, nothing. We tried everything the physicians suggested, and it's like Quentin never existed for me at all. I don't remember meeting him. I don't remember falling in love with him. I don't remember our wedding," she said, and sniffed. "I remember a wedding. I remember Oliver. But all the small, intimate moments that relationships are built off have been stolen from me. I'm afraid to sleep or dream in case I forget him all over again before he returns."

"Nothing should stop you from dreaming," Ella said, and handed her a handkerchief.

"It's not fair." Madame Monet gripped the necklace tight and took a deep breath. "I should feel things when I think of him, shouldn't I? Or his scent should be familiar? I should at least know his face and see it in Oliver's."

"It *isn't* fair. Losing people changes us," August said, chest tight and eyes burning. August didn't even want to consider losing his remaining memories of his mother. The ones he had were already fuzzy and fading. If he lost them, he would lose her for good. "But your husband is coming back to you. He's crossing the kingdom for you. You can certainly grieve what you have lost, but you can still make new memories together."

"I notice there's no promise to return my memories in that speech," muttered Madame Monet, clutching her locket.

"We don't make promises we're not sure we can keep," Martin said plainly.

Ella's lips pinched together, but Madame Monet nodded. Even after so many years, August recognized the open honesty and worry on Ella's face. She was terrified for the people of Fresne.

"Well, at least you're honest." Madame Monet took a deep breath, settled her hands against the table, and locked her gaze with August's. "What else do you need to know?"

"It would help if we could speak to Oliver," said August.

"He should be home soon."

"Soon?" asked Ella.

"Any minute now," Madame Monet said. "He was tutoring one of my students this morning. The boy's close to stealing my job entirely."

Ella twisted and glanced out the window, clutching the music sheets in her hands. "Forgive me. I didn't realize we had been talking for so long. I need to head out. I told Lady Tremaine that I would be home early."

August still recognized that unease in her voice, too.

"Of course, dear," said Madame Monet, and her lips pinched together. "You do whatever it is you need to."

"Let me walk you to the door," August said, and rose before she could protest.

She didn't accept his offered arm and wouldn't look at him as they left the room.

"Stepmother is very particular about punctuality," said Ella once they were alone. "She's very strict, you know, because she wants the best for her daughters."

"Ella, it's fine," he said, caught off guard by her frantic reasoning, as if she feared he would challenge her for having her own things to do. She nervously stepped from one foot to the other, like a bird about to take flight. He feared if he didn't say the right thing in this moment, she just might. "You were doing us a favor. You don't need to explain yourself."

"Thank you." She stopped and slowly reached out as if she might touch his arm, but she hesitated a hairsbreadth from him. "I'll be honest and say that I really don't know how I'm feeling about you returning. It's a shock to see you again without warning."

"I would have written a letter, but I didn't want another angry missive from Lady Tremaine." He shrugged, hoping it wasn't too soon to joke about the death of their friendship. If they were ever going to get past it, they had to address it. Humor seemed like the easiest route.

She inhaled sharply. "I didn't realize she wrote to you."

"Only once. I don't really remember the details," he said. "Honestly, I only decided I would be coming the morning before we left. I think I would have arrived before a letter. Anyway, I'm here now, so if you want me to avoid you, I can."

He didn't want to, but maybe no friendship would be better than this situation they were in.

"No, I don't want that. I'm sorry," she said, shaking her head. "I shouldn't be distracting you from work, though. Tell me, Sir Schooling, how many of us must forget someone before a fairy offers a wish to fix it?"

Good. He could deal with light teasing. That was a step forward.

"I *wish* I knew," he muttered. "Fa—the king is writing to the fairies to see if they can help."

"That will make people feel a lot better," she said. "I should probably leave."

"Ella," he said softly, "can we see each other again while I'm here?"

"I'll introduce you to the others and show you

around town," she said, and moved out of his grasp. "I'll come find you, all right?"

He sighed. That wasn't what he had meant, but they had to start somewhere. He took a breath and tried to keep the disappointment from his voice. "That would be great. Thank you."

She smiled, shooed him back inside, and waved goodbye, August watching her go until she rounded a corner down the street.

"Better than nothing," he muttered, and went back inside.

Martin and Madame Monet were discussing how her day-to-day life had changed after the memory loss. August took his seat, letting them speak. All they needed now was Oliver's version.

Soon enough, there was a knock on the ajar door.

"Mother?" A slender young man with dark brown skin, wide black eyes behind silver spectacles, and his hair in meticulously ordered twists poked his head through the doorway. "Oh, hello?"

"Oliver! Perfect. These are the men sent to investigate the memory loss." Madame Monet's face broke out into a wide grin, and she beckoned him inside. "They have some questions for you."

"Of course," he said, and glided into the room. He was lithe and light-footed, and he held a well-worn but equally well-cared-for case against his chest. A silver charm in the shape of a music note clinked against its handle. He was a good head taller than his mother, but up close it was clear he had inherited her broad nose and easy smile. He set down his case and then offered his hand to them in turn. "It's a pleasure to meet you both. I'm happy to help."

"We'll do as much as we can ourselves and then return to court to get whatever help we need." August took his hand, surprised by Oliver's calloused fingers. Music had never been one of his strong suits. "I'm—"

August's arm bumped the case, and it tumbled from the table. Martin, moving faster than August had ever seen him move, grabbed the handle before the case could hit the floor. A moment later, Oliver's fingers grasped Martin's hand. Oliver yanked his hand back and laughed awkwardly. Martin set the case back on the table.

"Sorry about that," said August, and he gestured to Martin, eyeing the ruddy spots of color on Martin's cheeks. That was interesting. "Allow me to introduce the Honorable Martin Tremblay."

"Thank you," said Oliver, bowing his head slightly to Martin. "It's a pleasure."

Martin nodded back in stony, suspicious silence.

August grinned. At least one of them would be kindling a friendship in Fresne this week.

~ 4 ~
A Dream, A Wish

*M*ADAME MONET and Oliver had been a good starting point for the investigation. Oliver's perspective didn't provide any definite solutions or many answers. He wasn't sure exactly when the forgetting happened, no more than she was, and he hadn't noticed any other odd things about his mother. He was worried about what would happen when his father did return, uncertain if either of them would be too disappointed to face each other when meeting again didn't return her memories. She wasn't a different person without her memories of Monsieur Monet, but she wasn't the exact same either. His concern for his mother made August all the more eager to figure out what was happening.

Oliver had told them Blaise lived near the center of town on the ground floor of a building that had been divided into separate living quarters on each floor. The door was shut, but bright scents of honey and fruit wafted into the street through the open shutters. August knocked on the wall beside one of them.

Blaise was one of the only people in town who knew who August truly was. After decades as a guard in the royal city, they had retired to Fresne when August was still young. Blaise had always been discreet when it came to August and his family, and had even joined Father on a hunt or two ages ago. August could still remember the way their eyes had crinkled with restrained laughter when he had tripped up introducing himself once.

"Hello!" Blaise, sprightly and small with a bun of white hair wobbling at the top of their head, beckoned them inside with a wide, crooked smile. "You're new faces."

August was about to reintroduce himself and Martin when Blaise narrowed their eyes at him.

"Not new," they muttered, and leaned in close. "I didn't expect to see royalty today."

"You haven't. I'm just August today, and I'm a little surprised you recognize me still," he said, smiling. "We're here on behalf of the royal court to investigate the memory loss."

"I would have been a poor guard if I didn't

recognize you," they said, and pointed to a table. "Sit! I took up bread making since leaving my post, but I'm guessing Joan did most of the eating, because we haven't been spending much time together lately and I've got bread piling up in every corner. Picard refused to take any off my hands."

Before either of them could protest, they were all seated at the table with rose hip tea and jam on slightly too dense bread. The jam was good. The bread would not put the old baker Monsieur Picard out of business any time soon. Blaise turned away to remove a pot from the small fire burning in the fireplace.

"Thank you for talking to us," August said, trying to get the last chewy piece of bread from his teeth without Blaise seeing. "So, your friend Joan is the one you forgot?"

Starting with that would hopefully ease them into the questions.

"Joan Bardin is a person-shaped hole in my memories." Blaise wiped the flour from their hands and picked up a ring with an arrowhead on it. "Joan told me we got matching ones of these since we retired around the same time and that I used to wear mine every day. I remember why I wear it but not that it's part of a pair. You know, I would almost think . . ."

Blaise shook their head and shrugged.

"Could you walk us through the day you forgot?" August asked so that they didn't have to linger on whatever thought had stopped them. "Include even the smallest of details."

They nodded, and Martin pulled out his notes.

"I woke up early. I hadn't done any baking in a while, so I figured I'd spend the day doing that. Couldn't get my damned ring off and flung it under the table," Blaise said, laughing hollowly. "So, I'm scrambling on the floor, still only in a nightshirt, and then this stranger came swanning into the room. I shrieked and knocked my head on the table—not hard enough to do any damage, mind you—and she laughed like it was a joke. I asked her what she was doing, and she said she was there for breakfast. I asked again who she was. After a bit of back and forth, she introduced herself as Joan and asked if I knew about some people in town losing their memories. I realized, then, what she was getting at. I don't know about you, but if I make a beautiful woman cry before dawn, I start questioning my life.

"Three people lost their memories before me, and sure, the first time most of us thought it was a fluke, but three is hard to argue with."

"What happened the day before you forgot Madame Bardin?"

"We had dinner together the night before, according to her, but if anything special happened, she didn't tell me."

Both Blaise's and Madame Monet's memory loss had occurred on the same sort of nondescript day, and neither had done anything out of the ordinary beforehand.

"Would Madame Bardin be willing to talk to us?" asked August, reading Martin's notes over his shoulder.

Blaise hesitated. "She's a bit put out by it all. We've been friends for years. She's been helping, you know, but I don't blame her for needing a break. I lost her, and in a way, she lost me, too."

August swallowed. Each conversation was dragging him down into the depths of unfathomable despair. There were still three others left to speak with, which he would do without complaint, but his heart ached with each new revelation. No one should have to suffer through this.

"I'm sorry," August said. He rose, and Martin followed his lead. "We'll be staying at the inn. If you remember anything else that might be important, you can find us there."

Blaise wouldn't let them leave without a basket of rolls, and August tore into one as they began their walk back to the inn. Food often helped him think better.

"Oh, these are good," he said through a mouthful, pleasantly surprised.

Martin sighed and shook his head. "Focus."

August didn't know what to make of the memory loss. He couldn't figure out why anyone would want to cause memory loss or what someone could do that would even cause it.

"Most of what we investigate, no matter how odd, usually ends up being motivated by greed. More money, power, or prestige. I don't see how making people forget someone could result in any of those," said Martin, checking his watch. "Of course, the other motivator is love."

August glanced around. Despite the time of day, no one was outside.

"If this was intentional, then we need to talk to the others to see why," said August. "If someone did want one of these people to forget whom they loved, it will be hard to find out who was the target and who was collateral."

From what they had discussed with Madame

Monet and Blaise, neither had any enemies, spurned lovers, or rivals.

Martin scowled and hesitated as they neared the inn. "We're no closer to knowing what's happening than we were yesterday."

"Martin, we got here a few hours ago. Of course we don't know anything yet," said August, holding open the door to the inn for him. "Don't let anyone from Fresne know that, though." August didn't want to make people worry more.

Blanche was on her way out, waving goodbye to the lone girl working, and she stopped them in the doorway.

"Henry is on his way. Along with Monsieur Segal, the person Lucie Renaud forgot. Lucie is refusing to talk to you, so he's as good as you're going to get for now," said Blanche, looking a bit harried.

"Is everything all right?" August asked, noticing her worried expression.

"Someone's saying there's a monstrous cat on the outskirts of town, so I'm going to deal with that."

"Do you need our help with this cat?" August asked. It sounded interesting and solvable, which would be fantastic for morale.

"No, sit. Let Mary know if you need anything,"

she said, and slipped past them. "Probably some puffed-up mouser."

The pair sat at a table in the far corner. The server, Mary, brought them bowls of garlic-and-leek soup and wished them luck, and August set the rolls from Blaise on the table. He peeled the crust from his bread and dunked it in his soup. Martin placed their notes between them.

"Your stomach is a void, I swear," Martin said without any malice, and picked at his own food. "It must have been nice to see Ella today."

August narrowed his eyes at Martin. "Yes, it was."

"I remember you writing to her every week for years until you stopped talking about your mysterious letter recipient altogether," Martin said. "Whenever I brought it up, you would even get that little twitch under your eye like you're getting now."

"I still don't know why she stopped writing me, if that's what you're getting at," August mumbled. "She's still reticent."

"You always get verbose when you're nervous."

August hated frowning so much, but he couldn't help it. Martin, the oldest of four siblings and kind despite his sarcastic exterior, would want to fix whatever had gone wrong between August and Ella, and August wasn't sure outside help would be useful. Martin had already taken on August as a misplaced younger brother. August adored it, except for all the times it made him feel foolish. If he failed to rekindle his friendship with her, he didn't want a witness.

Martin looked around before whispering, "And you never told her you were the prince?"

August shook his head. "No one knows."

It never felt good lying, but his father and mother had explained it to him as more like playing pretend. That had made sense to him as a child, and he liked the way Ella and the other people in town treated him as if he were normal. It was a feeling he never got in the city. But now that he was older, his deception felt heavier.

"Are you sure you have no idea why she stopped writing?" Martin asked. August hadn't hidden his letters from his peers at school, and Martin had been privy to August's reaction when the letters had trickled off years ago.

"We grew apart. That's all."

Martin made a face, and before August could defend himself, the door to the inn opened.

A young man in a sharp black uniform, one hand clutching his hat and the other a cane, hesitated in the doorway. August didn't recognize him, but he nodded to August and Martin and made his way over to them. He looked a few years older than August, stood taller than lanky Martin, and was drenched in freckles despite his pallor. Up close, his clothes looked to be those of a valet and were lovingly cared for. Even the buttons had been shined recently. He made his way to their table.

"Sorry, you're the pair the court sent, yes? Blanche said they would be here," said the man, and August nodded. "Oh, good. I'm Henry Heroux."

August offered him a seat and pushed his finished meal away. "August. This is Martin. Thank you for coming so quickly."

"Oh, once everyone knew why I needed to leave, they were happy to pick up the work left behind," he said, taking a seat and leaning his cane against the table's edge. The silver grip was in the shape of a wolf's head. "Blanche said you're leaving in five days, though. That means Danielle probably won't be able to speak with you. She's a lady's maid, and her lady is visiting a friend."

"That's fine." Martin flipped to a clean page

in his book. "You're the first person who lost their memories. Could you describe what the day was like for you?"

"I fell down the stairs and hurt my leg one day. I came back to work a week or so after the fall, and had no idea who Danielle was. We worked in the same household at the time. She was a maid and I was a footman. We assumed the memory loss had something to do with the fall."

"What was your relationship like with Danielle before the fall?"

"Well, we worked together, of course. But between you and me, by the sounds of it, I was carrying a torch for her before forgetting her. She's kind and serious, and she says I used to never look her in the eye, so I'm guessing I was afraid I would blush and give it away." Henry prodded his cheek. "I go red as poppies. Completely embarrassing."

"It's not embarrassing at all," said August, smiling. "So, you believe you liked her romantically?"

"I think, but it's not like I can say for certain," Henry said, and shrugged. "The memory loss was bad, even when it was only me and no one knew it would become all this, but it brought us together. Danielle and I became friends because we talked so often after

I forgot her. We wouldn't be married if not for this, so it's not been all bad."

"And to think, all you had to do was talk to her," said August lightly.

Henry chuckled. "True, but it was sort of like meeting her for the first time, which helped."

They spoke briefly of what he remembered from the time around the memory loss, and August tried to find any similarities between Henry and Danielle when compared to the others. There was the obvious overlap since they all lived in Fresne, but nothing stood out to him.

"You know, I thought relearning to walk was going to be the largest obstacle that year. My friends had Nathalie make this for me," Henry said, taking his cane. He stared at the wolf-head grip. "Then I forgot Danielle." He smiled sadly. "Turned out getting to know her again was a blessing."

They spoke for a few more minutes, August probing for any clues and discovering nothing. Henry Heroux wished them luck as he rose to leave.

"We might need it," said August, watching Henry leave. "Do you know what worries me?"

"Nothing as much as it should?" muttered Martin.

Usually, August would have taken the bait,

but he was actually worried about this memory loss.

"If this was a targeted attack, then why did the perpetrator wait so long between them?" August asked. "This has been going on for years, with the shortest time between memory loss events being months. And why is the time line accelerating now?"

August thought back over Madame Monet, Blaise Jullien, and Henry Heroux. If someone was profiting socially or romantically, August couldn't tell how. None of the three had reported making new connections except Henry, and that was with Danielle.

"Random and completely unprompted." Martin flipped through his notes on Henry. "Who's Nathalie? And Picard. Blaise mentioned a Picard."

"Nathalie's a merchant, I think, but I never met her, and Monsieur Picard's a baker. He's lived in Fresne for ages," said August. "It's a small town. I imagine all of them spoke to the same people."

Martin nodded, opening and shutting his pocket watch in a steady rhythm. "Monsieur Segal is on the way. Perhaps the perspective of someone who was forgotten will shed new light on things."

Soon enough, an older man stomped into the room. His clothes were worn and patched, and when he turned to August's table, there was a glint of gold in his scowl. He dragged a distant chair to their table despite there being two empty ones nearby.

"Where do you want to start?" he asked, offering no greeting or preamble.

"Monsieur Segal?" August asked. The man had the air of someone who thought breathing was a waste of time. "Your neighbor, Madame Renaud, forgot you?"

The man sniffed, mouth twisting up. "Thought Blanche sent you a letter?"

"She did."

"You not read it?" asked Monsieur Segal.

He sighed and laid his hands on the table, continuing before August could answer. "She's lonely. Frustrating, too. Used to come talk at me day in and day out, and for the life of me, I've got no idea why. She's sunny as a summer day, and chattier than songbirds. I knew the morning she didn't come calling that something was wrong."

August glanced sideways at Martin. "Do you know what she was doing the day before she forgot you?"

"You know, I can put up with a lot of chatter. She's interesting most of the time," he said, and pulled out a pair of leather gloves. "But she started this new thing, gifting me all sorts of nonsense and not accepting anything in return, a while back. Don't understand it, so I don't care for it. The day before she forgot me, she catches me on the road and gives me a pair of leather gloves. Said she noticed mine were worn out. No idea why she bothered. I can buy my own gloves!"

From the corner of his sight, August saw Martin make a face and resisted the urge to laugh.

"Has she ever been married?" asked August. "Does she have family or friends?"

"No, and no idea why not. It's just her now." Monsieur Segal shook his head like she was the most frustrating person he had ever encountered. "She left a little bit after giving me the gloves. Seemed disappointed, but I was in the middle of fixing a post. No time to talk. Last time she stopped to talk at me while I was working, I knocked my thumbnail off with the hammer. Don't know what she did for the rest of that day, but the next day, she didn't come by. Knew something was wrong."

He threw the gloves on the table, but his frown didn't seem like anger at Madame Renaud. August would have said the older man was disappointed if he didn't think Monsieur Segal would scoff at the idea.

"She doesn't believe a word I say. Smarts, to be honest," he said. "Now, you got questions?"

"A few, if you don't mind," August said.

He huffed. "If I did, I wouldn't be here."

August ran through the questions they had asked everyone else, though there were a few blanks since Madame Renaud thought everyone was lying. The memory loss had almost certainly happened overnight, and she had no memory of her "new neighbor" even when others insisted they had been living next to each other for over fifteen years. Monsieur Segal had insisted he was pleased she wasn't bothering him anymore, but once admitted missing their chats. He couldn't stand the gifting.

"Used to drink and complain about everyone else in town once it got dark, you know," he said. "Do miss that. She would've told me if she met anyone new or was doing anything."

Monsieur Segal left with as little pomp as when he arrived. The gloves he gave to them, claiming they only reminded him of the memory loss now. With him gone, they were the only two around, and August whistled.

"Do you think he'd figure it out if she proposed?" August asked.

Martin looked over the gloves and pocketed them. "He would probably assume it was only for tax reasons."

"So, we agree that there's a pattern?" asked August. "He's obtuse but likes her well enough, and she definitely was flirting."

Spouse, friend, coworker, and neighbor—so far, Blaise and Madame Bardin were the only outlier, but the others all had some sort of romance in common.

"Blaise did refer to Madame Bardin as a beautiful woman. Perhaps there is something there," August said.

"Fair point," Martin agreed.

"Exactly," said August. "I'll go see if Monsieur Allard is home, and you can organize our notes and look over the information from Blanche we didn't read thoroughly yet. See if there's anything interesting in there. We should turn in soon, anyway, so you can get ready for bed without me around."

The light in the inn was starting to dim, and August suspected that if people were as skittish at night as they were during the day, then everyone would turn in as soon as possible.

"Sounds good." Martin stood and gathered up all the notes. "The travel this morning did my mind no favors. The words are starting to swim together."

August grabbed an orange from the inn's kitchen. He dug his nails into the pith as he walked, enjoying the sharp bite its scent added to the air. Monsieur Allard, the cobbler for Fresne and the surrounding area, had already closed up shop. The shutters over the upper-floor windows were drawn, too. August half turned, raising a sliver of orange to his mouth. A flash of gold hair caught his eyes.

Ella, at the far end of the road, caught sight of him and startled. August kept his head down and pretended he hadn't seen her. She turned on her heel and took a side path between two buildings. August frowned.

Was she avoiding him?

After walking around the other side of the building, August emerged onto the other road and peered down it. The sun was setting, casting long shadows over town, but Ella's silhouette was unmistakable. She was hurrying toward him with her head bowed. She hadn't seen him yet.

August started walking down the street, keeping her in the corner of his sight, and she finally saw him. Ella hurried down another side road and out of sight. He bristled.

She was avoiding him!

August ripped another section from the orange to redirect his displeasure. Uncertain as to how he would explain his circuitous path, August backtracked and cut her off in front of Monsieur Allard's house. She froze at the sight of him.

"Ella?" he asked softly.

Her head jerked up, and for a brief moment, she frowned. Then, she schooled her expression.

"You saw me, didn't you?" asked Ella.

"Immediately." He held out an orange slice and smiled when she took it. She seemed embarrassed more than upset. "I was hoping to speak with Monsieur Allard, but he's in for the night, and then the dying light glimmered in your hair."

She snorted. "Did it, now? I needed to see Monsieur Allard, too. He's been embellishing a pair of Lady Tremaine's boots and repairing some other shoes for the family. How is your investigation going?"

"Slowly."

Ella peeled the thin skin from the orange slice with her nails, and August noticed soot under their edges.

"Let me walk you back to the road, and you can get your new shoes tomorrow," he said, and glanced down at hers, but she took a few steps that kept them out of sight under her dress. "I can't believe Monsieur Allard is still working."

"I know! I think he's made every pair of shoes I've ever owned." She ate the orange slowly, an expression of pure bliss wrinkling across her face, and sighed. "Thank you for this."

"Of course," he said. "How was the rest of your evening?"

"Fine."

She offered up no more information. August tried to think of a safe topic of conversation and landed on Madame Monet and Oliver. She clearly liked the woman, and maybe she would let slip why she had seemed anxious about crossing paths with Oliver earlier. Sometimes, melting a layer of ice was easier with cool water, not boiling.

"How long have you known Madame Monet? She was very nice, and Oliver seemed all right," he said. "Have you known him for a long time, too?"

"They moved to Fresne when Oliver was younger, and we met around then," Ella said, nose crinkling as she thought about it. "The whole family is lovely, and it's so rare anyone moves here and I get to meet new people. Oliver took over some of his mother's lessons, as you know, so I see him more now since he's tutoring my stepsisters. He's been very worried about his parents, though. I don't even want to imagine what that sort of stress is like. I've been making sure his favorite tea is available during lessons, but I'm not sure he's even noticed."

Kind and responsible. He was happy to see that part of her had not changed.

"Well, I hope Martin and I can do something to ease his worry," August said.

"Perfect," she said, "because I've never known him to be so tense."

"And what about you? Are you doing much embroidery these days?" he asked. Sewing was a safe topic. She loved it. "That marigold on your waist isn't ribbon embroidery, is it? You used to go through endless thread and fabric when relaxing."

"Oh, yes. Quite often, actually. It's probably my favorite part of the day, even if part of it is work." She lit up, smiling and swishing her skirt to show off the small yellow flower at her waist. "It has been a bit of a chore recently, because while Nathalie has many good qualities, identifying well-made fabric is not one of them. Drizella was getting a new dress made for this dinner a while ago, and the fabric was so . . . well, I ended up hiding how it pleated with some ribbons. If I didn't know Nathalie better, I would have assumed she did it on purpose, but I've seen some of the things Drizella likes. She does not have her mother's good taste."

The tone was off, as if Ella wanted to say more but couldn't, and she scrunched up her nose.

"Lady Tremaine did choose your father," August offered.

Ella hummed. "And he chose her. That's what I always come back to. My father married her because he thought she would be a good mother to me."

There was something about those words that hooked into his mind, but he couldn't figure out what it was. It made him think of their letters.

"Was it hard to suddenly have a stepmother and two new sisters?" he asked, and touched her arm. "I remember how excited you were to meet them and then how anxious. How are they now?"

"Trying," she said.

"It's good they're putting in the effort," he said, "if not a bit late."

Ella stared up at him through her lashes and shook her head. "You're still too nice for your own good."

"You know, Martin says the same thing, and I

don't want to say you're both wrong, but if the shoe fits . . ." He shrugged. "Really, Ella—how are they?"

"Families are complicated, and my stepsisters lost their father when they were quite young. We're not a perfect family, but we are family," she said softly, and looked up at the sky. The first stars of the night were beginning to twinkle above them. "Lady Tremaine is trying to prepare Drizella and Anastasia for their first season, and it is difficult. Lady Tremaine's been quite on edge."

"What about your debut?" he asked.

"Not to brag, but I had a wonderful dance tutor as a child, and her son was my dance partner. He was quite good, if I recall." She smiled at him, and he was struck by a blurry memory—the warmth of her hand on his shoulder and weight of her feet atop his as they cheated. "I'm taking a bit of a break from studying. I'll be fine. Everyone has to help out, and I'm doing that by helping run the estate. It's far more interesting to actually run an estate than to simply listen to someone talk about how to do it."

"But that doesn't really answer the question— what about your debut?" he asked. "When we were children, you were so excited to fall in love and have a family."

She flushed and muttered, "Managing an estate doesn't make me un-marriable."

"Of course not. Sorry," he said quickly. "I just mean, what are your sisters doing to help?"

"My stepsisters will help out by marrying upstanding young gentlemen. Or the prince. Every girl dreams of marrying into royalty, I think."

He cringed at the mention of the prince, and she elbowed him.

"Rude," she said, but she was grinning. "You don't even know them."

"Do you dream of marrying the prince?" he asked, and instantly regretted it. What if she hated him? Worse, what if she didn't?

"Oh, yes. Fairy tales, dreams, wishes—that's the point of them all, isn't it?" she asked, sighing. She touched his arm. "They give us hope that one day all of our problems will be solved and our hard work will have been worth it."

"And the answer to all of your problems is the prince?" he asked, painfully aware of her fingers gently curled around his forearm.

Ella had been by his side during his worst moments, and she didn't know he was the prince. Maybe he was the answer to some of her problems.

"Don't be ridiculous," she said quickly, but her glance at him was bright with fondness. "Hope is the answer. That's what the prince represents."

"Oh, my mistake."

Well, he could still solve that one if she ever asked.

"August?" Ella tightened her grip on his arm. "It's difficult to see you now, educated and working, successful in all the ways you wanted to be, and I'm still here. Just Ella."

"Just Ella?" He laughed, because the statement was too ridiculous not to balk at. "You've never been just anyone."

She shook her head, and he swallowed, pulling the collar up on his shirt to hide the blush creeping down his neck.

"I went to school, yes, and I do work for the royal court, but the things I have actually accomplished are raindrops in the ocean. And that's with all the advantages I had to make going to school and working easier," he said, spinning to face her. "You haven't even scratched the surface of all my faults."

She rolled her eyes. "I'm not asking you to bare your failings. I'm only saying that I have no accomplishments to show you, and you're . . ."

She gestured at him with one hand and shrugged, and he caught her sleeve.

"You are standing before me with some of the most delicately done embroidery I have ever seen, and I imagine you have even more wonderful creations at home," he said. "Your accomplishments—your family's estate, your family, your perseverance— aren't something you should dismiss. Everyone in Fresne knows you, so it's harder for them to see what you've built. To them, it's a given. To me, you're very impressive."

She stared up at him, the dusk sky glittering in her eyes, and smiled. "Thank you."

"You're very welcome." He nodded to the path, and they kept walking, her arm tucked into his.

He didn't want to say anything that would ruin the relative peace, so he kept quiet. Ella fiddled with a loose thread on his sleeve.

"I didn't know how to write you again and say hello without simply dumping all my problems at your feet," she whispered. "You never did anything wrong. Everything was wrong. I didn't feel like I could talk to anyone about anything."

"I wouldn't have minded."

"I knew that, deep down," said Ella, tying off

the loose thread. "My parents would have been disappointed in me for not answering you."

"I doubt that," he said softly. "I may not have known what was happening at the time, but you were going through a lot, to put it lightly. My mother would have been disappointed in a few of my responses to you."

August startled at the casual mention of his mother. He had feared what returning would be like emotionally, and yet he had just been able to think of her without the usual stabbing pain in his chest that followed.

"I doubt that," Ella mimicked, and laughed softly. Sadly. Like she wasn't sure what else to do. "I only remember the one letter that was not very nice."

Had he not sent those others? That time felt like ages ago.

"Then I think we're both in the clear," said August. "Can we stop avoiding each other?"

They reached the edge of town and the split in the road that would lead her home. Ella stopped first, slipping her hand from his arm, and turned to face him. August flexed his left hand.

"Yes," she said. "I'm sorry. No more avoiding each other."

August grinned.

"I can't convince you to let me walk you all the way, can I?" he asked, inexplicably bereft already.

"No, I'm afraid not," said Ella. Her arm twitched, and she clasped her hands behind her back. "You need to speak with Monsieur Allard?"

He nodded.

"Meet me in the market at dawn. I'll reintroduce you when I bring him my errand. His wife left for a while due to the stress of it all, and he's burying himself in his work, so he keeps earlier and earlier hours," she said. "Does that work for you?"

"Perfectly," he said, and inclined his head.

She smiled, moving as though she wanted to embrace him but wouldn't let herself. "Dawn, then."

～ 5 ～

Better to Have Loved

*A*UGUST WAS used to waking up at dawn. He had been forced to become an early riser during his school years and carried on the habit once he returned home. The meetfasts with his father kept him in practice, since court started early. Somehow, though, Martin was already outside when he left the inn.

"I saw a short-toed eagle!" Martin said, not bothering to keep his voice down since he was the only person on the street. "I walked around the whole place, and there are so many more birds here than on the royal grounds!"

Bird-watching was one of the few things that made Martin smile, and even with the seriousness of everything, August couldn't help grinning in return.

"Did you bring your list?" asked August. "You can come back after the end of the week, you know. Perhaps someone else in town likes birds."

Music and birdsong weren't so different. Perhaps Oliver enjoyed both.

Martin wound his pocket watch and turned around, but August still caught the slight stutter when he spoke. "Where is Ella meeting us?"

"The market," said August, knowing exactly why Martin brought her up, so he changed the subject. "Monsieur Allard is the last of those who forgot their memories, so hopefully we'll learn something new before we begin retracing everyone's steps."

"Since the town is so small, it will be easy to find places where their paths crossed," said Martin slowly. "It will also be difficult to determine if anyone else was there and, if so, then why didn't they forget someone?"

There were a few people walking the streets today—the market was smothered in shadows, but August would have recognized Ella's eager stance regardless of the dark. As a child, she had always stood on her tiptoes when excited, as if preparing to fly away. She seemed to stand like that constantly now.

"August!" Ella waved and darted to him. "Good morning."

He smiled. Another layer of ice gone.

She stopped before him, hesitated, and then patted his arm.

Close enough.

"Good morning," he said, returning the pat. "Thank you for doing this."

"Oh, it's nothing. I told you that I need to see him, too," she said, and nodded a greeting to Martin. "Let me run into the bakery before Monsieur Picard gets into a mood, and we can bring Monsieur Allard breakfast. He's usually testy before he eats."

August and Ella led Martin to the narrow building on the corner of the main street. It wasn't attached to the other buildings on the street, a thin little stone wall separating its steaming kitchens from its neighbor. The wooden walls were washed a light color, and the door was thrown open. Inside, August could make out the counter covered in freshly baked breads. It had seemed so much taller when he was young. Otherwise, nothing had changed in the last decade.

Even Monsieur Picard seemed frozen in time, still the same old man August remembered. All he could recall about the baker other than his wrinkled face was that the gruff man hated thieves and laminating. August still wasn't sure what the latter meant, but he perfectly remembered the sharp *whack* of the man's rolling pin against his sticky fingers as a child.

"Good morning!" Ella swept inside first, homing in on a large ceramic bowl shaped like an ash tree, the branches full of steaming rolls. She picked out five. "Can you put aside a crown for me once they're done?"

Monsieur Picard was folding dough atop a small table. Two huge ovens flickered behind him, and he grunted without looking up at Ella. August paid for it all before Ella could.

"You're helping us out," he muttered. "So really, the court is buying."

"The court sent *you?*" Monsieur Picard's gaze cut to August, and he snorted. "Oh, we'll be safe in no time, then."

Martin tensed.

"Monsieur Picard!" August said quickly. "How lovely that you remember me!"

"Remember you running wild with her as a child," said Monsieur Picard, pointing at Ella. "I remember your mother, too. Good of you to come back, I suppose."

"I wanted to help," August said, feeling like a student being inspected by their new teacher.

Monsieur Picard glanced behind August, to the

people milling about outside, and beckoned for him to lean in close.

"You figure out why folks are forgetting?" he whispered.

"We're still investigating theories," said August.

"There's got to be something connecting the people who are forgetting," said Monsieur Picard, grabbing August's arm and pulling him so close he was leaning across the counter. "That boy, Henry, was the first. You tell me what he said. What's the memory loss like?"

August stiffened—aware of Martin tensing further a step away—and held up a hand. "When we have news, we'll have Blanche alert the town, monsieur."

The baker leaned back, eyes still blue slits, and turned to Ella. "I'll set a crown aside, but if you're not here in two hours, it's going to the first person who walks in."

"Thank you!" Ella smiled despite the tension between Monsieur Picard and August, and she looped her arm through August's. "Let's go."

The three of them left the bakery in silence. A chubby older boy with honey-colored hair and a half-donned white apron sprinted past them into the bakery, and Ella sighed.

"Robert's always late," she muttered.

"I wouldn't have thought anyone would want to apprentice with Monsieur Picard," said August. "He's so intense."

"That's a word for it," muttered Martin, clicking the latch of his pocket watch repeatedly.

Ella pulled her gaze from Martin's pocket watch, winced, and untangled her arm from August's. "Monsieur Picard's all but given Robert the bakery, but he doesn't want to quit altogether. I could live happily eating only freshly baked bread from his bakery, and butter. And maybe apple preserves in winter."

"That's three things," August pointed out. "Though I won't fault you for wanting more than bread."

"Wouldn't that be lovely? All the bread I can eat, and it's always perfectly baked, free of mold, and never stale."

Why in the world would Ella ever be worried about moldy bread? She had a whole farm on her family's property.

"You wish for that, and I'll wish for cheese," he said. "Then we'll both be perfectly happy."

"Oh, to be happy," Martin said, and sighed. "I wonder what that's like?"

"No, you don't. You were born scowling," said August, suddenly remembering that he and Ella had an audience.

They reached Monsieur Allard's shop a few moments later, and Ella took the lead again.

"Monsieur Allard?" she called, knocking on the door and walking inside. "Do you have a moment?"

An older man with tanned skin, rusty freckles, and brown hair peppered with gray bustled out from a back room and welcomed them all inside the shop.

"I always have a moment for you, my dear," said Monsieur Allard.

Ella handed over the breakfast she had gotten from the bakery and laid it out on a kerchief, buttering some bread for Monsieur Allard. He accepted it and sent a fond smile her way. August couldn't help grinning.

"Lady Tremaine's shoes are much improved, if I do say so myself, and her daughters' boots should be just as she asked now." Monsieur Allard set a pot of tea on the table and gestured for them to serve themselves. "If she says anything about them, remind her that I did exactly as she asked."

He loaded three pairs of shoes—one pair of red velvet boots with glass forget-me-nots on the front, and two of yellow with blue floral embroidery—into Ella's basket and set it on the table.

"I think they look lovely," said Ella, sipping her tea.

Monsieur Allard's smile widened, and he held up a finger. "Now, I know you said that yours are fine, but these were turned over to be used for parts and all they needed were new soles and laces to be functional again. I've taken care of the soles."

He pulled a fourth pair—a pretty set of dark blue shoes that weren't as elaborate as the others—from his workbench and held them out to Ella.

"Oh, they're wonderful!" Ella took one and turned it over, inspecting every part, then handed it back to Monsieur Allard. "They're much too lovely for me to take when I have a perfectly good pair already. Thank you, but I couldn't possibly accept."

"I shall keep them for now, but if no one else buys them, then they are yours," said Monsieur Allard, and August got the feeling that he wasn't going to try very hard to sell them. "You've been far too kind to me these last few years."

Ella flushed, and Monsieur Allard set the shoes aside.

"Now," he said, turning to August and Martin.

"Unless I'm much mistaken, you're the two here to investigate the memory loss. August and Martin?"

"That we are," said August, dragging his gaze from Ella. "Do you have time to talk now?"

"That's why I made tea," said Monsieur Allard. He patted a teapot and gestured to the multiple cups on the tray next to it.

Ella hesitated near the door. "I could leave if you prefer to keep it private."

"No, my dear, you're no stranger," said Monsieur Allard. "Where do you want to start?"

Martin opened up his notebook. "Please describe the day on which you believe you forgot your wife, Denise, in as much detail as possible."

Monsieur Allard sighed. "I know exactly the morning I forgot her, because I woke up in bed with no idea who she was or why she was there. Terrible time for both of us. I can't really blame her for needing a break, given that nothing's worked to make me remember her. It was a few days after you brought Lady Tremaine's boots in and she made me redo the embellishments," he added, nodding at Ella. "I must have gone through Nathalie's whole stock looking for something she'd like before I found those glass forget-me-nots. I remember you leaving them on the steps for me to grab when I returned from a walk, but now I know it was Denise that took them inside and set them on my table."

His hands twitched, and Ella handed over a roll. Monsieur Allard picked it apart as he spoke, never eating it but tearing the bread into smaller and smaller pieces as he recounted the day he forgot his wife. His memory loss was exactly like the others, and it concerned another beloved partner.

Ella nodded. "You've been married for so long and worked together for so much longer. In your mind, without your memories of her, did you have any help working?"

"Not at all. It was always just me," he said. "Alone."

August inhaled. He didn't want his sadness at such a statement to make Monsieur Allard feel worse.

"I can write to Denise if you want. She's with her folks," said Monsieur Allard.

"Thank you. We'll keep that in mind and let you know if we do need to speak with her," said Martin, and August nodded. "We should take our leave anyway."

They left and emerged into the sunlit streets, blinking. Ella hefted her basket onto her shoulder.

"I wonder," she said slowly, scrunching up her

nose. It was the same expression she used to make when trying to remember a dance step.

"Go on," August said.

"Do you think it requires that they're asleep?" she asked. "I hadn't thought about it before, but it seems like each instance occurred overnight."

She wasn't wrong—Monsieur Allard, Blaise, and Madame Monet had mentioned waking up one day without their memories.

"It's a good thought," said August. "When we retrace people's steps today, we can try to determine if there's a trigger for the memory loss and how sleeping could be related."

"I think it best if we split up. Let August walk you home," said Martin, tone soft and unassuming and—to August, who knew him well—wholly unlike his usual manner. "You're carrying far too much if you still need to pick up things from Monsieur Picard, and August thinks best when he's not looking at the problem."

"Oh," said Ella, spinning to August, "you don't have to."

"Martin's right," said August, seizing upon his opportunity to spend more time with Ella. "You don't mind if I join you, do you?"

"Well, no, I don't mind."

"Wonderful," Martin said, walking backward away from them. "While you're walking, see if you can find anything odd about the places they went in the days before they lost their memories, and I'll do the same on the other side of town."

Martin checked his pocket watch, pulled out his notebook, and walked away with his nose to the page.

Ella laughed. "He's . . ."

"Obvious?" August offered. "Clear as crystal?"

"I was going to say focused," said Ella, shaking her head. "I need to stop by the butcher, then the market for strawberries, and then the bakery again."

"Perfect," said August, "because the market and the main road are the only places the others went that they have in common. Madame Monet and Blaise visited the market, and Henry and Monsieur Allard walked down the main road. I'm assuming Madame Renaud bought those gloves from someone at the market, but since she won't talk to us, we can't confirm."

"Perhaps she purchased them from Nathalie's, which is off the main road," said Ella, pointing down a side path. "She doesn't open until later in the day, though. She keeps the oddest hours."

"That's definitely possible. The others mentioned gifts from Nathalie's as well, so it would be a good place to check out," he said, and silently thanked Nathalie. August wanted an hour or two with Ella and without work.

August followed after Ella happily. She spoke of how she was teaching herself accounting to better help care for the estate, how she had finally mastered brewing the perfect pot of tea, and her recent attempts to preserve one of her mother's old dresses so that she might wear it later. At the market, they gathered up bones for a beauty concoction for Drizella, purchased strawberries to fade Anastasia's freckles, and traded some eggs for a cut of pork. Ella saved the bakery for last, holding open the door for an older woman. She let Ella go ahead of her. August waited near the door.

Monsieur Picard handed Ella a ring-shaped crown loaf wrapped in cloth and nodded to August. "What did Monsieur Allard say, boy?"

"That's between Monsieur Allard and us," said August, trying not to let his dislike for the question show.

Monsieur Picard opened his mouth, and the woman behind Ella clucked her tongue. "Leave him be."

She took Ella by the arm and led her outside, gesturing for August to follow.

"He's gotten so ill-tempered," Ella said once they were outside. "I wish he would say why."

"Never mind him," said the woman. She stopped in the street and shook her head, the white curls falling out of her tie. "If he's going to be like that, I don't need any bread today."

"Thank you," said August, "but you didn't need to do that . . ."

He trailed off as she stuck out a scarred hand with the nails chewed to the quick.

"Joan Bardin," she said.

August took her offered hand, noting the large ring on her finger that matched Blaise's. "August. Nice to meet you."

"Well, I'm sure you heard enough about me already," she said. "Sorry I missed you yesterday. With everything happening, I've been taking on some odd jobs to keep out of Blaise's hair and my mind off everything."

"I doubt they consider you in their hair. They only spoke kindly of you," August said. Maybe Madame Bardin could confirm any romantic feelings for Blaise if prodded.

"Of course they did, even with me cut from their memories," she mumbled, spinning her ring. "Blaise has always been a smooth talker, but in a good way. They're always sincere. Always complimentary. It was very confusing at first, because I thought they were always joking—well, making me the butt of the joke—but they weren't. They have a much better sense of humor than that and a much more tender heart."

She swallowed, a flush slowly spreading across her face.

"Well, they seemed very sincere when they called you beautiful," said August, and Madame Bardin startled. "May I ask if anything noteworthy happened the night before Blaise forgot you?"

"We had a nice dinner. Shared some stories. Nothing that I think would make them forget," she said, blushing a bright red.

But something that would make her blush.

She nodded to him, then to Ella, and sighed. "I hope Blaise's bake is edible today."

Madame Bardin headed off toward Blaise's, and Ella elbowed August gently.

"You're thinking something," she whispered. "What is it?"

He smiled down at her, gesturing for them to continue their walk. "That is between Madame Bardin and me."

"Sure it is," said Ella. "You know, I once saw her jump off the roof of the inn."

"Why?" August asked, aghast.

"She was demonstrating how to land properly after a fire had trapped some folks upstairs and they were too scared to jump, and . . ."

Ella spoke of the town on the walk back home. August was glad to hear about her life in Fresne these past few years, but each tale made his chest ache with a homesickness he hadn't expected. The sight of her home was an even sharper pain.

They entered the estate from the back, crossing through the fields that surrounded it. The château's sharply slanted towers cut dark figures against the morning sky, standing out starkly against the white stone beneath them. Glass windows glittered in the light, and a spiral of smoke rose from the kitchen's chimney out back. It was exactly how he remembered it save for the ivy creeping across the front. August glanced at the empty stables near the kitchens. Major, Ella's horse, was sleeping in the shade.

"Odd how some things don't change," he said.

"Oh, trust me—things have changed," said Ella, stumbling into the kitchen and dumping her wares on the large table in the center. "See? The walk wasn't so bad."

"Do you trade off on chores with your step-sisters?" he asked.

Ella turned away from him and set a large pot of water atop the brick oven, where a low fire burned. "They're focusing on their studies right now so that they can debut. Lady Tremaine is very strict with them. Going into town is frankly a nice break from the house."

"That's good, then," August said, glancing around the kitchen. It was well lived in, but there should have been a scullery maid or cook in it right then. There was only one cup of watered-down coffee on the table, and he rubbed his face as Ella sipped from it. "Ella, do you do the cooking?"

"It's been fun learning how to cook! There's more science to it than people talk about, and it's nice to be able to do something and immediately enjoy the results," she said. "Better me than Drizella. She would set fire to a pan trying to boil water. Here, bring me those apricots," she said, nodding to a cheesecloth-covered bowl.

There was nothing wrong with working; there

was something wrong with how only Ella seemed to be doing it.

He grabbed the bowl and joined her at the fire. "Why?"

"You need some way to be useful," she said. She removed the cheesecloth and layered the apricots into a large pot with honey. "There are some sprigs of lavender hanging up. Place them in a sachet and tie it off, too, please."

"I shall be the scullery maid to your cook any day," said August, grabbing the lavender. The sachet tie was quite small, and he struggled to close it. "How am I supposed to do this?"

"Really?" She stared at him over her shoulder, one side of her mouth twitching as she tried not to laugh. "How do you lace your boots?"

"I hired someone to follow me around and do it for me whenever I need," he said, grinning, and knotted the sachet shut. "Ha!"

He tossed it to her, and Ella caught it without looking. "Not even Drizella has made someone do that yet."

"Is their only contribution attempting to marry well?"

"That's all they've been taught to do, and all

society will allow them to learn. You know, no one ever even considered teaching me to make jam until I taught myself, and that's a travesty. Do you know the secret to good jam?" She dropped the sachet in the pot and glanced at him over her shoulder.

He shrugged. "They took it off the curriculum after a terrible prune accident."

She shook her head. "Travesties upon travesties."

"What else can I fail to help with?" August asked.

"Honestly, not much," she said. "We're having a late breakfast. Lady Tremaine kept them up all night practicing how to walk in their new gowns. Coffee for her and chocolate for them, with some bread on the side. Lady Tremaine is very strict about everything, including what they eat. . . ."

Ella bustled about around August, and he tried to wrap his mind around the concept of keeping children up late for something like that. He speared a strawberry with a dull knife.

"Ella," he said gently, and pulled her to a stop, holding the strawberry before her mouth.

She eyed it. "That's for Anastasia's face."

"If you don't eat it, it will be on *your* face," he said, and tapped her nose with it.

Ella sighed. Slowly, she opened her mouth and let

him place the strawberry on her tongue, then closed her lips around it. Her eyes fluttered shut. August stilled.

"Pity they're going on her face," mumbled Ella, licking her lips. Her smile was a soft pink stain. "I don't think I'll have time to see you again today. We should plan to meet again, though. Before you leave."

"Yes, please," he said, and cleared his throat. His skin felt hot and flushed beneath his shirt, and it had nothing to do with the heat of the kitchen. "I mean, that's fine."

August looked away from her, trying to find a distraction.

"The jam!" He pointed to the pot she had removed from the heat a little while before. "You never did tell me the secret."

"Oh, yes!" She grabbed a spoon and a mouthful of the jam. "It's not set yet, but trust me, it will. What you're tasting for is brightness. A bit of lemon juice cuts the sweetness, but you have to add it early or the jam might not set correctly."

Ella approached him slowly, cheeks freshly pinkened from the heat of the stove, and held the spoon up to his mouth. August swallowed and carefully ate the jam. Never before had he been so aware of how easy it was to get food on his face. He couldn't even feel his face, and . . .

"Well?" Ella pulled the spoon away and stared up at him expectantly.

"Well," he repeated, and stopped. The jam was good—it wasn't too sweet, and the sharp bite of lemon perfectly paired with the softer floral from the lavender. "It's delicious."

"Really?" She beamed, smiling so widely her eyes briefly closed, and spun. "Perfect!"

Her joy made his breath catch in his chest.

A terrible yelp interrupted them, then a cat yowled. The chickens outside the door clucked up a storm, feathers and dirt fogging up the air. A fuzzy monster of a cat leapt over the bottom of the half door and smacked into Ella's legs, knocking her away from August. He barely caught her wrist.

"Why, you!" She righted herself and shooed the creature away.

Something hit the bottom of the kitchen door and yelped again. Two large paws clawed at its top, and August darted to it as an old hound dog tried to crawl over the short panel.

"Bruno! You're still around, buddy," August said, and hauled the dog into the room. He held on to Bruno despite his frantic wiggling. "I can't believe this old man is still running around."

"He's not that old," said Ella, ensuring the cat was gone. She came over and rubbed Bruno's head. "He's distinguished!"

Bruno licked her hand, August's face, and everything else within reach of his tongue.

"Good boy." August set the dog on the floor but kept a hand on him. "Down."

Yawning, Bruno growled and circled twice before lying down on the warm kitchen floor at Ella's feet. August ruffled the fur about his neck.

"Never grew into those paws, did you?" he asked.

Ella laughed. "I keep hoping he'll age into dignity and grace, but that may be asking for too much."

"He loses his balance, and you lose your hope," said August. "So poetic."

Ella rolled her eyes. "That's such a silly saying, don't you think? Hope isn't something that can be misplaced or dropped."

August had never really thought of it like that.

"Lady Tremaine says hope is for the weak-willed. Those who want, do," said Ella, putting on a slight accent and dragging out the sounds.

August chuckled at her impersonation. "And what do you think?"

Ella smiled at him. "It's never really gone, is it? We hope and hope and no matter how hard the world tries, it doesn't ever really take all of it from us."

"I certainly hope not," he said, and felt better when she returned his smile. "Lady Tremaine isn't stealing your hope, is she?"

"No, I try not to give anyone that power," she said, and squeezed his shoulder. "And I think I've taken up too much of your time."

"I have some to spare," said August. "Is everything all right?"

"Of course, it's my general worries about everything. Who will be next? When will it happen? What if the memories never return? It's a terrifying amount of uncertainty."

August had similar worries. There was so much at stake, and the guilt of sharing this moment with Ella hit him suddenly. The lingering taste of jam on his tongue soured.

"We'll do our best to figure this out, Ella."

"I know you will," she said softly, and nodded down the road. "And then you'll be off on your next adventure."

A pit settled in his stomach. The rest of her sentence hung silently in the air between them. *And she would still be here.*

"Martin is waiting for me," he said, and cleared his throat, unsure of what to do or say or if he should do anything at all. He watched her closely for any indication that she wanted him to stay, but she gave him none. "I should go."

With only a few days remaining in the investigation, he had to focus.

"Of course. Thank you for your help." She smiled, but it did not reach her eyes.

And despite wanting nothing more than to do the exact opposite, August left.

~ 6 ~

Impossible

UGUST'S MALAISE lasted his entire walk back to town. Monsieur Picard was waiting for him in the middle of the road as he approached town, pacing back and forth so quickly he'd made a dent in the dirt. He stopped when he saw August and crooked a finger at him. August followed.

"It's happened to me," said the baker once they were safely ensconced in his rooms over the bakery.

"You forgot someone!" August tamped down his shock and shook his head. "You weren't mentioned in Blanche's letter, and you haven't said anything."

"Why would I want to tell anyone? He's mine." He paused. "Was mine."

No wonder he had been trying to get August to share information about the memory loss. Monsieur Picard was so private, so singular, that August was surprised all over again and didn't know what to say.

"I don't know. I wouldn't have noticed I forgot

him if I hadn't . . ." He blinked and shook his head. "I've always kept journals, you see, and one of them caught my eye when I was putting the latest up. I keep everything, and I found these letters and sketches in my chest. A lock of hair. Dried wheat stalks. A little bell for a cat's collar. They were old, but they weren't rotting or dusty, and so I went looking back through my diaries. You don't know odd till you find keepsakes you clearly treasured and can't figure out why you loved them."

He shook his head again.

"I learned his name was Immanuel, and he died nearly thirty years ago, when we were still young. We never married, but we were together from fifteen till I put him in the cemetery," said Monsieur Picard, sniffling. The older man wiped his face and took a shuddering breath. "Thing is, I don't know when I forgot him, so I'm as likely to confuse you as I am to help you."

"It's all right," August said, and handed the man his handkerchief. He couldn't help being struck by the fact that love was at the center of Monsieur Picard's story as well. After the crying had lessened and Monsieur Picard seemed ready to continue, August asked, "So no one in Fresne would know Immanuel?"

"Some might if pressed, but not really. I'm older than most of the folks in Fresne. Lord Moreau sent his regards when Immanuel passed. He's done that for every widow and widower since his wife died." Monsieur Picard sniffed again. "I feel like I've lost someone again, even though he's been dead for years."

"May I ask something personal?" August asked, mouth suddenly dry. This was almost exactly the fake scenario he had considered asking his father about a thousand times.

Monsieur Picard snorted. "You may ask."

"Is it better not remembering how much it hurt to lose him the first time?"

Monsieur Picard scoffed, head tilting to the side. "Different kinds of love breed different kinds of grief, none of them good or easier to handle than another."

That wasn't what people had said to August at his mother's funeral. They had uttered condolences with the same mouths that whispered, "Pity he's old enough to remember this."

August had no desire to forget his mother, but sometimes he did want to forget losing her. While things hadn't gotten better since her death, they had changed.

Not better. Different.

He still woke on her birthday and wandered to her quarters with a bouquet of roses the same deep red of her hair and pink of her blush; when in court or listening to the Grand Duke drone on, he still leaned over as if to whisper a joke into her ear before realizing there was no one beside him; and on the worst days, he dreamed of her and woke up thinking she was still there. The grief stopped him in his tracks and took hold of his heart. It wrung a little more joy from his life each time.

"There's no shame in grief or sadness," Monsieur Picard continued, "and there's none at all in wanting to forget. For some, I'm sure this would be better. It's not for me. It's a purgatory. I cannot trust myself to know what I really feel about Immanuel, and I can never find out because he's the only person I could ask. I think those memories of him were a comfort. I want them back."

August nodded. "I'm sorry."

"Don't apologize. Fix it," said Monsieur Picard.

"I'll do my best," said August. "I have a few more questions, if you don't mind. Write down your normal routine. Any and every detail you can think of. Did you do anything different in the last few years, meet anyone new, or receive any items you didn't have before you forgot?"

Monsieur Picard grabbed a dip pen, ink, and a scrap of paper. "Sit, boy. This might take a while."

He wrote down far more than August expected. His notes on his routines were detailed—including monthly visits to the memorial that he had stopped taking several years ago, suggesting that he had lost his memory after Henry and was either the second or third to do so—and he listed everything he had purchased in the past few years that was out of the ordinary.

When August was done speaking with Monsieur Picard, he made his way to the inn to meet Martin. His friend was at a corner table talking animatedly to Oliver Monet, and August lingered a few steps away so as not to interrupt. If romantic love was involved in the memory loss, then this was a bad time to nurture such affections, but he didn't want to crush Martin's heart. The older boy spent so much time taking care of work, August, and his siblings that he rarely focused on himself.

"Most people think birds sing when they're happy, but their communication is a bit more complicated than that," Martin explained to a rapt Oliver. "It can often be territorial in nature."

"Unfortunate," said Oliver. "When I hear a bird singing, I usually stop and listen instead of leave."

This was good. August couldn't stand bird facts anymore after so many years of them.

"Do you sing?" August asked.

Martin spun around, and even Oliver looked chagrined.

"August!" said Martin in the most suspicious tone August had ever heard. "Oliver offered to show me around Fresne, and since I needed to retrace people's steps, it took a while, and I didn't want to discuss the job details since so much of memory loss is personal, so we started talking about birds. How are you?"

August took a seat across from Martin. "I couldn't find anything of importance by checking out the town. We ran into Madame Bardin at the bakery, but she wasn't ready to speak. On my way back from Ella's, Monsieur Picard pulled me aside."

"The baker?" Martin asked. "Why?"

August hesitated, uncertain how much he wanted to reveal to Oliver. He was already involved since his mother had forgotten someone.

"Please keep this between us. Don't even tell your mother," August said.

"Of course," said Oliver, dark eyes widening. He leaned in and whispered, "I won't say a word."

"Monsieur Picard has also forgotten someone, and it falls in line with our working theory." August glanced at Martin and nodded. "He keeps journals, and I would place his forgetting after Henry but before Monsieur Allard."

"Well, that opens the door for others who haven't come forward," Martin said with a sigh. He scribbled something down and slid a sheet of paper over to August. He had taken all their notes and boiled them down to a single chart of facts. There were dates, locations, ages, birthdays, and occupations listed, and he had even included what each person had been wearing and doing when their memory loss was noticed.

Madame Monet had been tutoring a local student. Blaise would usually have been baking, but had taken a break. Madame Renaud, who still refused to talk about her experience, had been seen by a few dozen folks picking up her latest gift for Monsieur Segal from Nathalie. Monsieur Allard had been putting the forget-me-nots on Lady Tremaine's shoes.

Madame Monet's necklace, Blaise's and Madame Bardin's rings, Monsieur Allard's forget-me-nots, and Henry's cane—Monsieur Picard had also noted some odds and ends from Nathalie's shop.

"Is Nathalie the only merchant in town?" August asked.

Oliver nodded. "Unless one comes through, but she fixes things and trades with folks, too. She nearly lost everything opening the store a few years back, but it's taken off now."

Even if it wasn't anything, it was worth looking into.

"Also, this came for you." Martin pulled a thin letter from his pocket. "A courier dropped it off before you arrived."

"Let's see, then." August cracked open the blue wax seal. The paper was iridescent and nearly translucent, as if a thin sheet had been cut from a large pearl. Silvery blue ink glittered in the light. "'I regret to inform you, Your Majesty, that the information I can provide will be of little help. Due to the personal nature of wishes and magic, we reveal information about them only when the person who made the original wish requests it. I can say, however, that while the occurrences you are describing are magical in nature, no fairy has granted a wish in Fresne. Please remember that neither magic nor wishes are simple matters. They leave marks.'"

"What does that mean?" asked Martin.

Oliver pointed to the paper. "Wait—'Your Majesty'?"

"The king wrote a letter to her and sent the response to us," August said, and shook his head. "So, not a wish, but for a letter telling us that she can't say much, she said a few things."

He flipped the letter over, hoping against hope that there was more information, and groaned.

See you in three days was scrawled on the back in his father's hand, the *three* circled and underlined.

"Comforting," Martin mumbled as he checked his pocket watch, flipping the cover open and shut repeatedly.

"What kind of marks does she mean?" Oliver inspected the letter, eyes narrowed in curiosity. "My mother doesn't have any new marks, and I think we would have noticed."

"No, not like that. What was that thing we learned? That was ages ago . . ." August tapped his fingers against the table and closed his eyes, thinking back to their school years. It had been so long ago, and as interesting as he had found the lessons on magic, they had been few and far between. "Wishes channel magic into action, but if there's leftover magic that didn't get used by the wish, then it can leach? Yes, that's it! The leftovers leach into what's around when the wish is made! That leftover magic is much easier to manipulate."

"So you think the memory loss could be caused by excess magic that's leached into Fresne?" Martin asked slowly. "Why memory loss specifically, though?"

August shrugged. "We'll figure it out. With this new information, magically tainted places or items makes sense. Maybe a wish was granted here ages ago, and that's why the letter didn't mention it."

"Wouldn't we notice magical items?" Oliver asked. "I can't even think of anyone in Fresne who's ever seen magic. Would they stand out?"

"They wouldn't, actually," said Martin. "Magic doesn't glow or have a distinct look. It's simply there. Glass holds it quite well. Metal and gems, too. Living things, like plants or even wood, don't."

"Like if your father was granted a wish and your mother was next to him, all the magic the fairy summons isn't used up, so some might leach into the buckle on his belt or her locket," August said.

Her locket . . . it was perfect for that. The rings, too, and the flowers Monsieur Allard had used were made of glass. Henry's cane was wood, but the wolf-head grip was metal. The gloves didn't make sense, though. They were leather.

Still, though, this was at least something they could pursue, even if it proved to be a dead end. Nathalie might have sold or reworked a leached object accidentally and spread the magic around.

He was about to ask if Martin still had the gloves on him when a hand touched his shoulder. "I see you have found my wayward son."

The three of them looked up from the table, and Oliver winced. Madame Monet was standing next to the table, shaking her head at her son. Her locket flickered as she moved.

"Sorry," mumbled Oliver.

"He's been very helpful," said Martin.

"He's supposed to be studying for the university entrance exams," she said, fiddling with her necklace. "I suppose I cannot fault him for helping you."

Martin seemed surprised by this information, and Oliver's cheeks reddened. August was impressed—it was difficult to get accepted to university. Oliver must have been modest about his accomplishments.

"This is going to sound silly, but your locket . . ." August said, and pointed to where she was twisting the chain. "Have you found that having a physical reminder of your husband helps?"

"It's helped, but I think only in the emotional sense," she said slowly, dropping it back to her chest. "It's proof he does love me and that no one is lying about that."

Oliver made a choking sound, and his mother rolled her eyes.

"Yes, yes. You're proof as well, and trustworthy, my little capriccio," she said. "My point is, I don't think it's helped me regain any memories, as I still have none."

"Well, I imagine Nathalie would be happy to make keepsakes for people if necessary," said Oliver, tapping the wooden brooch holding a fresh rose to his shirt. "She made this brooch out of one of my grandfather's old harps. Mother gave her the harp, and she had this done in two weeks. That's what most people do. They bring in old things that don't work anymore and have her fix them up.

"She's nice. She used to travel almost exclusively, but her mentor got mixed up in something illegal, apparently, so she settled in Fresne with barely anything. Cut some deal on rent with the building's owner," said Oliver, shrugging. "I imagine Nathalie is still paying them back."

"Why did she settle in Fresne?" August asked.

"The great-aunt who raised her is buried here. She used to visit that memorial every morning until she got too busy around the shop a few years ago," said Madame Monet. "I would see her walking that way when I went to the Tremaine estate."

The Tremaine estate? It definitely belonged to Ella.

"She continues to threaten to fire me," muttered Oliver, pouting.

His mother clucked her tongue. "To be fair, she did agree to pay *me* for teaching them music, not you. Though she has fired everyone save for Ella. I didn't meet Lady Tremaine until after her late husband passed, but I imagine that was quite the blow, emotionally and financially."

"I've been trying to convince Ella to take a job elsewhere. She's wasted as a scullery maid. You know Ella, though," said Oliver, and it was clear he was frustrated. "She refuses to leave Lady Tremaine's service and won't tell me why. She won't even really talk about it anymore since I've been going over there."

"Dear, you cannot fault her for not wanting to discuss her life. You were hardly friends until recently," Madame Monet said. "The girl doesn't really talk to anyone in town so far as I can tell, and to be honest, for the longest time I thought she was Drizella and Anastasia's older sister."

August twisted his hands together, his vision tunneling to a single point as rage flooded his body.

Scullery maid. No relation.

Oliver huffed, glanced at his mother, and dropped his voice as if Ella or Lady Tremaine would hear them. "She asked me not to say anything about it to anyone, but you visited her there today, right? She does everything—cooking, cleaning, upkeep for the estate, and tailoring all of their clothes. They're running her ragged. I mean, they used to have a cook at least, but they fired her, too. Ella's the only one they haven't gotten rid of."

"They can't get rid of Ella. Why would . . ." August rubbed his face and tried to decide if he should say more. Ella definitely didn't want him to know this, and for some reason, Oliver and his mother had no idea that Ella was Lady Tremaine's stepdaughter.

Monsieur Picard, Monsieur Allard, and Blanche all knew who Ella was, though, but if they didn't know what was going on in the house, then would they assume she was simply taking care of her own estate? They had no reason to visit it or gossip about Ella. But if she was asking people not to talk and hiding things, then something worse was going on than her taking extra work.

"Poor girl never stops to talk much these days," Madame Monet said. "Niceties, yes, but if you ask her about anything, she's off. I'm glad she's been spending time with you."

August had to talk to her and find out what was really happening.

Martin fiddled with his watch, and August caught a glimpse of the time. Nathalie's shop would be open by now.

"Excuse me," he said, and rose. "I have a meeting, but Martin can stay. I'll be back shortly."

Investigation first. Then, he could talk to Ella.

～ 7 ～

Possible

ATHALIE, WHO called herself a trader of trinkets, trifles, and everything in between, had set up shop near the market square. August had learned she was a merchant with a penchant for fiddling with knickknacks and fixing small treasures, and had originally been apprenticed to a merchant who worked throughout the towns of southern Charmant. Travel hadn't agreed with her, though, if the cozy nature of her storefront was any indication. Every shelf, stand, and windowpane was decorated with something for sale—jewelry of every imaginable shade and quality, ornate clocks with mother-of-pearl faces, and rare quill feathers as long as August's forearm.

The work he had done with Martin up until this point had been about finding a pattern, be it in the people, the area, or the records in question. And for whatever reason, the pattern seemed to point to Nathalie's shop.

"I'll be with you in a moment," Nathalie called from her stool at the counter.

August picked up a set of collar pins. Seed pearls were gathered like grapes on the vine along the golden chain connecting them, and a few slivers of green glass glittered in the place of leaves. They wouldn't have been out of place at court.

"Take your time," he said.

It had been a smart idea to open such a place. Before, most people had waited for a relative to travel to the city or for a merchant to travel through every few months if they needed goods. Nathalie seemed to do good business repairing what most would consider beyond saving.

"There we go!" Nathalie said, and whatever she had been working on tolled. "Now, what can I do for you? Purchase, repair, or trade?"

"None of them, though these are all nice," said August, setting down the pins. "I know this will seem like a non sequitur, but I'm here investigating the recent memory loss some people have experienced."

"Oh, I know," she said, grinning. She pushed a pair of large spectacles to the top of her head and patted down her curly silver hair. "I'm happy to say I have all my memories intact, August."

"You know who I am?"

"Gossip moves faster than introductions," she said. "I know everyone who's lost their memories, but I'm not close to them. Not enough to fill in any gaps, at least."

"That's fine. I understand," said August. "You made the locket for Madame Monet?"

"I did," said Nathalie proudly. "Had an old but nice one lying around and found an apprentice to do the portraiture for a good price. Monsieur Monet liked the idea of them having matching keepsakes."

"Well, I think there's something to be said for that." August stepped up to the counter. "It's been really helpful for her to have proof that Monsieur Monet is real and they're in love."

Nathalie caught on and tilted her head side to side. "Doubt Henry Heroux will need a trinket, seeing as I sold him their poesy rings. The Allards, though, have had a rough go of it, and Madame Renaud will come around eventually. I made those gloves she got Monsieur Segal, and she's particular when it comes to things. She had me put steel tips into the fingers of those gloves, you know, to keep him from hammering his thumb again. Should be easy enough to think of something for her."

"The gloves had metal in them?" August asked. That would do it. "That's odd."

"Not if you know her. She values function, so a pair of gloves that would make it harder for her neighbor to hurt himself is the perfect gift so far as she's concerned. She picked out the leather, and I used some of the leftover steel from Henry's cane top," said Nathalie, sighing. "I'd a feeling she was about to meet with rejection, so I tried to talk her out of it when she stopped by to see if I had any nice boxes."

Nathalie kept talking about the process of making the gloves. He glanced behind her at the small shelves of things being repaired, each labeled with a little tag. There was an open door that led out into a narrow alley, and it let in a cool breeze. A few strips of silk and leather rustled on the shelves. An open, unused lockbox kept them from fluttering off.

He didn't want to accuse her of anything with so little evidence.

"Fresne had nothing like this when I was here," August said softly.

"When was that?" she asked, spinning one of her tools in her hand.

"Over a decade ago, when I was a kid," said August, and he nodded to some of the repaired cups on a shelf. "This would have saved me from a talking-to when I shattered my mother's favorite cup."

Nathalie laughed. "That it would've. I can't tell you how many folks I've had come in begging me to repair something quickly so no one knows they broke it."

"You made Blaise's ring, too?" asked August.

"I did!" Nathalie smiled and held up her hands. "With old metal like that, you have to be careful when you're reshaping it. I didn't want to add too much and have it look all patchwork, but I wanted the whole thing to be a keepsake and comfortable to wear around. I think it turned out nicely!"

She lit up when she talked about her process, and it reminded him of how Ella looked when she discussed sewing and embroidery. He hoped Nathalie wasn't truly involved with any of this.

"I know it's a long shot, but does where you bought the ring have anything in common with the leather, Henry's cane, or Madame Monet's locket?"

The tool she had been spinning stopped.

Her gaze cut to something beneath the counter that he couldn't see. "I've been getting things from my usual supplier, who is Lord Moreau, if you must know. He travels far more often than I do, and he brings back all manner of things that he sells to me to remake for Fresne."

That complicated things. Technically, Fresne was a part of the baron's holdings and his responsibility, but he hadn't been the one to request the court's aid.

"And to your knowledge you've never dealt in anything magical?"

Nathalie jolted as if she had been slapped.

"Everyone in Fresne purchases things from me. Has things repaired by me. Sells old pieces to me. I'm the only person here who does such a thing, and it took a while to catch on, but it's going well now," she said, swallowing. "I have what I have and buy what I can to try to create pretty things people can afford. I've never sought out magical items. Wouldn't even know where to get them. If something magical is floating about Fresne, it's not from my store. Definitely not."

August hesitated, and she looked at him desperately, fingers twitching against the counter.

"You understand how even a rumor that my store

could somehow be involved in this could be damaging."

August blinked. "Of course, I completely understand. I assure you our investigation will be discreet." He took a step back. "If you do see anything odd, please let me know. Sometimes magic accidentally gets in places it shouldn't be."

She nodded.

"Do you mind if I buy something? I need a birthday gift."

Her smile returned. "I'd never turn down a paying customer."

Martin's birthday wasn't for four months, but she didn't know that.

August perused the items but kept her face in the corner of his sight. She watched him study the pieces, and as he neared the front of the store, she stiffened. August picked up a ring, and she didn't react. An eyeglass chain. A vase. A bookend.

Then, the collar pins, and her skin blanched.

"These, I think." August carried the pins to the counter. "They're perfect."

Martin would actually love them, but they would have to figure out why they made Nathalie react like that before he wore them on the slim chance these were related to the memory loss. It also seemed love was a necessary factor, and since neither of them was entangled in any sort of romance at the moment— Martin's brief flirtation surely didn't count—that added another layer of safety.

"These old things," she said, laying a hand over them. "Are you sure?"

"Absolutely," he said, flashing his most princely smile. "Using green glass to represent the leaves and the pearls as grapes is gorgeous, and they'll fit right in at court."

She blinked at him and then squared her shoulders. "Let me get something to put them in so they don't tangle."

She slipped from her stool, ducked behind the counter, moved something, by the sound of it, and then reappeared with a small cloth in hand. The rest of their interaction was utterly banal, and August pocketed the collar pins carefully. He left Nathalie's with a smile and glanced back through the open door once he was halfway down the street. She had vanished from behind the counter.

Martin was in the dining hall of the inn, alone this time, and large books took up the entirety of the table. August joined him.

"We have a lot to talk about, but first, I've gotten

you a gift," August said, and laid the pins on the table. "They're a double-edged sword."

"They look like grapevines to me," said Martin, admiring the pearls. "Not that I don't love them, but why did you get them for me?"

"They're from Nathalie's shop, so they're more work for us," said August. "And don't you have a birthday coming up?"

"So, we need to find out where she bought the parts from," said Martin. "I'm guessing these interested you for some reason?"

"She acted like she didn't want me to buy these but would tell me anything about the other pieces," August said, and sighed.

"Here are the town records Blanche gave me," said Martin. "Perhaps they'll help."

August pulled the nearest book to himself and checked to make sure it was the most recent. "Not even tax records are always true, though."

Unfortunately.

August scoured the records for any indication of a sudden windfall or change in fortune. Anything out of the ordinary that couldn't be explained, he took note of. One family started paying their taxes on time, but after he looked into it more, it was clear they had inherited that wealth. There was a year of excellent crop yields, but August knew that had been kingdom-wide. There were no disasters or miracles.

He couldn't resist peeking at the records for Ella's estate, though. Lady Tremaine had neglected to pay taxes after Ella's father had died, citing a mourning period. She had inherited several properties from Ella's father and purchased more that she also paid taxes for, and it looked like she had raised the rent for most of them in the past few years. The estate should have been doing fine financially.

A shadow fell over the book. "What are you doing?"

"Ella!" August snapped the book shut and turned. "What are you doing here?"

Martin snorted. His back creaked in protest, and August realized he had read through most of the day. Ella had her hair bundled up beneath a kerchief, damp strands stuck to her neck, and there was a red flush across her face. She sat down next to them, smelling of lye and lavender.

"Drizella wants poached pears tomorrow as a reward for practicing her music, so I had to come back to town to get some," she said.

"At the inn?" asked Martin, shooting August a look he didn't care to decipher.

"No, but I thought . . ." Her gaze drifted over the records they had been studying and then up to Martin's shirt. She nodded to the collar pins. "Are those new? They're familiar."

"I bought them at Nathalie's shop," August said.

"So, you got the chance to visit her?" Ella asked.

"Everyone who has lost their memories obtained something from her shop. She didn't want to sell the collar pins, either, and she kept glancing behind her counter when I asked about them. She was clearly unnerved by whatever she realized when we were talking.

"The next thing I think we need to do is read Nathalie's ledgers. She said that the baron is her biggest supplier, and I shall follow up on that, but she was not happy about my asking where she got the supplies for those items. I don't think she was entirely truthful."

Softly, Ella asked, "It was the flowers on Stepmother's shoes that did this to Monsieur Allard, wasn't it?"

"Maybe," said August, heart breaking. "We can't know that for sure yet."

Ella's face fell. She took a deep breath, and her lips pursed, the gleam in her eyes shifting from teary to determined. "I'll help. What if I distract her while you two sneak around back?"

"Are you sure?" August asked.

"I am. I want to do this."

They discussed what they would do as they walked to Nathalie's, and August suggested Ella go in while Martin and he went around to listen at the back door of the shop.

"All right," Ella said, nose wrinkled. "I won't push her to share, but I'll try to ask things that might reveal she knows something is wrong. I can't imagine she would have something to do with this. Forgetting loved ones entirely? It's cruel."

August and Martin made their way to the back of the store. Nathalie had opened the small door in the back and was loading empty boxes into a handcart. She counted them up.

Then, glancing around, she pulled a rolled-up slip of paper from her coat and tucked it into one of the boxes. Her hands shook.

"Nathalie?" Ella called from inside the building. "Are you still here?"

"Coming!"

Nathalie bustled into the building, leaving the cart unguarded and the back door open. August hesitated, and Martin nudged him in the back. August held up his hand.

"What can I do for you, Ella?" asked Nathalie, and August heard the scrape of a stool against the floor. "Drizella after a new trinket to draw wealthy, handsome eyes?"

Ella laughed. "Close, but not quite."

With Nathalie distracted, August crept to the cart. Martin followed and kept an eye on the street while August moved toward the letter. Most of the boxes were as empty as they had looked from afar, dinged with little scuffs and nicks from constant use. But in the nearest box sat a pile of papers and small packages under a small cloth purse.

"I've been thinking about Madame Monet and her husband, you know, and how unlucky it is that she lost her memories of him while he's away," said Ella softly, as if more to herself than to Nathalie. Still, her voice carried.

Nathalie hummed, and August heard the tap of her fingers. Her nails caught the wood. "You've always been a kind girl."

August opened the purse. There was a good

amount of money in it—a little more than what he had paid for the collar pins—and a small box no larger than his palm. The box was tied with string he wouldn't be able to undo and retie quickly, so he left it and fished the scroll free. It was little more than a scrap smeared with a hastily written note:

No more.

How utterly unhelpful but so enlightening. Nathalie wasn't pleased with whomever she was sending this note to. Was the money their cut of the sales?

If it was the baron, then would she dare speak so plainly to him?

August flashed the note at Martin, and he made a face. Investigations like this were never easy. August rolled the note back up and replaced it, leaning against the wall so that he could hear inside better. Martin crouched next to him.

". . . something elegant like her mother has, you know that pendant, so that she looks more mature and regal," said Ella. "She mostly only told me moods and said something expensive, so do you have a few things I could show to her?"

August peeked inside through the door, and beyond the small back room, he watched Nathalie's back go ramrod straight.

"Do you have anything that might go well with green emeralds set in gold? They're earrings." Ella leaned away from the counter and looked around. "Green glass, perhaps?"

Nathalie relaxed. "Green glass? Like sea glass?"

"Oh, that would be lovely, especially if it's been shaped into something like a dolphin or flower," said Ella, pacing before a shelf. "Not a fish, though."

"I have just the thing," Nathalie said. She hopped down and scurried after Ella. She pointed to something August couldn't see. "This isn't personal, but it is a lovely piece. Sea glass reshaped to look like a necklace of ivy."

"Oh!" Ella let out a delighted trill. "It looks almost magical! And glitters!"

Martin whispered, "Not that Nathalie would admit to magical conspiracies in this conversation, but that's still a good segue."

August nodded. Ella was clever and kind, and wistfulness pinched his heart.

"I would say good art is a magic all its own," said Nathalie, and Martin's snort distracted August from his thoughts.

"You don't happen to have anything magical, do

you? A powder puff that gets rid of spots? A hair ribbon to prevent hair loss?" said Ella.

She was exquisite, asking things to get them a little more information.

"No, nothing like that. I imagine I'd be the richest person in town if I did."

August leaned forward into the building. The counter was littered with tools and scraps, and a large accounts book rested near the stool. A pair of scissors sat on top of it, and August slowly crept farther into the doorway, stepping lightly so as not to rattle the stool's contents. Nathalie had taken the empty lockbox from the shelf sometime after he left. It was closed and hidden under the counter now.

"Oh!" Ella said. "What's this?"

Nathalie whistled and scurried over to Ella. "Now that's an interesting story . . ."

Nathalie started explaining the history of a cameo. August slunk inside, keeping an eye on Nathalie's back. Ella was facing him, keeping Nathalie's attention on her, and Martin began going through the little crates and baskets used to repair and make trinkets. August went through the accounts stored beneath the counter.

"Well, given the nature of everything, I was thinking I could get something for Lady Tremaine, as well, to remember my father if the worst comes to pass," said Ella. "He gave her the green earrings, you see, and a set might be nice."

"Lady Tremaine?" Nathalie stilled. "You want to buy something for her?"

"Yes, for her."

That was another odd reaction.

"I don't think I have anything in line with Lady Tremaine's tastes," Nathalie said slowly, thinking over each word. "Unfortunately."

"I see." Ella hummed, fingers on a green vase. "I thought her emerald pendant was from you?"

"I—" Nathalie swallowed audibly. "Yes, however, I was lucky with that one, and at the moment I don't think I have anything that would please her."

"She can be so particular, I know," said Ella gently, reaching out to touch Nathalie's arm.

August returned his attention to Nathalie's accounts. The entries looked remarkably accurate, including even his recent purchase of the collar pins. Next to the entry was an odd notation of four unconnected lines, as if someone had drawn an X and removed the center, that he had never seen in any of his accounting lessons. He scanned the last few pages, and her notation system looked like most others he had seen save for that single mark. He couldn't figure out what it meant.

Then he found it again, marking Monsieur Monet's purchase of his wife's locket. Nathalie had recorded every single detail about the sale—the time and cost of using an old locket to create two new necklaces, the price for finding a painter for the portraits, and even the minuscule amount she charged for a decorative box to gift it in. The mark was only next to the final price that Nathalie had charged, and so far as August could tell, it didn't reference any other information she had recorded.

He could find every bit of information about the necklaces except what the mark meant and where Nathalie had purchased the original locket, in fact.

"Martin," August whispered, flipping through the pages and skimming each line. "She records everything about what she repairs, makes, and sells, but look—there's this mark next to the collar pins, the Monets' necklaces, and the gloves Madame Renaud bought. I cannot find it referenced anywhere else, and I also can't find where the pieces she reworked to make them are from."

The pearls and chain from the collar pins, the original locket, and the metal used in the gloves were all unaccounted for.

Martin looked over the accounts, brow furrowing. "I see the sales for Henry's cane and Blaise and Madame Bardin's rings, but I don't see where she got the materials from."

"That's because, unlike everything else she's sold, there's no recording of that," said August. "And she marked those with this notation, too."

"I can guess where the records went." Martin ran a thumb down the center of the book. "There are pages missing."

August yanked the book up and peered into the dip of the spine. Martin was right. August had missed it in his haste to read the entries, but there was a cleanly cut page. August glanced through the earlier pages and found slivers of paper where more pages had been fully removed.

"She was cutting out pages," said August. "That's what the scissors were for."

She had clearly wanted to hide her removal of them. August peeked over the counter. Ella was still distracting Nathalie, but the slant in the woman's shoulders implied it wouldn't work for much longer.

"Every single sale related to the memory loss is marked by this notation, but a few other sales are, too," said August. "We need to find those missing pages and these other items."

The notation marked the sales of the collar pins, the cane, the gloves, the rings, the lockets, something labeled only as *embell.* to Monsieur Allard, a basket for Monsieur Picard, and two odd entries that had no sale prices at all, as if Nathalie had given two items away. Seven sales, two gifts, and nine entries in total with the odd four-line mark.

August placed the book back where it had been and left with Martin. They waited for Ella around the corner. Soon enough, she emerged from the shop with a small ribbon in hand.

"I couldn't leave with nothing," she said. "So, did you find anything?"

"Everyone who lost their memories purchased something from her that she marked with a unique notation, and unlike all her other items, she didn't record where she got those items and their parts. She said that the Baron of Ghent sold her most of what she used from his travels, but she cut out some pages from her accounts. She's hiding something."

Ella sighed, sadly tucking the new ribbon away.

"I was really hoping Nathalie wasn't involved. Maybe it's an accident."

"Maybe," said August, though he was doubtful. "We need to find out more about the baron, I think."

"We can't show up and immediately act as though we suspect him of something," said Martin.

"True," August muttered. "I can still ask for a meeting and see what he says. Ella, what are you doing tomorrow?"

She hesitated. "Some chores. More than usual. Oliver will be teaching my stepsisters, so I'll have the day to get more done."

And Oliver had no idea that Ella was family and not a maid.

"Let me help you with chores." August nudged her gently. "The baron most likely won't get back to us until past noon, and I need a less somber sounding board to discuss Nathalie with."

"Lady Tremaine is the only other noble in the town," said Martin. "It might be useful to talk to her."

August and Ella shook their heads. He wanted to figure out why Ella wasn't telling Oliver who she was, and if the others who did know were privy to how much work she was doing, but he never, ever wanted to speak with Lady Tremaine again after that letter.

"She won't talk to you, and trust me, she doesn't know anything. She never comes into town. She only knows about the memory loss because of Madame Monet," said Ella. She looked at August. "I don't think she knows the Baron of Ghent well, but I could find out? If you want to help me with my errands, I won't stop you."

"I'll see you at dawn, then," August said, and smiled.

There were two mysteries in this town he was determined to solve, and Ella's estate was one of them.

～ 8 ～
Work Song

*D*AWN LOOKED brighter and warmer with the promise of seeing Ella soon. August had spent the evening after Ella left staking out the cart with Nathalie's hidden message, and then Martin had taken his place. No one had come to claim the note while August was there, leaving him plenty of time alone with his thoughts. He had mentally drafted a letter to the Baron of Ghent while waiting and then written it after retiring to his room. On his way to Ella's estate, he dropped it off with Blanche to be given to a messenger. He wanted to talk with the baron soon.

Slowly, Ella's home appeared on the horizon. August touched one of the fruit trees lining the circular path to the front door. The grounds were lush and green. No part of the exterior betrayed financial troubles that would call for reducing the staff.

There was some neglect on the grounds here and

there—overgrown weeds, bags of feed stacked near the side of the house, and limbs leaning a touch too close to the glass windows—but it was the back of the house that revealed the family's financial distress. The goats and chickens were well cared for, though their pens were not. A few poorly cut and nailed patches looked like Ella's handiwork.

August hadn't registered it when he was there yesterday, but now that he was on the lookout for it, it was obvious.

The kitchen door was open. Through it, he could hear Ella bustling about and the pops of a new fire. He knocked the toe of his boots against the little stone step before the doorway, and she spun, a chipped cup clutched in her hands. Her hair was hidden behind a kerchief again, and the skin under her eyes was a now-familiar deep lavender. Her face lit up.

Perhaps their relationship was salvageable.

"What do you need?" he asked, smiling. "I'm at your command."

Ella waved him inside. "I already left their tea and food at their doors and gathered the washing, so while they eat, I need to do laundry."

August glanced around. The kitchen was as he remembered it, but looking closer, he could see the dishwater-gray stains at the knees of Ella's apron as she swished about and tried to hide them. A bucket of water and rags that hadn't been there the day before rested by the door leading up into the house. Was she keeping the whole house clean as well?

"I need to wash the household linens and their clothes," she continued. "Then, the goats need to be moved to a new part of the estate. They keep trying to fight these grebes who've taken up near the pond."

"My friendship with Martin requires me to ask what kind of grebe they are," August said. "He keeps a journal of all the rare birds he spots."

Ella laughed. "I have no idea, but he's welcome to see them before he leaves."

"I can help you with the laundry; then we can deal with the goats. I imagine they'll get us too dirty to touch the linens?" asked August.

"Given Marguerite's love of headbutting people and Jacqueline's mudslinging, good call," said Ella, leading him outside. "Have you ever done laundry?"

"Only when traveling," August said, and followed her. "I doubt you want me to wash your linens in a river."

"I'd like to see Stepmother's reaction to that, but

no," she said. "This is the wet laundry. It takes me ages to move the water myself, so I haven't started on stain removal yet."

They stopped before a small building near the kitchen. One wall had three large copper pots with fires going beneath them, and the other was lined with a wooden counter. A small contraption with two metal rollers stood in a corner and was far less unsettling than the larger, odder version of it in the back. Two carts full of towels and sheets rested near the door.

"Anastasia has been practicing her calligraphy, and she's got ink stains all over her sleeves," said Ella, and she laid an outer dress on the counter. "Put buttermilk on the spots, and once it's soaked, work it out. I'm going to deal with the perfume on Drizella's dress. She spritzes it everywhere."

August got to removing the ink, treating the dress sleeves far more gently than he did his own clothes.

"So," he said softly, "you're running the estate until your stepsisters have their first season and get engaged."

She nodded, rubbing at what looked like a strawberry smashed into a pillowcase.

"What's after that?"

"What?" she asked, and scrubbed at the cloth so furiously strands of pale hair tumbled from her bun. They curled around her flushed cheeks.

"What will you do after they marry?" he asked, and angled his head so he could see her expressions. "You stopped your lessons for them, and you haven't been to court. What do you want to do?"

"Oh, I guess . . ." Her vicious scrubbing subsided. "I'm still quite good at sewing, you know, and while I haven't done anything fancy in some time, I do enjoy it. I think I would like to do that."

"You always had such lovely ideas," he said, nudging her with an elbow. "Dressmaking, then?"

Ella wasn't noble like Lady Tremaine and her daughters, and dressmaking could take her far, especially with the right customers.

"I think. If I could get started, you know. It's quite expensive," said Ella. "I think I would start with friends and family, and then maybe I would open a small stall at the market so that I could sell some pieces. Then, a storefront. Maybe it'll be 'A Stitch in Time,' and I can give every ninth customer a discount or something fun. That's far off, though. I won't be able to afford any of that for a decade at the very least."

"Unless you find a business partner," he said slowly. "Perhaps a mysterious benefactor is out there waiting for you."

Ella rolled her eyes. "Who would make an offer like that to me?"

"To the actual lady of the house, you mean?" asked August. "Oliver Monet thinks you're a scullery maid and doesn't know you're related to Lady Tremaine and your stepsisters. Why did you ask the Monets not to say anything about your homelife to the rest of town? I know they moved here after your father died, but have they never spoken to anyone else in town about you?"

"No, people don't speak of my father often. They know it upsets me. I don't want people gossiping about my family, August, and Oliver's assumptions are hardly my fault." Ella's hands stilled, and her voice cracked. "It's complicated. The estate needs help. If I weren't doing this, then we would be in a much different situation."

"But Lady Tremaine—"

"Is family," said Ella sharply. "She is my stepmother. Her daughters are my stepsisters. They are my only family left, and I will not abandon them."

Like he had abandoned her.

"Do you think they would do the same for you if the positions were reversed?" he pressed.

"I hope they would, but if the positions were reversed, we wouldn't be who we are right now," she said. "I know you think I'm naive, but hoping and seeing the best in people doesn't make me naive. Hope is not the opposite of reality."

Ella took the cleaned dress from his hands and tossed it with hers into one of the copper pots. The water wasn't quite boiling.

August opened his mouth to speak.

"Don't ask me to abandon them," she whispered.

He swallowed his next statement. He watched her throw several more articles of clothing into the pot and stoke the fire. He reached for her, and she didn't pull away. His fingers closed around her wrist.

Pulling her away from the fire, he asked, "What now?"

Ella took a deep breath and closed her eyes. Still, she didn't pull away from him, and he ran his thumb along the calloused edge of her palm. Ella opened her eyes, looked around the room, and shook her head.

"Now, we need to dry the linens I already washed," she said.

August laughed and let his hand fall away from

hers. Right—it was the middle of her workday, so of course she didn't know he was asking what this meant for them.

"With you here, I can use the box mangle," she said, and clapped, grinning. "That will make everything so much easier."

"Use the what?" he asked, and chuckled.

"The box mangle," she said, as if that explained everything. "It mangles boxes."

"Obviously," said August.

"Obviously," she repeated, though her smile cracked slightly.

She had always been like that. Pranks and jokes weren't her thing, but little digs or bits of wordplay were. Dry, his mother had called her once. She was far drier now and clearly trying to move on from their conversation about her family.

She gestured to the machine and waited for him to join her, both brows arched.

Quieter but not gentler.

"You look like you've got two grasshopper legs on your face when you do that," he said.

"You love grasshoppers," she said, and waved away his comment. "Anyway, it takes two people to use this, and I never knew that before. I thought the laundress had to burn the clothes we ran about in."

He laughed. "Any mud you got covered in you came by honestly, with no help from me."

"Sure I did," she said, and grinned. "Now, come over here and help me do this. I tried to make it work alone and asked Nathalie if there was a way to do it, but nothing worked. It will be worlds faster than ironing tablecloths, though, so what we need to do is wring them out with the mangle"—she pointed again at the smaller machine—"and then press them smooth." She nodded at the large machine.

He stared at it. "With the box mangle?"

She nodded.

"I'm sorry," said August, mind reeling. "That's a mangle and that's a mangle, and they look similar but do different things?"

"Obviously," said Ella, and she tried very hard and very clearly to not raise her brows at the same time. She failed and ignored his chuckling. "They're basically the same, except the small one wrings out water and the big one makes dry clothes smooth. So come on."

They set to the laundry like old cats after young mice, persistent and a touch ungraceful. He didn't press her any more about Lady Tremaine, and she didn't ask anything about his mother or how he'd been after that. They talked about everything she had learned since taking over the household, and her tone slowly slipped from guarded to wistful. She talked about wanting a family with more desperation than she ever had before, the way she used to talk about adventuring beyond Fresne. Her dreams were smaller and bigger all at once.

It was painfully relatable. He wanted to be kind and good like she already was. He had been taught how to do so many things deemed necessary for royalty—accounting and statecraft and etiquette—but what could be more important than actively caring about people? When they were young, Martin had told him that princes needed better, more global goals, but August didn't want to be an ambitious king. Anything more and greed might take hold of him, and kingdoms suffered when the greedy ruled. To be a good king and have a family were his greatest dreams.

He couldn't explain all of that to Ella, though, so he described it in terms of helping people through his work.

"Wanting to do right by people and have a family isn't simple or silly," Ella said, picking up an armful of freshly folded towels. "If being kind were easy, everyone would—"

A bloodcurdling yowl cut her off. The cat from the previous day shot into the laundry between Ella's legs, moving so fast it was only a gray smear. Ella shrieked and stumbled, and her foot stomped down near the cat. It clawed her leg and fled through one of windows. Ella ripped her foot off the ground.

And went falling backward into one of the copper pots full of soaking linens.

August lunged, dropping the towels he had been folding, and grabbed her wrists. Ella used his arms to hold herself out of the water, but overcompensated and shifted her weight. They knocked into each other, and he collapsed, her chin smacking into his chest. She fell into his lap with a huff. Her armful of towels covered the floor.

"Ouch," Ella muttered. "Are you all right?"

"Are you?" he asked, raising his head.

Ella's lashes tickled his cheek. She was closer than she'd been in ages, so close he could make out the little indent of her teeth in her bottom lip. Ella had always been beautiful, but up close she was breathtaking. He could make out the little freckles on her nose and the curl stuck to her cheek. He wanted to brush it aside.

He was still holding her wrists, the thin skin warming beneath his own, and she laid her forehead against his shoulder. The odd fluttering in his stomach spread to his heart and stole the air from his lungs. Her breath ruffled his shirt.

She mumbled something against him.

"What?" he asked gently.

She turned her head. He didn't want to let go of her. He wanted to stay like this. He wanted to help her up.

He wanted, more than anything, not to leave her alone ever again.

Ella lifted her head and sighed. "Did the laundry survive?"

The words were ice. Right—laundry.

"I'm afraid not," he said, and let her go.

Tripping over himself trying not to shift while she got off him, August helped her up with the least amount of contact possible. She didn't seem to notice his discomfort, and he didn't say a word about it. Attraction would complicate their already confusing lives.

The laundry room was warm, what with the heated pots and everything.

"The cat." August pointed to the half dozen

muddy paw prints in the doorway, dragged his finger toward the pristine towels covering the floor, and then gestured to the paw prints that continued on the other side of the towels. "That was the one that Bruno was chasing. When did you get a mouser?"

Ella frowned. "We didn't. That was Lucifer."

"The devil?" he asked.

"As good as," Ella muttered darkly. "He's Lady Tremaine's cat and the most miserable creature I have ever met in my entire life."

"A house cat is the worst creature you've ever met? That's bold."

"He's bold!" She stomped and mock-clawed at her face. "Oh! He's a monster! He's always doing things like this and antagonizing poor old Bruno."

A sad woof sounded outside the door, and slowly, a muddy hound dog slunk into the laundry. Ella put her hands on her hips.

"How did this happen?" she asked the dog. "Never mind. I know exactly how it happened. You have to stop letting Lucifer rile you up."

Bruno lay down, tail between his legs as if he understood exactly what she had said, and August grinned.

"Bruno!" August laughed and hefted the old dog

up in his arms. He carried the dog outside and set him down far from the kitchen. "Go shake off somewhere far away, buddy."

Bruno slunk off, and August returned to the laundry.

"That cat was well taken care of," August said when he came back inside. "Bruno's looking a bit worse for wear, though."

He hadn't noticed it before because he hadn't even thought to compare them, but Bruno wasn't just old. He looked like he slept outside.

"There isn't some grand conspiracy afoot," said Ella, dumping the ruined laundry into a pot and grabbing the few towels that were still clean.

"Isn't there?" he asked softly. "People think you work here. People who should know you're Lady Tremaine's daughter are letting you work yourself to the bone for her."

"Letting me?" She whistled and led him back into the main house. "They're not saying anything because, unlike you, they understand that it's embarrassing but necessary."

August winced. She was right—he couldn't understand. They were family. There was no reason for it he could condone. The inside of the house was utterly different than how he remembered. New wallpaper filled in the spaces between the tall windows glittering in the morning light, pristine save for a few inches above where Ella could reach. Portraits of family members he didn't recognize stared down at them. Ella gestured to a small door at the end of the hall.

"Lady Tremaine's study. She only comes in here after supper, and they can't hear us from this side of the house," she said, expression flat. "Come."

"Ella, this isn't . . ." He hesitated in the entry.

She ignored him and opened the door. The study was cold and empty, lacking in any sort of decor. There was no personality beyond the organized desk and two portraits on the wall opposite of the desk.

"Lady Tremaine and Drizella," Ella said, gesturing to them. "Rather mean to leave out Anastasia, if you ask me, but she won't."

She pulled a logbook from the desk.

"Here. See for yourself. We won't survive the year without sacrifice."

August flipped through the book, his stomach sinking. He hadn't meant to drive her to this, but he couldn't leave it alone. The expenses and income of the estate were sobering, and August tried to find the entries from around the death of Ella's father. The book didn't go back that far, but even a year out from his death, the estate's savings were far lower than they should have been. The expenses for Ella became fewer and farther between as he read toward the current day until it was as though the estate had only three family members and one servant.

Ella seemed to have nothing to her name. There were calculations in the expenses to ensure there was plenty of food for three people, but she bought no clothes or anything else that wasn't absolutely necessary. Lady Tremaine didn't seem to consider her part of the household expenses at all.

Every expense, no matter how small, was logged dutifully with an explanation, and every bit of money brought in was written down with a note about where it had come from. Just as they'd learned from the town records, Lady Tremaine had inherited properties in Fresne and collected monthly rents. The rents had been raised in the past few years so that she was collecting more and more, but if August's calculations were right, she shouldn't have been in financial distress. He said as much when pointing out the income.

"She's not pocketing the money. It goes toward her own expenses, which she logs in her personal books," said Ella, tapping a line in the accounts. "This is just for estate records, and Father used to record the rents in here, so she kept doing it to keep everything straight."

"What are these, then?" August asked. "She has seven instances in which she logged herself being paid, but why not put these in her own personal accounts, then?"

The seven sums weren't large, but they were unlabeled.

"She's had her hands full with Drizella and Anastasia, so perhaps she . . ." Ella's voice trailed off as she read through the seven entries. They spanned the last five years. "She sold quite a lot, honestly, to repair and refresh the house after Father died. I helped. Living with everything as he left it was like living with a ghost. These might be from that?"

August swallowed and tried to think of something to say but couldn't.

"My father picked her," she said, still reading. "She's who he picked to be his wife and my mother. He chose her and her daughters. He trusted her. If I don't, what sort of daughter am I?"

Except the break in her voice, the little warble like a dying songbird, was more a plea than a certainty. If the people who were supposed to love her didn't, what did that mean about her? August had never doubted that his father loved him. His family was bombastic in their affection, even in public. He didn't know how to navigate this.

"Not loving you is too difficult to do," he whispered, and hesitated.

She opened her mouth to speak, her eyes bright with unshed tears as she stared up at him, and he shook his head.

The work he had helped with today was barely a dent in her duties if no one worked on the estate. Those responsibilities were far more than any kind of daughter could hope to accomplish.

Ella moved to hand him back the book, but a loud knocking echoed through the house. She shoved the book back and ushered him into the hallway.

"Who would be visiting now?" Ella muttered, half running down the hall. "Come on—Stepmother hates it when lessons are interrupted."

She led him through the house and his own distant memories. The layout was the same, but the colors and portraits were all new and cold. Once, the pale blues and silvers of the house had felt inviting, and August had spent whole summer days investigating the knickknacks Ella's father had collected on his travels. They were all gone, the halls oddly empty of life despite more people living here than ever before. He waited near the front doors while Ella answered them.

"Martin!" She beckoned him inside. "What do you need?"

"I left my post," he said, shooting August a look. Martin had been watching to see who came for the letter, but it was unlikely anyone would during the middle of the day when they were likely to be seen. He knocked the dust from his boots and stepped into the entry hall. "I've received word from the Baron of Ghent. Apparently, he has dinner plans tonight and is heading to the city in the next few days."

"I don't suppose you know who he's dining with?" asked August. They didn't need to meet with him for long. "We could visit him anyway and beg forgiveness after."

"Yes, I'm sure he would love that," Martin said flatly.

August sighed and turned back to Ella. "You've never met him, have you?"

"Oh, no," she said, shaking her head. "Lady Tremaine has met him once or twice, but she mostly keeps to herself."

"Martin, what do you . . . Martin?"

For once, Martin wasn't frowning. His head was tilted back and his eyes were closed. August grinned.

"Developing an appreciation for music?" he asked, and flicked Martin's ear.

"He's giving them an ear for what it should sound like," said Martin, shaking his head. "He's very good."

"He's quite a good tutor, but I don't think he enjoys it as much as playing," Ella said. "They must have left the door open."

A girl was attempting to sing the song now, accompanied by someone else on the flute. Both were too loud.

A soft voice August couldn't make out said something, and Oliver stopped playing. The girls' music trailed off.

"Drizella, why don't you practice your piano while Anastasia sings?" asked Oliver. "That way, you can rest your voice."

"No."

"That's Lady Tremaine," whispered Ella. "She's set on Drizella learning to sing, but the poor girl doesn't have the voice for it. Worse, she would be perfectly fine at piano if she practiced."

Oliver seemed to agree, because he said, "I don't think singing is her forte, but the piano might be."

Martin snorted.

Lady Tremaine let out a loud sigh. "Your mother was in the middle of perfecting Drizella's singing voice."

"I understand that, my lady. However, she cannot continue teaching. Part of a music tutor's job is to ensure that the student is given the best chance for success."

"I know, and I do miss her effort dearly," said Lady Tremaine softly. "There were just certain things she understood, and others she knew she would never understand and simply had to take my word for, like the demands of society upon upcoming ladies. I learned singing and the flute as a girl, and it's important that my daughters, ladies of the court, excel at those. I want to give them the best chance at success, as your mother and I gave you this chance to tutor them."

Ella stiffened.

"My heart flutters at the very thought of what's befallen your mother, and it would be best if you dedicated more time to her care, would it not?" Lady Tremaine asked. A chair scraped against the ground. "Your poor mother, with your father so far away and her mind . . . well, I can't tax your family any longer. I am sure there is another tutor with experience instructing peers."

"Another?" asked Oliver stiffly. "Who?"

"Oh, don't worry about us. Worry about your mother," said Lady Tremaine. "Now, I think this is as good a time as any to call an end to this session. You can treat your mother to an early lunch. Consider it a gift."

That was a cold dismissal.

The door creaked. "Of course, my lady. I shall inform my mother. Good day."

His footsteps hurried away.

"But, Mother!" one of the girls cried. "You said I would learn how to sing. How am I going to do that without a teacher?"

"Shush, Drizella." Lady Tremaine kicked over what sounded like a music stand. "I shall take over your teaching."

"Does that mean I'll learn to sing, too?" the other, Anastasia, asked.

"You will play the flute, dear."

Drizella cackled. "Only pretty girls can sing."

"And yet you are not a great singer yet, are you, my dear?" asked Lady Tremaine in such a venomous tone that even August winced. "I shall play, and we shall start at the beginning."

Ella nudged August and Martin out the front doors.

"We can talk to him outside," she whispered. "Let's not get caught by Lady Tremaine, though."

They waited off to the side of the house and out of sight of any windows. Oliver emerged from the house after a moment, expression stormy. He carried a music book rolled up in one hand.

Ella darted forward. "I'm so sorry!"

"It's hardly your fault." He laughed and caught her in a quick hug. "I can't believe she's letting me go. I know she's strict about what they learn, but this is beyond that." He hesitated, as if not quite sure he should say what he was thinking, and shook his head. "It stings, is all. My mother is already tired of me hovering around her."

Oliver stepped back from Ella and glanced at August and Martin.

At Martin for slightly longer, August noticed.

"Apologies for eavesdropping, but we were with Ella," Martin said, and cleared his throat. "Tragedy befalls everyone at some point."

August winced, and Martin looked as if he wished the floor would collapse beneath him.

"Like you right now?" asked Oliver, his lips falling into a half smile.

Martin nodded.

The front door cracked open, and one of the stepsisters came sprinting down the front steps, a pale pink day dress fluttering behind her. She stumbled to a stop before them. "Wait!"

"Anastasia, what are you doing?" Ella asked. "Lady Tremaine hates it when you end early."

"I told Mother I needed a moment to catch my breath, and she told me I could leave if I wasn't serious," said Anastasia, and then her expression tipped. "I don't have to explain myself to you!"

She turned back to Oliver, ignoring August and Martin completely.

"Thank you for teaching me how to sing," she said uncomfortably, as if the words were utterly unknown to her. "I really did enjoy it."

Oliver smiled tightly. "You're welcome."

"I like it more than the flute," said Anastasia. "Anyway." She gestured to herself, forgetting the flute in her hand, and knocked it against her shoulder.

Her cheeks pinkened. "Enjoy your time with your mother."

Ella narrowed her eyes, and even Oliver waited. Anastasia glanced at both of them.

"What?" she asked.

"Did you come down here to thank him?" Ella asked, and Anastasia nodded. "Well, that's nice."

"I can be nice. You don't know me." Anastasia scowled and crossed her arms over her chest. "You don't know anything."

Ella sighed. "I know Lady Tremaine is going to be in a bad mood now that you've been gone for so long."

"She was going to be in a bad mood today no matter what," Anastasia said, and she tried to look down her nose at the taller girl. "She always is before she sees the baron."

"Lord Moreau?" Ella asked. "The Baron of Ghent?"

"Yes, the old man. She even bought a gift. Didn't you know she was meeting him tonight?" Anastasia looked thrilled to know something no one else did, especially Ella, and she raised one shoulder like a child trying to feign an adult's disinterest. "Anyway, I have to go, and you still haven't brought me my riding dress for tomorrow."

"I shall finish ironing it shortly," said Ella, "but you should get back before Lady Tremaine gets upset."

"Don't tell me what to do," Anastasia said. "Did you really not know? I don't think she told Drizella, either."

She said her sister's name the way an old person in church would utter a curse word, and August muffled another laugh against his shoulder. Anastasia reminded him of the younger girls at court. He wouldn't have been surprised if she was too young to debut this year, even though her mother was pushing it. As bratty as her tone was, it almost sounded put on.

Like one of the wallflowers trying to copy the girl who hated her.

"Ella is too nice for them," August whispered to Martin. "She'd give her last pea to a mouse. She's far too nice for her own good."

"Like you." Martin shrugged. "What good is a single pea to a person? It's much more important and useful to the mouse."

August stared at him. "That was almost hopeful."

"She didn't even tell Drizella?" Ella asked with an exaggerated gasp. "Lady Tremaine must trust you a great deal to tell you that. Did she mention anything else?"

Ella had gotten better at subterfuge since they last met.

"Well, no. Only that this isn't the first time she's visited him and that she got him a gift this time," said Anastasia.

"Lord Moreau must truly enjoy her company."

"I know! He's turned down twenty marriage offers in the last decade, according to Mother, but he's invited her back." Anastasia sniffed. "She didn't tell me why she was meeting him, though."

"Well, maybe she will after tonight," said Ella, and she glanced up the stairs toward the music room.

Anastasia startled and scurried away without another word.

"Why on earth would she be meeting with the baron?" Ella spun to them. "She can't be considering marrying Anastasia or Drizella to him, can she?"

August snorted. No one was that cruel. "Surely, if marriage were the goal, then she would be the bride."

Ella stared sidelong at him.

"We could investigate," said Martin before she could respond.

"Like eavesdropping?" Oliver asked. "Like you definitely weren't doing to me?"

Martin turned away, hand on his chest, and said, "I have no idea what you mean."

"Well, at least we know who his dinner partner is now," said August. "He's always been so reclusive. Why dine with Lady Tremaine?"

"Don't say reclusive like it's an insult," said Ella. "Lord Moreau's perfectly nice. He's just sad. Did you know he had been fighting with the court about his inheritance since he doesn't have an heir?"

August did, thanks to his position on the court. His father had complained about the baron's insistence on not remarrying, until August's mother had passed. He had never brought it up again. The issue of inheritance, though, was the court's latest worry.

"Perhaps there's a way to circumvent needing an invitation to this dinner," said August.

Martin's expression fell. "You mean sneaking in?"

"Is it really necessary to sneak in?" Ella asked.

"Maybe not, but I want to know why Lord Moreau is entertaining Lady Tremaine," said August. Spying seemed like a good place to start, especially if there would be discussions of marriage. Finances always figured into those conversations.

He clapped Martin on the back. "Let's walk around to the side of the house, where no one will interrupt us. You can stay in town with Oliver and find out if anyone ever gets that note and if Nathalie does anything odd, and I'll help Ella with the rest of her work. Then we can find a way into the baron's estate tonight when Lady Tremaine visits him."

Martin lifted his head, an odd brightness to his dark eyes. "That sounds fine, but who's Oliver?"

They all went silent. August yanked his hand back, the very idea of Martin's being affected making him shake. They had only been here a few days, and Martin's feelings were still new. He couldn't have forgotten Oliver.

Oliver chuckled, unsmiling and tense, and shook his head. "That joke's in bad taste, but I'll let it slide since I'm distraught upon my dismissal."

August had never known Martin to joke.

Martin laughed uncomfortably, and August held him back as the others walked ahead.

"It *was* a joke, right?" August asked, gripping Martin's arm tightly.

Martin nodded at Oliver ahead of them. "August, I don't know who that is."

Once, in his first year at school when he had been

a few years younger than the other students, August had tried to get a book from the top shelf in the library and fallen from the top of the ladder. The breath had been knocked so hard from his lungs that he thought he'd never breathe again.

"Martin, we met him days ago," said August. "Do you not remember Oliver Monet?"

"Monet?" He shook his head. "We talked to Madame Monet, but her husband is still traveling, and she lives alone."

August glanced at Oliver and Ella. He wasn't sure he would be able to explain what was happening without being sick.

"By the green tinge to your face, I'm guessing that I forgot him," said Martin, "but it can't be related to love, then. I would have just met him. Did just meet him?"

"At least you remember enough to know you've forgotten someone. My apologies in advance for treating you like a subject and not a friend." August squeezed Martin's arm and let him go. "I need to ask you some questions to confirm what you remember. I bought you collar pins yesterday. Why?"

It took everything within him to stop his voice from breaking. He could not, would not, let emotion make him stumble. He had to see this through. He had to figure out what was causing the memory loss and stop it, for Martin and everyone else, and being upset wouldn't help.

"Because we think Nathalie might be selling the items causing the memory loss," Martin said, and pulled the collar pins from his chest pocket.

"And what did you overhear from Ella's stepsisters' music lesson?"

"Lady Tremaine dismissed the tutor." Martin shook his head. "I don't know who they are, but it's not Madame Monet."

"It's Madame Monet's son."

"Oh," said Martin. "Two people in his life forgot others. That's going to be terrible."

"Focus on yourself for now." August took a deep breath. Oliver and Ella were at the side of the house, heading for a shaded space out of sight from the house's windows. "Come on. No point in putting it off."

August led Martin to them, not quite willing to let his friend go, and Ella looked at him first. She must have recognized his expression.

"What?" Ella asked, eyes wide. "What's happened?"

"Martin wasn't joking," said August, hesitating. He tried to give Oliver as apologetic of a look as possible. "I'm sorry, Oliver. He has no memories of you."

Oliver's face fell and he shook his head.

"That quickly?" she asked.

August nodded. "It would appear so."

"Wait, I thought people were forgetting who they . . ." Ella covered her mouth, her eyes wide.

August shrugged. "Well, we're not completely certain as to why people forget others, but it was our leading theory." August didn't think Oliver would appreciate a lie, anyway, when so much of his life had already been tipped on its head by the memory loss plaguing the town. However, the boy didn't seem to have heard any of it. "Oliver? Are you well?"

"Is it me?" whispered Oliver, eyes wide but unseeing. He opened his mouth a few times, but the sounds got choked up in his throat. The thought had clearly been haunting him. "Did I do this to my mother? To him?"

"No," said Ella, taking his hand in hers. She looked up at August.

"She's right. It's not you," said August, and Oliver closed his eyes in relief. "We were investigating a possible lead, and it was apparently far more likely than we thought. So, this is bad news and good news. You didn't cause anything."

This made talking to the baron all the more urgent. The pins from Nathalie's were somehow connected to this. He let go of Martin and patted his arm. "Perhaps, given everything, you shouldn't join me on this scheme."

Martin huffed but nodded.

Oliver turned to him, an odd expression coming over his face, as if the puzzle pieces were sliding into place. "I'll keep Martin company. We probably should talk and fill in the gaps, shouldn't we, Martin?"

Martin swallowed, speechless. Oliver had recovered from his moment of panic, at least.

"He would love that, and he'll agree when he figures out how to speak again," said August. "Thank you."

Oliver held out his hand to Martin. "Oliver. Pleasure to meet you again."

Martin slowly took his hand. "I hope you don't mind me asking a lot of questions."

"I don't at all," Oliver said, and smiled. "After you."

He offered Martin his arm, and the pair walked back toward town, chatting as if they were old friends and one hadn't forgotten the other entirely.

Unbelievable. August shook his head.

"That's rather cute," said Ella, watching them walk away. "So, I guess we're partners now."

Partners—that was what they had been as children when sneaking burned loaves from Monsieur Picard's bakery or eavesdropping on their parents' plans for their birthdays. He smiled at her, the image of them as children racing through his mind. She didn't grin, but she didn't scowl either. Was she remembering the same antics he was?

"Partners in crime," he said, and she did smile slightly at that. "I can't quite recall the punishment for trespassing."

"Well, if Lady Tremaine is going there tonight, then it doesn't really have to be a crime," said Ella.

"Would she introduce us?" he asked.

Ella gaped at him.

"We're not going to ask her," she said slowly as if she were teaching Bruno a new trick. "I'm going to go get invited, and then we'll figure out what to do with you."

"Oh, of course," he said, and bowed over his arm, gesturing back toward the house. "Teach me how to leave this life of crime behind."

~ 9 ~

Better Together Than in Bad Company

$\mathcal{E}$LLA'S PLAN was simple but elegant: she would attend to Lady Tremaine as a lady's maid, insisting that her favorite dress was too fragile to be worn without someone on hand to fix it, and August would take the place of their usual footman. One of them would surely be able to find out what the meeting was about and, if they were lucky, any further information on the source of the baron's supplies to Nathalie.

"I trust you implicitly, but please remember that I have met the baron before. It would be best if he didn't see me sneaking around." August borrowed a coat from some of the spare clothes left behind at the estate over the years and smartened up as best he could. "I can try to eavesdrop through a window. It's perfect weather for that."

She smacked his hands away and fixed his collar. "Do all court investigators rub elbows with nobility?"

"Some of them *are* nobility," he said, and looked away. He didn't know if there would ever be a good time to tell her he was *the* Prince August. "Usually, it's us rubbing our hands together in the cold, await-ing orders."

"I'll have to make you more mittens," she said, and grinned. "We usually hire a carriage, and the driver, Charles, has committed to not speaking after an ordeal about it with Lady Tremaine. So, you won't mention it, will you?"

Ella and August were waiting with the carriage in front of the château. The driver had stopped before the doors, slumped back, and covered his face with his hat the moment he had arrived. At Ella's question, he raised his hands in mock surrender.

"How could I see anything suspicious when I have my nose in everyone else's business?" he asked. "All I asked was how she was doing!"

Ella patted his arm consolingly.

"Won't Lady Tremaine notice I'm not the foot-man she hired?" August asked.

"Oh, no. She doesn't pay attention to the help, so long as you look and act right," said Ella, nose wrinkling.

August could barely make out the voices on the

other side of the front door, but Ella leapt to attention and dove to open them. Lady Tremaine, Drizella and Anastasia trailing behind her like ducklings, walked through the entryway without even glancing at Ella. She dismissed her daughters with an exasperated look and glided toward the carriage. August bowed his head and opened the door.

"Ella, do hurry up. I cannot be late," she said as Ella shut the front doors of the château. "We already wasted enough time making you look presentable."

Ella, dressed in a neat black dress and white apron, followed her into the carriage with a frown.

"Good luck," August whispered, but condolences would probably have been more relevant. The ride to the baron's estate was a good hour.

For August, that hour passed quickly enough. Dusk fell in a haze of warm purple, softening the cacophony of the countryside to a dull thrum of crickets. He could make out the sounds of Ella adjusting, sewing, or fixing Lady Tremaine's various accoutrements, and he didn't care for the dismissive tone Ella's stepmother took with her. Even if she was pretending to be a handmaid for the evening, no one should speak to another person like that. He was still stewing when they came to a stop on the baron's grounds.

The soot-colored wooden house blended into the evening sky, and candles flickered high in the narrow windows, the glowing glass glaring down upon them. A lone figure stood before the open front door at the top of a wide set of stairs, and August was so taken aback by the breach in protocol he nearly flew off the driver's bench when the carriage stopped. He stumbled down to the ground and opened the door for Lady Tremaine. She emerged with a sniff.

Ella stepped out after her and carefully lifted the bottom of Lady Tremaine's dress from the carriage. Lady Tremaine's gold and porcelain chatelaine clinked, the keys catching on the lace overlay. Ella fixed it before her stepmother even noticed.

Lady Tremaine carried on up the stairs and curtsied, saying loudly, "Monsieur de Ghent, thank you so very dearly for hosting me yet again. There was no need for you to meet me outside on such a night."

The baron, head tilted back to study the sky, shook his head. "It's a pleasant evening. Allow an old man his indulgences—let us not waste time on propriety. Come, eat, and tell me of this opportunity you wish to discuss."

"As you wish," she said. "I think you'll be quite pleased."

They vanished into the large house. The driver of the carriage collapsed back into his seat and was snoring in seconds.

"Now, I'll be inside with her," said Ella, lifting her skirts. "I'm assuming there's a waiting room where I'll be stuffed until she needs me, and I should be able to sneak out or crack the door enough to hear. She's even given me the gift for the baron."

Ella pulled a small box from her pocket. It was wrapped in burgundy velvet and a black silk ribbon. Whatever the gift was, it was no bigger than a pocket watch.

"She had me wrap the box in the carriage, but I couldn't see what was inside. I don't have time to redo it," said Ella, placing it back in her pocket. "However, I shall have to give it to her and should have a good view as to what it is."

"That's good," said August, entranced by how quickly and perfectly her fingers moved.

"What are you going to do?" Ella asked. "You're the only problem left I can think of."

"Tell me what you really think of me, Ella," he said, and her answering smile warmed his heart. "It's a nice night, so the windows will be open. You should go before she notices you're still here."

All places like this had the same general layout. There would be a plethora of windows overlooking a courtyard or garden that he could spy through. The whole point of countryside estates was to see the country.

She nodded. "I'll talk to the servants, too. See what they have to say about the baron and if they have information on what he sells to Nathalie."

She ran off to the servants' entrance. Sure enough, the main building was surrounded by meticulously kept gardens of climbing roses and fragrant lilies. A kitchen protruded from the back of the house, and August quietly walked around it to the back of the estate, pausing near one of the open doors. The dining hall was on the second story of the château right above them and had a large balcony leading off it—August could only just see inside if he stood on tiptoe a few steps back from the balcony. The glass doors were thrown open to let in the evening air and let out the voices of the occupants. The balcony was far too bright and open for him to hide there. From the ground, however, August couldn't hear them.

But two smaller balconies extended on either side of the larger one, both leading to brightly lit rooms, and a small handkerchief embroidered with roses hung from the window on the right.

A few workers passed through the gardens, carrying trays to a stairwell that must have led to the dining hall. He tried to stay in the shadows, keeping his pale clothes out of the light, where he'd glow like a ghost, and climbed over the hedges separating the path from the side of the house. He picked up a small twig and threw it at the window. It clinked against the glass.

A slender hand snaked out of the window, and Ella pointed toward the opposite balcony. That one must have been the safe one. Ella's pointing grew more frantic.

He waited for the area around him to clear and then darted over to the other side of the dining room balcony and shinnied up the wall. August peeked onto the small balcony. It was washed in light from the brightly lit room connected to it, but that room was blessedly empty. That didn't mean it would stay that way, though.

He climbed onto the balcony and lay down on the very edge of it. Anyone who walked into the room would be able to see him, but no one walking below would.

". . . self-evident," Lady Tremaine was saying in the dining room. "I hear your cousin has had some recent issues, small issues, with gambling debts?"

The baron huffed. "I know I said no propriety, but you do cut to the heart of things, don't you?"

"I find clarity more beneficial than subterfuge," said Lady Tremaine. Silverware clinked against porcelain. "You were traveling recently, were you not? That's dangerous for someone without an heir."

The baron laughed, and it sounded like he took a drink. "I enjoy travel and riding. They are invigorating, and if I avoided anything and everything that could kill me, then I would hardly be living. I enjoy seeing the craft and artistry of other provinces as it develops. Do you travel much, madame?"

"No, I'm afraid not, though I am sure my daughters wish we would," said Lady Tremaine. "My eldest, Drizella, is quite fond of art."

"What kinds of art does she prefer?" the baron asked. "I recall your playing the flute."

"Oh, I had hoped no one recalled such a thing," said Lady Tremaine with a delicate laugh, but having heard her several times with Ella, August didn't think it was sincere. "Drizella prefers singing, but she is a quite accomplished flutist."

"I have always been thankful that the Monets returned to Fresne. But such a tragedy to have befallen them," the baron said gently.

"Yes, it has been very inconvenient." Lady Tremaine's glass clinked against the table. "You haven't been affected, have you, my lord?"

"No, thankfully my household hasn't been affected, and I must admit that I have no one to forget. Yet," he said quickly. "The court sent investigators, however, so hopefully it will be handled soon. I shall be traveling to the city soon and shall be able to speak with His Majesty about it as well."

He didn't sound like he wanted to stall the investigation. So why had he declined to meet with them and instead hosted this dinner?

"I see," said Lady Tremaine, voice becoming far more friendly. "Do you go to court often?"

"Only when it's necessary," the baron said. "I enjoy my solitude, and the hunting is better here."

"My Drizella finds hunting such an impressive undertaking," said Lady Tremaine. "She adores riding."

"Do you?" the baron asked.

Lady Tremaine laughed. "I'm happy to indulge my daughter."

The pair exchanged pleasantries after that. The

baron had plenty of interesting stories about his decades of traveling, but none of them hinted at magical items or his late wife. August had met the man only a few times before, but he was certain that Lord Moreau had traveled the whole kingdom *with* his wife, not alone.

Stranger, though, he and Lady Tremaine seemed to be talking around each other. Every time the baron tried to ask about her interests and life, she provided a new hyperbolic detail about Drizella. The baron was becoming frustrated by the lack of answers to his actual questions, by the sound of it. He rose with a rattling at the end of the meal.

"I am curious," he said. "After everything, you are amenable to marriage?"

"Well, my opinion is hardly the most relevant," said Lady Tremaine. "You need a wife, and eventually an heir, whom you can trust to care for your estate and family name when you are gone, not some distant cousin you have never met."

"A good if blunt point." A chair scraped against the floor. "Come, madame. Let us take a turn about the gardens. I'll hear out the proposal you wrote me of, and we shall talk."

The side chamber's door began to open, and

August rolled off the balcony. He landed face down in the dirt, air knocked out of him, and groaned. That hadn't been silent.

He peeked over the hedge toward the path. A pair of scullery maids were hurrying away in the distance, but they didn't seem to have noticed him.

The real question was where in the gardens he could hide so he could hear the rest of the baron's conversation.

August ran to the shadows beneath Ella's window. Through the opening, he heard a door slam.

"Your sewing leaves much to be desired!" hissed Lady Tremaine. "It ripped in the middle of dinner. I haven't been able to lift my arm all night."

"I warned you it was too fragile to hold," Ella said.

"Does that statement fix your mistake?" Lady Tremaine asked.

August scowled. Lady Tremaine walked the line between truthful and hurtful with practiced steps.

"There," said Ella. "Seam repaired, but take short strides. Since I didn't make this dress, I have no idea how strong the beading on the bodice is."

Lady Tremaine sniffed. "Stay."

Like Ella was a dog.

August began his search for a path into the gardens. There was another set of doors on the west wing of the house, and they led out to a large fountain. The gardens were on the wilder side, though a hip-high hedge maze separated the château from the woods out back. Two silhouettes appeared at the doors. August crouched down a little way into the maze, making sure he wasn't at a dead end.

The baron offered Lady Tremaine his arm. "I suspect that you are about to propose marriage?"

"Astute as always," said Lady Tremaine. "Why not? It makes perfect sense—you need an heir, and Drizella needs a husband."

The baron spluttered and stumbled. "Her? I . . . Forgive me, I was under the impression that you were proposing that *we* marry."

"What?"

"You wish for me to marry your daughter?" He made a sound not unlike gagging. "She's a child."

"She's about to debut!" Lady Tremaine said with a gasp. "She is young and educated and lovely, and she would make anyone, even you, a lovely wife."

"I do not know her. I know you," he said. "I cannot believe your daughter would agree to this."

"Drizella would consider herself lucky to be

married to a man of such standing." The rest of Lady Tremaine's response was covered up by a gust of wind through the flowers.

The baron scoffed. "My standing will not keep her company when she is thirty and I am long dead."

"No, it won't," said Lady Tremaine, "but she will not be dead, and you will have your inheritance protected. Your legacy will persist."

"Does your daughter wish to marry someone, or does she wish to inherit my title?"

"Please," said Lady Tremaine. "Let us not pretend either of us is a stranger to a marriage of convenience."

"I certainly am," the baron said. "I had thought you were as well."

"Interesting to see young Ella isn't the only one playing pretend tonight," said someone quietly behind August.

He froze.

"No need to run. Young Ella's already wooed the staff and learned a great deal more about my lord's personal affairs than I'm sure he would be comfortable with, but I'm uncertain as to whether she is working with Lady Tremaine or you. Turn around, please."

August did. An older man with silver hair and narrowed eyes, wearing a plain all-black suit, sat on a low bench with a cane across his legs.

"I'm René Castillon, my lord's butler," said the man, frowning. "Though you, I'm unsure of."

"I'm August. I'm investigating the memory loss in the town."

"The lads who wrote. Yes. My lord was confused as to why you wished to speak with him, but you must have a good explanation for this?" Monsieur Castillon gestured to the garden and looked August over. He sighed when August nodded. "Come on, then."

Monsieur Castillon led August to a more secluded part of the garden nearer to the road.

"Why did you feel the need to do this?" he asked August. "And why is Ella pretending to be a lady's maid? One of Lady Tremaine's plots?"

"Ella couldn't muster ill will if her life depended on it. She's simply doing Lady Tremaine a favor tonight," August said, and snorted. "As for me, I was left with no choice but to visit unannounced when Lord Moreau refused my invitation, and you see, another has lost their memories—my traveling companion."

"That's the first we've heard of a traveler being afflicted." Monsieur Castillon's eyes sharpened with surprise.

"It has increased the alarm around needing to bring this investigation to a close. We've traced the items we believe are causing the memory loss, and Lord Moreau might have some information on them."

To August's surprise, the man flushed. "I fear my lord did not reject your invitation. I did."

"Why?" August asked, and tried to school his face to keep his shock from showing.

"My lord is a private man." Monsieur Castillon glanced around despite the darkness, and he rubbed his jaw. "He wouldn't want anyone to know if he were aware of it, and I wanted to protect him."

"Protect him from what?" August asked, leaning in slightly.

"He's been acting odd," said Monsieur Castillon, and he rubbed his knee. "I thought he took these meetings with Lady Tremaine because he found them humorous, but I realized he was taking the proposition seriously after the last one. He never did before. He swore off remarrying."

August exhaled, saddened that he was right. "You think he forgot his late wife?"

"He did, but when I attempted to speak with him about it, he grew quite upset," Monsieur Castillon said. "The other staff and I confirmed a few days ago what had happened, but given his acceptance of Lady Tremaine's approach and the pressure from the court recently—"

"You feared others would take advantage of his vulnerability, so you kept it a secret," August said. This changed a few things. "That's very understandable, but in order to help him, I need to know several things. Do you know when he forgot?"

"It's difficult to say. He already did not speak of my lady often," said Monsieur Castillon, shaking his head. "If I had to pick a date, I would place it sometime between his first and second meeting with Lady Tremaine, a month or so ago. I didn't suspect anything until he agreed to tonight, but he would not have humored her if he wasn't going to marry her."

That would place him between Madame Monet and Martin. The time line truly was accelerating.

"And has he supplied anything to Nathalie recently, or received anything from her?"

"Nathalie? He has plenty of things she's made over the years. Why?" asked Monsieur Castillon.

August couldn't think of a way to prevent

suspicion. "Nathalie sold several items of untraceable origins recently, and everyone who lost their memories had one."

"He's not her sole supplier, and frankly, he's been traveling less, so she's turned to others." Monsieur Castillon glanced back toward the house, and his fingers tapped along the top of his cane. "She's repaired a number of curiosities for his curio as well."

"Tonight, Lady Tremaine gifted him something," said August. "I was hoping to see what it was."

"Yes, her second gift," he said, pensive. "Meet me at the carriage."

The older man hustled back into the house through a side door, and August returned to a snoring Charles at the carriage. Servants were bustling about and whispering. Distantly, he thought he could hear Lady Tremaine shouting.

Monsieur Castillon returned a few moments later with a box in one hand.

"He refused it since he refused her offer of marriage to Drizella." Monsieur Castillon gave the unwrapped box to August. "I admit that the piece is familiar, but I do not think it is one my lord sold Nathalie. Lady Tremaine's first gift to him, a glass brooch that he adores, was not something he sold to

Nathalie, either. It is not familiar to me at all, though."

August opened the small box. A brooch of gold stamped with a falcon in flight rested on a black velvet cushion, and it looked familiar to August, too. So many families used birds in their heraldry.

"I don't suppose I could see the glass one?" he asked. "Did Lady Tremaine ask for it back?"

"She would never be so uncouth. It is in my lord's closet, and he would notice if it went missing. I shall try to convince him to speak with you and part with it for a time. He's fond of Nathalie. If she did know of this, he'll be devastated."

Monsieur Castillon left August at the carriage, and August sat on the back step, trying to figure out where he knew the falcon from. It wasn't newly forged. The gold was of good quality but old, and the falcon wasn't on a field, which was unusual for heraldry.

"August!" Ella came striding out of the side door. She caught his collar with one hand and held out her other, two small tarts clasped in it. "Try one. They're divine. Louisa is a lovely cook and gave me some. Also, I saw the gift!"

"So did I," he said, taking one of the tarts.

"How did you see it? Lord Moreau's butler took

it from me." She popped the other tart into her mouth, closed her eyes, and sighed. "I love blue plums."

In that moment, August would have bought her every blue plum in the world.

"You should have eaten the other one, too," he said, cheeks flushing.

Ella cracked open one eye and pursed her lips, whispering, "I ate five."

He grinned, and she laughed. It was the first time she had laughed—loud and uncontrollably—since they had reunited, and it made something deep in his chest tighten. She sounded so happy.

"Ella." August grinned.

"We make a good team." She smiled up at him. "So, the brooch?"

"Here," he said, and showed her the falcon brooch. "The butler gave it to me. Do you recognize it?"

"Not really. I couldn't do anything more than peek at it inside." She turned it over in her hands. "You should ask Blanche about it. She knows everyone in Fresne and all of the old family sigils."

The realization shot through August with a shiver—the Fauconnier family.

The front doors to the château opened again. Lady Tremaine and the baron emerged, making their way to the carriage. August slid into position, and Ella stepped aside. She glanced at him.

"It's Blanche's," he mouthed as the baron helped Lady Tremaine into the carriage. Her family had been falconers before they owned the inn. It was her last name. How could he not have seen it?

Ella's eyes widened.

August could picture it clear as day in his mind. Ella's teary eyes gleaming in the sunlight as she stared up at the statue protecting Fresne's cemetery and clutching a crown of flowers in her hands. She had pointed to a thick gold cuff on the statue's spear, and he had been so overwhelmed with the sight of that statue glittering with grief-soaked trinkets that he had closed his eyes. She said it had taken Blanche years to decide what keepsake she felt right leaving at the memorial. He hadn't understood that at all. He had known instantly.

The cuff had been there long before August's mother had died.

Until someone had stolen it and supplied it to Nathalie, who had used the falcon for a brooch and then sold it to Lady Tremaine.

The Good Little Mouse

AUGUST OFFERED a stunned Ella his hand to help her into the carriage, but before she could take so much as a step, Lady Tremaine grabbed the door and shut it.

"Move!" She stomped.

Charles glanced back at Ella and August still waiting on the lawn.

"Lady Tremaine?" Ella asked.

"So help me, boy, if you do not get this carriage moving in the next breath," said Lady Tremaine, reaching through the window and motioning for Charles to leave.

The carriage took off. Ella seemed to wither, sinking in on herself with an exhale, and August offered her his arm. August's fury cut through his confusion like a blade.

"Come on," he whispered. "We need to see the statue to prove the falcon cuff is gone, and it's a shorter walk to the cemetery from here than from your home, anyway."

"She's doing us a favor leaving, then." She laughed hollowly and took his arm.

August would be leaving her again soon. Given how thoroughly she had isolated herself from the rest of Fresne, she would be all alone with Lady Tremaine and her stepsisters. The idea crept over him like an icy chill. One more day—that was all the time he had left with her.

"Her mood is no excuse," said August. "Has she done anything like this before?"

"No, she's never left me anywhere," she said, and glanced up at him. When she caught sight of his scowl, she leaned against him and sighed. "She's never taken me anywhere, either. We don't really go places, and she's very strict with Drizella and Anastasia. She doesn't leave them alone for long."

August could believe that. She seemed controlling, desperately pushing her daughters to pursue what she wanted. There was a special kind of hurt in that, which August knew well. Being royalty came with expectations and little room for change—though it also came with plenty of privileges—but his father still supported him, even when they didn't agree.

They started walking to the cemetery. The night was warm and thrumming with the songs of hungry owls and rustling field mice. The road back to town was winding and far too long to take on foot, so August tugged her into one of the barley fields alongside the road. Cutting through it and its neighbors would get them closer to the southern hills they had played in as children. Ella let her head fall back to study the stars as they carried on.

August tried to smother the warm feeling her closeness awoke in his skin. He tried to ignore the brush of her hair against his nose. He tried to think about anything other than the comfortable feeling of her tucked against his side.

And failed at it all.

He sighed, and he tried to think of what to say, of how to convince her to leave. She deserved better.

Ella looked at him, eyes narrowed, and shook her head.

"I know that look. Are you going to try to talk me into leaving?" she asked. "Leave my family. Leave Fresne. Leave my problems, but no one ever asks me what I want and if I want to leave. I can't imagine wanting to leave. No adventure could be as comforting as my childhood home."

She slipped from his grip and turned to face him, walking backward.

"I know every step, nook, and secret in that house. I know that the hallway rug feels softer underfoot than the entry one, and that if I open the door to the study while lifting it slightly, then it won't squeak. I know how many mice live in the walls and which one is coming to steal my crumbs based on the sound of their little feet," she said, smiling up at the night sky. "I know Fresne better than I know myself. Why would I ever want to leave?"

She walked with an assurance he had never possessed back home, and a loving, gentle envy seeped into his chest. She was right—it wasn't fair to ask that of her.

"Blanche walks around town every morning, and she calls it a constitutional, but it's so she can clean up anything on the roads before everyone else is up and traveling. Picard will hem and haw about his 'wayward apprentice and his newfangled ideas,' but he'll taste every single experiment that boy bakes, even the ones with almonds. He hates almonds." Ella laughed and shrugged, throwing her arms out. "And Oliver, clever and kind and bored because he's far too smart for the work he's doing, will return to Fresne after university because he doesn't want to leave his parents.

"And most importantly," she said, "I know that next we'll be walking through a beautiful lavender field with a little stone bench on one side where people can sit to take in the sight. The farmer who owns it says he didn't put it there, but he did."

"If you wanted to take in the sights, you only had to say so." August followed after her, plucking a fallen twig and twirling it in his fingers. "You shouldn't have to leave to feel safe."

But if she didn't, what future awaited them? With him in the city and her in Fresne, they would only be able to visit occasionally. They could write constantly; the day of travel was nothing for messages even if it made meeting when not working frustrating, and perhaps it could be like when they were younger.

She tucked her hair behind her ear, close enough to touch yet still so far. His chest went cold.

Ella reached out and touched his arm. "You're staring."

"At where you should be staring," he said, smiling. "You're about to trip."

Ella hesitated, heel a hairsbreadth from a stone.

"Once upon a time," she said, "you would have let me fall."

"Once upon a time, I was a child with a child's sense of humor," said August. "I'm not that August anymore."

He didn't want things to be like they were before.

"What do you hope will happen if you stay?" he asked, curious as to what Ella wanted.

"If I stay? That's easy," she said. "Drizella will spend tomorrow in bed crying about how her mother promised her the baron despite Lady Tremaine never having done that, and Lady Tremaine will say that the baron is not worthy of her. Drizella will demand hot chocolate for her nerves. But she'll forget to drink the chocolate."

Ella winked at him.

"I'll drink it. Then, everything will repeat. Lady Tremaine will find someone else to offer her daughters to, and eventually, someone will agree. It's not as if Drizella and Anastasia are devoid of good qualities; she's nurturing the bad ones. Lady Tremaine will spend far too much on Drizella's wedding and only too much on Anastasia's, and Anastasia will notice. She won't say anything, but she will be nice to me while I comfort her. Then, they'll be off with their new families."

He waved the twig on her right, and she stepped

over the little hill of earth marking the start of the next field. Then, without looking or waiting for input from him, she perfectly navigated to a small makeshift bench overlooking the rustling lavender behind her.

"Lady Tremaine doesn't care for the country. She'll want to leave the moment she can, and I shall not go with her," said Ella, collapsing onto the bench. "For now, I shall endure, and eventually, I shall be in Fresne without my stepmother. I'll be able to get work with the tailor or start doing specialty embroidery for people. I might be able to have a relationship with my stepsisters. Perhaps even Stepmother. I think distance will make our relationships easier."

August sat next to her. "You shouldn't have to endure anything, though."

"It's really not that bad," she said. "It could certainly be worse."

If *this* wasn't that bad, what would Ella put up with, and what had she already endured to make this acceptable?

She reached one hand out to brush the lavender blooms and let a cricket crawl into her palm before it jumped away.

"When my father and Lady Tremaine got married, he made me promise to treat them like family.

And that means not giving up on our new family even when it gets hard. I won't break that promise."

"All right," August said, even though he wanted to ask if they were trying at all to treat her like family.

He had tried a few times, and it wasn't his place to do anything more. She could be right about all of it. All he could do now was offer an escape if she ever did need it.

"You know you can write and ask me to return, and I shall."

Ella went still. Her eyes fluttered shut, and August worried that he shouldn't have brought it up.

"Would you have come back then? I know you offered to, but everyone offers to do things," she whispered. "They don't always mean it, especially when they're a child who couldn't even stand to return to the town their mother was buried in."

She turned slightly, staring at him from the corner of her eye, and August flinched.

He *hadn't* wanted to return to Fresne. He hadn't wanted to face the cemetery or the statue or his mother's grave, and looking back, he hadn't tried very hard to find out if she really wanted him to stay away.

"You did ask me to stay away," he said slowly. "Though, you are right—I didn't really want to return to Fresne. I would have, but I shouldn't have made you ask that of me."

"And I should have said what I wanted." She sighed. "Children aren't great at communicating."

He laughed. "No, we were not, but we're not children anymore."

"True."

"Ella," he said, and turned to face her. There were stars in her eyes, flickering as she met his gaze. "I don't want us to lose touch again. Whether that is visiting or writing letters or both."

She nodded, nudged him to turn back so that they were both facing the field, and laid her head on his shoulder. "I knew if I pushed and asked, you would come. Even when we hadn't written in years, I knew you would still answer. I'm sorry that I didn't answer you. I won't do that again. I do want to see you again. I don't want to simply write letters. I want this."

August took in the horizon, the weight of Ella tucked into his side unfamiliar but comforting, and rested his head against hers. She threaded her arm through his.

"What will you do when you leave?" she asked.

August hummed, tempted to say *Solve this issue*

and then move on to the next one, but the night called for honesty. "Fight with my father."

Ella startled. "What? Why?"

"He is desperate for more family, and I am his only avenue for that," said August. "So I've taken any and every job I can these last few years to avoid going home, because I don't want to marry and love and then end up like him when they die."

"August," she whispered, "that's not how . . . Do you not want to fall in love?"

"Oh, no, I do. The fear isn't really that strong anymore, honestly. I have been avoiding it for a while, but it's much easier to solve everyone else's problems and pretend I don't have any."

"Until you have to go home," she said.

He squeezed her arm. "Until I have to go home."

Ella took a deep breath and withdrew her arm from his, squaring her shoulders toward the stars. "Well, the first step for both of us, then, is to stop avoiding our fears."

She held out her hand, and August took it without hesitation. Together, they rose.

"Agreed," he said, tightening his grip on her hand. "No more avoiding anything, though I would say this conversation was necessary."

Hand still in his, she glanced back over her shoulder and smiled. "I look forward to when the mouse plays start arriving."

Night had fully sunk over the fields, and it settled around August like a shield. They could do this. They could mean something to each other again.

"I fear I'm a retired playwright," he said, and brought her hand to his mouth. "I still have all of your letters and those mittens."

It wasn't a kiss—her skin never touched his lips—but it was a promise. She stumbled and nodded. He placed her hand back at her side.

They walked slowly. The night was quiet and still, the chirps of birds and crickets a distant dirge. Neither spoke. August tried not to think of the memorial statue standing empty-handed in the night. His mother's bracelet gone. Every token of joy and sadness ripped from Fresne like the memories had been.

He knew Ella was thinking of the same thing. She had left her father's pocket watch there. Would anything be left of it?

Soon enough, the white stone of the statue guarding the front of the cemetery came into view. They looked alive at night, every ripple of moonlight granting their hands movement and glittering across the goods draped over them. August froze, a hot and sticky taste like vomit coating his tongue, and Ella grabbed his hand. The memory was fuzzy, their conversation lost to time and grief. Unwanted images overtook him.

Ella, small as a mouse, clutched a crown of purple and white flowers to her chest. August swallowed as the heady floral scent drifted over him, and the wind upset a necklace dangling from the statue's neck. Gold and silver glinted in the painfully bright light as the morning sun overtook the Fresne memorial, and his gaze stuck to a pair of glass flowers resting atop a steel box at the soldier's feet. They reminded him of the heavy, heavy bracelet in his hands. It took him ages, long after Ella crowned the statue and left, to look away. He couldn't remember how long he lingered or what he said as he raged against how unfair it was.

Only that he had left his mother's bracelet on the statue's wrist.

"We can do this," she said, squeezing his hand and interrupting his thoughts. "I remember seeing a gold chain, a necklace of seed pearls, and two enameled boxes, and I left my father's pocket watch. Blanche left the cuff on the soldier's spear."

August swallowed. "The pearl necklace broke,

and there was a steel lockbox at the statue's feet. You used it to reach the statue's helm."

They approached the statue together. There were little purses and boxes, each of them closed, at the statue's feet, protecting their items from the elements. Withered flowers and rotting cloth fluttered from the soldier's arms. August's gaze rose to the soldier's wrist. It was bare.

The words wouldn't come. They stuck in his throat, sharp as knives, and his chest tightened. He had, foolishly, thought that one day he might return for his mother's bracelet, but that choice had been taken from him. He wouldn't be able to keep his promise to his mother.

"His watch isn't here," Ella said, slipping away from August and pacing around the statue. "There isn't much on the ground, either. That's where most things would have fallen. It would make sense for some things to go missing, to be taken by nature, but not everything."

August leaned forward and opened one of the purses—empty save for one coin to weigh it down. Fury filled the hole in his heart.

"Someone stole the offerings," he spat. "They stole everything!"

"Who would . . ." Ella touched the statue's empty hand and swallowed. "No one in Fresne would do this."

This was the worst wound of all—everyone in Fresne knew how beloved the memorial was and the unspoken rule of leaving it undisturbed. No one would dare steal from it.

Yet someone had.

"They weren't even careful," said August.

Ella sniffed and wiped her face. "How did no one notice? The bracelet, the necklaces, the pocket watch—those aren't things that just fly off in a gust of wind."

"Whoever did this probably did it slowly," August said, checking every box to be sure. "I bet they started small, and then as time went on and no one noticed, they got more confident. Was your father's watch engraved?"

"Only with a date. My birthday," said Ella. "I don't know if Nathalie would recognize it. She might not recognize any of it, since she's not from Fresne."

So maybe she wasn't aware. But then why not say so?

"The cuff wasn't changed that much, but the locket was fairly common and split in half. The rings and wolf head were probably melted down from other objects." August touched a threadbare cloak hanging from the statue's shoulders. "With all the wear on some of the items, I bet Nathalie had to entirely rework some, and no one would go into her store looking for the objects left at the memorial. If they saw something similar, would they even say anything? Or would they assume it was grief making them see things?"

"For a while, every pocket watch I saw made me cry, so I avoided looking at them. I don't know if I would have noticed anyone using my father's until recently."

August nodded. "I would only recognize my mother's bracelet because it's unique—as a bracelet. If the glass beads were split among several things, I might not."

Even though he wanted to think he would, he had seen dozens of glass beads in earrings and necklaces over the years and never once even considered it. It wasn't far-fetched that no one would recognize their offerings to the memorial.

"Maybe the stealing is what did this," he muttered. "Maybe the memory loss is a punishment for stealing from the memorial or something."

Ella stared up at him. "Is that possible?"

"Maybe," August said slowly. "The memorial

stood for centuries, collecting trinkets and prayers and probably wishes from the grieving. Maybe enough magic had settled in and around the memorial over the years to affect people."

"Then, would returning them end this?" she asked. "We could do that, I bet. We can try to make a list of everything that's been left here in the last twenty years or so, but that will take time."

"Any solution will take time," said August, reaching out to take her hand. "But no matter how long or how difficult, we'll get the items and memories back. We have a good lead now. We can do this."

~ 11 ~
So Little Time

HE NEXT morning dawned red and late, licking at the dark edges of the sky like flames. August hadn't slept a wink. He had tossed and turned all night before giving up entirely, and it had taken all his self-restraint not to wake Martin up so they could speak more. He had told Martin everything once he returned, and they had agreed to watch the memorial and Nathalie the next day. Today.

Their last day in Fresne.

August's time was up. They had only just figured out that the items causing the memory loss were from the memorial. There was still so much left to do—figure out Nathalie's supplier and whether Nathalie had known anything, and make a list of all the items from the memorial and return them.

"Martin?" August said softly. "Martin, wake up."

"August?" Martin groaned and rolled over. "How long have you been awake?"

"I didn't sleep," he said, and tossed a damp cloth to Martin. "We have a lot to do and no time to waste."

Martin crawled out of bed and wiped his face. "Good morning to you too, Your Brusqueness."

August clapped and stood. "Let's handle this quickly, then. We'll go see the memorial, and then talk to Blanche about what we learned. Anything else?"

"Prepare to leave?" Martin asked.

"I'll get to that this afternoon," said August, gesturing for them to leave. "Father will understand given the nature of everything, and worse comes to worst, you can come visit Oliver until it all blows over!"

Martin didn't look convinced, but he followed August out the door.

"So, you and Oliver?" August began. "I know the memories aren't back, but you only knew each other for a few days. Do you feel like you've recovered some of what you're missing?"

"Yes and no," said Martin, unable to meet his gaze. "I think it will be much easier to reestablish what little relationship we had, but I can feel something missing. Like a loose thread in my chest."

"That's sweet," said August as they descended the stairs of the inn. Perhaps love had simply made a poet of Martin.

"I know myself, and while I understand why I was inclined to forget Oliver in the first place, I wouldn't call it love," Martin said. "It couldn't have been. We barely knew each other."

August hummed. He adored stories of love at first sight and wanted to believe in them, but they had always felt too fantastical to be true. "Mutual romantic attraction? Will that spare your feelings?"

"You're lucky that I'm admitting to having any feelings," Martin said, and rubbed the back of his neck.

They made their way out of the inn. Much like the other days they'd been here, the town was barren.

"Blanche must be out doing something," August muttered, looking up and down the streets. "So we'll head to the cemetery—what do you think about the theory I shared with you last night about the memory loss being a punishment?"

"It's not unprecedented. There are old stories about places being punished for the greed of men, you know, and returning what was stolen heals the damage done," said Martin, pulling his collar up against the early morning chill. "Perhaps that is the answer to this."

Soon enough, Ella appeared over the far hill. Her

hair was bound back with a plain ribbon and covered by a blue kerchief. The basket over her arm was laden with eggs and her homemade jam.

"For Blaise," she said as she approached them. "They're trying to figure out how to make cakes now."

"How was Lady Tremaine last night once you returned?" August asked.

"She's ignoring me. Drizella, though, was inconsolable all night. I didn't sleep at all." Ella pulled a small flask from her basket and offered him a sip, grinning at his surprised expression. "She had me make chocolate, which she never drank, so this morning has gone fairly well, all things considered."

"Enjoy the fruits of your labors for once," he said, and shook his head. "With you around, my life is sweet enough."

Ella blushed and looked away. "What's your plan for the day?"

"We're going to go look at the memorial and see if I notice anything that you two might have missed last night," said Martin. "Then we need to talk to Blanche and confront Nathalie again."

"May I come with you?" Ella asked. "I don't want to be home while everyone is moping."

"That would be much appreciated." August offered her his arm, and they all started walking toward the cemetery.

August spent most of the walk avoiding the looming statue on the horizon. Despite seeing it and the evidence of the thievery last night, August's stomach rolled at the thought of facing the soldier again, even through the haze of dawn, and Ella seemed just as uncomfortable. August had made a list of every item that was missing so far as they could remember, and they went over it while Martin walked around the statue. Once he was done, they all found a spot where they could watch the statue from out of sight. No one approached the statue in the few hours they were there.

"Not that I expected the thief to be bold enough to rob it while we were here, but I thought we would be able to see people traveling to and from Fresne," said August as they returned to town. "Because of the hills, you can't really see anything from the memorial."

"Or the memorial from anywhere," said Martin. "Well, you can see the top of the statue, but someone could definitely have stolen everything and not been seen."

"Monsieur Picard said he used to visit every morning," August said, squinting at Fresne as they neared. "I suppose the path to the cemetery isn't one most take. It only leads out here."

"There are a few footpaths that lead away from the back of the cemetery, but no one really uses them anymore," said Ella. "One even leads through some of the lands near home. I only ever see badgers on it, though."

The trio entered Fresne a few hours after sunrise. Unlike the last few days, there were people walking up and down the streets. There was still a somber silence in the town, but a few people nodded to the trio as they passed. The bakery was open, Monsieur Picard shouting instructions to his apprentice, and the stalls at the center square were staffed for the first time since August had been back. Ella brightened up at that, and August smiled. Maybe Fresne would recover faster than he thought.

"Let's find—"

A scream echoed down the street.

Everyone within earshot went still and quiet, and Ella tilted her head into the breeze.

"What was that?" she asked, tugging August toward the sound.

He shook his head and stepped in front of her. "I don't know."

Another shriek tore down the street, sending most people scurrying back inside. Shutters slammed and doors locked, and August sprinted toward the shouting. Martin and Ella hurried after him, slipping through the dispersing crowd of people who had braved the market that morning. As the people fled, August caught sight of who had screamed.

Madame Bardin, Blaise's best friend.

Blaise was on their hands and knees, picking up the pieces of shattered cups. Their hair was neatly brushed and braided, and they looked to be in their best clothes. Now, the knees of their trousers were soaked through with tea. A red handprint marred their tear-streaked cheek.

"Joan," they said, voice shaking, "you've forgotten. You remember the memory loss, right?"

"You were in my house!" yelled Madame Bardin. Her eyes were wide with terror and rolling every which way, looking for some help from the few around them. "Why were you in my house?"

"You invited me to breakfast last night," Blaise said. They couldn't seem to look at Madame Bardin.

Each time they did, they flinched. "You said you were ready to face me again."

Madame Bardin huffed and stepped back, shaking her head. "No, I didn't, because I don't know you!"

She looked around again and glanced back at her door. It was wide open, pieces of what was meant to be breakfast spilled across the floor and leading to Blaise. Madame Bardin finally looked to August, Martin, and Ella. The desperation for help or explanation was heartbreaking.

"We just did this!" Blaise smacked the cobblestones, their fingers clenched into white-knuckled fists. "This isn't fair!"

Madame Bardin reared back at that, and August stepped forward to intervene. It was a miracle no one had been hurt since the memory loss started.

"Joan!" Blanche sprinted past August and skidded to a stop between Madame Bardin and Blaise. "Joan, look—I know you're confused and angry, and that's all fine. You can be those things, but something has happened. We should talk inside. Trust me."

Blanche held out her hands, shielding a crying Blaise, and started herding Madame Bardin slowly back toward her house.

Madame Bardin sniffed and wiped her face. "Something *has* happened. A break-in!"

"And we can talk about that," said Blanche. "Inside, though, and I can get everything cleaned up, too."

She gestured to the spilled breakfast in the doorway, and Madame Bardin nodded.

"All right," she whispered.

Blanche wrapped one arm around Madame Bardin, mouthed something to a distraught Blaise, and took Madame Bardin inside. Ella darted to Blaise.

"Come on," said Ella, helping Blaise to their feet. "It's all right."

"We should have collected the items we suspected immediately," August said quietly to Martin. He moved to help Blaise as well. "Up you go. I'll clean you up. Let's get you home."

"She forgot me," mumbled Blaise, utterly limp in their arms. "I thought . . . I'm nothing to her. No one."

"Not forever," August said.

He and Ella helped Blaise back to their place, and Martin cleaned up the spilled breakfast on the street. Consoling Blaise wasn't possible, so Ella cleaned off

their face and hands, and August made them some
tea to drink in bed. August slipped Blaise's ring off
and took it. Once they were done, they waited with
Martin outside. The streets of Fresne were completely
empty.

"Why now?" asked Martin. "Madame Bardin
has had that ring for ages, and I only had the collar
pins for a day."

"Maybe she didn't wear it all the time," August
said, and handed Martin the ring. "Regardless, we
should get hers, too, and we need to collect the others.
This is a terrifying confirmation of something I didn't
even consider."

"What?"

"That someone can forget the person who forgot them," said August. "Imagine if Monsieur Monet
returns home and has no memory of his wife? If
Danielle forgets Henry? And what happens if two
people forget each other at the same time? That's far
too much lost for others to fill in for them."

"We have to find the other items," said Ella.
"Before this happens to the whole town."

They waited for Blanche to finish speaking to
Madame Bardin. She emerged after a quarter of an
hour, sighing when she spotted them. She had them

return with her to the inn, and they sat in the back corner of the front room, away from the door and windows. Martin pulled out their notes, laying them before Blanche. She nodded.

"Do you know what's causing this and how to stop it?" she asked.

"We are fairly confident that we know part of what's causing it and how to stop the spread of it," said August. "It is going to be hard to hear, and it's going to require some very sad work."

Blanche nodded again. "I don't know what could be sadder."

"Everyone who lost their memories purchased something from Nathalie. She cut out the pages of her ledger that we think contain details about where those items were sourced," said August, carrying on despite Blanche's expression shifting from incredulous to furious in a blink. "We are fairly certain of where those items were stolen from, though, and we think that the stealing is what caused magic to do this to those who have the items."

"Someone stole things from somewhere, and magic just decided to do this to the people who have the items, not the person who stole them?" asked Blanche. "Did Nathalie steal them?"

"We don't know if she stole them herself or if someone supplied them to her," August said, "but magic isn't a person. Everyone who has forgotten someone they loved had one of the items."

"Sure," said Blanche, and she braced her hands on the table. "Where were they stolen from?"

"It took us a while to recognize them, but Ella and I saw something last night that made us realize where they were from," said August. "The pieces Nathalie used for her work were stolen from the memorial."

"No," whispered Blanche, shaking her head. "No one would do that."

"That's what we thought, but there's nothing much left on it," Ella said, laying a hand on Blanche's shoulder.

August nodded. "We checked. Someone stole all the offerings with any hint of value. We remember some of what's missing, but everyone in Fresne will need to make a list of what they've left there. Not all of it will have been stolen—I'm sure magpies made off with some—but to be safe, we need to find *all* the missing items."

"I can take care of that," said Blanche. She patted Ella's hand. "What are the items we know for sure Nathalie sold that were stolen?"

"She used stolen pieces in the collar pins August purchased the other day, the locket the Monets wear, the rings Blaise and Madame Bardin wear, the metal for the gloves Madame Renaud bought and the grip on Henry's cane, the basket in Monsieur Picard's, and the glass charms Monsieur Allard used for a pair of shoes," said Martin. "I'm unfamiliar with the memorial, but August and Ella found an item last night that was instantly recognizable as from the memorial."

Blanche inhaled sharply. "What tipped you off?"

"This." August took the falcon brooch from his pocket and carefully unwrapped it from the cloth, trying not to touch the metal.

Blanche reached for the brooch as if it might bite her and ran her fingers over the falcon. "This was my mother's. I left it at the memorial years ago, but it was a cuff. It was on the glove that she used with the birds."

"It was made by Nathalie and gifted by Lady Tremaine to Lord Moreau. His staff confirmed he has also lost memories of his late wife, and the item that likely caused that is still in his possession."

"There's no proof it's Nathalie who did the stealing, just that she bought the stolen items and reworked them," said Ella.

"And she wouldn't have been here when most of those funerals happened," said Blanche. "She wouldn't recognize them. They'd only be trinkets to her."

Ella agreed.

"That's, uh . . ." Blanche cleared her throat. "You mentioned yourself in all of that?"

"Yes, August purchased something from Nathalie and gave it to me, and I lost my memories of someone," said Martin, the tips of his ears ruddy.

"There are nine people who have lost their memories now," August said, and let Blanche digest that information. "Henry, Madame Renaud, Monsieur Allard, Blaise, Madame Monet, Madame Bardin, Martin, Lord Moreau, and Monsieur Picard. Monsieur Picard didn't want anyone to know, and it took a while for people to realize the baron had forgotten his late wife. We think it's a matter of how close someone is to the object and how much time they spend with it. And romantic love seems to play a role, but we're not entirely sure how. Everyone has forgotten someone they have had romantic feelings for."

"Most of that stuff had been at the memorial longer than you lot have been alive," said Blanche, wiping her face on her sleeve. "If some was melted down, this will be difficult."

"I know," said August. "I'm sorry it's not easier news to deal with."

"At least it's a place to start," said Blanche. "Will people regain their memories?"

"We're not entirely sure," Martin said slowly. "This is not a common occurrence, but we think that replacing the items might return everyone's memories."

"So the memorial's magical?" asked Blanche.

"Sort of," August said. "It's been around long enough that magic has leached into it, from items and people. When the items were stolen, the magic retaliated. That is the most likely cause, but we won't know for sure until . . ."

"You have all the items and put them back," finished Blanche. "Let's do it, then."

"We think it would be best if you spoke to people about the memorial," August said, and gestured to Martin. "We can approach Nathalie. We don't know where we should keep the items."

"I'll keep them." Blanche pocketed the falcon brooch, and rose. "Here's what we do—I shall get the items from the others and start compiling a list of items left at the memorial. Romance isn't my cup of tea, so I'll be the safest bet if romantic love is the triggering event.

No one else will lose their memories. You will approach Nathalie and ask her to cooperate. If she doesn't, she will be detained. Whoever robbed the memorial has to be found. Now let's go, and save my town from any more grief."

～ 12 ～

The Sweetest Sounds

UGUST ENTERED Nathalie's shop alone. A gold pocket watch, its cracked crystal removed and its insides scattered, rested on the counter unattended. There was a rustling from the back, and August quietly crept around and studied the items for sale. There were pieces missing, spaces where items had been removed. He stared at all the glass pieces—a pair of drop earrings, a flower brooch, and a spiral quill—so desperately that their outlines remained in his vision when he looked away. None of them looked like his mother's bracelet.

"Be out in a moment!" shouted Nathalie.

August neared the counter, trying to recall any memory of Ella's father. He could remember the man complaining about how his watch was always fast, but had it been silver or gold?

Nathalie appeared from the back and stopped in her tracks. "What do you want?"

"I need a truthful answer about where you got some of your items," he said. "Those collar pins I bought. You didn't want to sell them, did you? Where were they from?"

"I made them," she said quickly, and cleared her throat. "Just because you think you know something doesn't mean I have to tell you everything about my trade secrets."

"So it's a coincidence that the day after I handed those pins over to my friend, he forgot someone?" asked August. "The collar pins, the locket, the ring, the cane, the basket, the gloves, the brooches."

She flinched at the mention of the brooches.

"You know the ones, don't you? All of those items have something in common, and there are others in your shop like them, aren't there?" asked August. "I have the gold falcon brooch. You used a cuff from an old glove to make it, didn't you?"

Nathalie's head tilted, and her mouth opened. Was she wondering how he knew that?

"The person you gave them to lost their memories?" she asked.

That wasn't fear. She actually looked upset by that knowledge.

"It had barely been a day, but he lost them.

Madame Bardin lost her memories of Blaise, by the way," said August. "It all comes back to those items. I know one of the things they have in common, and I don't mean that they all came from you. Where did you get them from, Nathalie?"

She shook her head.

"So if you didn't get them from a supplier, did you get them yourself?" he asked, dreading the rest of the conversation. There was something holding her back from talking.

"I bought them," she whispered. "I didn't . . . I bought them."

"From whom, Nathalie?" asked August, but she didn't answer. "Did you know they were stolen?"

She steeled herself and shook her head.

"I don't . . ." Her voice grew higher and tighter. "I didn't know."

Her gaze flicked behind him. The door creaked open, and a set of footsteps slowly crossed the store.

"I got suspicious about how long this was taking because I was certain you would agree to tell him who sold you everything," said Blanche, frustration shaking through her. "Nat, tell me truthfully right now why a brooch made with the gold cuff I left at the memorial when my mother died was sold from your shop?"

Nathalie seemed to wither, shoulders slumping and face falling into deep, uneasy lines. "I didn't know where they were from."

"But you knew they were stolen. You figured that out after August talked to you, didn't you?" asked Blanche. "Why won't you say who else is involved? I don't believe for a moment you did it yourself."

Nathalie remained silent.

"You're going to be detained," Blanche said. "I'm not telling anyone why. No reason to break their hearts yet."

Blanche escorted Nathalie to the town's guardhouse, keeping the whole procession inconspicuous. August remained in the shop and searched behind the counter. The accounts had been moved, and even more pages were missing now. The lockbox he had seen the last time they were there had been hidden in a crate and covered in papers. August covered the pocket watch on the counter with a cloth and dropped the lockbox next to him. He had no idea what the combination might be. Martin and Ella arrived a few moments later.

"Blanche said Nathalie was holding her tongue?" Martin asked before he was even through the door.

August nodded. "If Nathalie was stealing,

Blanche wants Fresne to handle that part, not the court. We need to hand over anything we find to her."

"People are going to be furious when they find out," said Ella.

"Which is why Blanche asked us not to say anything about it," August said, laying his hand over the cloth-covered watch. "Ella, I can remember every anecdote your father told us about it, but I can't remember what metal his pocket watch was."

She smiled. "Silver."

"That's right," said August. "I haven't seen it yet."

She joined him at the counter. Her fingers brushed the cloth. "Did you ask that because there's a pocket watch under here?"

"It's gold," August said, removing the cloth.

She touched his hand. "Thank you."

After that, they went through everything. None of them was sure they would be able to identify anything from the memorial, but it was still worth it to double-check in case there was another item as recognizable as the falcon. Ella found no items with glass beads like the ones on his mother's bracelet and no pocket watch. Martin and August went through the remaining records to try to find the code for the lockbox.

The only new thing August noticed, though, was

that Nathalie's rent was steady—she paid it out in two small amounts every month—and that she was either a terrible accountant or giving away money without recording it. Her sales didn't match up with her income at the end of a handful of months. The five pages were still missing from the book, and he couldn't find them despite searching every nook of the shop. A few more pages had been cut out, too, including the ones with the sales for Madame Monet's locket and Martin's collar pins.

"This is the only thing we can't get to," said August, setting the small lockbox on top of the counter. "I'm betting the pages are in it."

He hated the idea of finding his mother's bracelet, and he hated that he hadn't. He had left it unprotected at the memorial so long ago that he couldn't imagine something so fragile lasting this long.

"Obviously," Ella said, and she dropped her elbows onto the counter to study it.

The box had one of those odd dial locks that August had only ever seen on important doors and chests because of how pickable the cheaper versions were. However, those usually had only three dials; this one had six. Six numbers they had to find out from Nathalie or puzzle out themselves.

"What has six numbers?" she asked.

"Too many things," said August. "Come on. Let's go see if Nathalie has talked to Blanche and if she'll open this box."

Martin carried the box, and August hesitated when offering Ella his arm. Grabbing her wrist, closing his fingers fully over the warm, delicate skin, would be too much. Her arm, too forceful.

Everything felt too intimate with her after last night, and his chest tightened. He didn't want to leave.

Thankfully, she settled his uncertainty by threading her arm through his.

At the guardhouse, Nathalie and Blanche were sitting across from each other at a table, and Nathalie had somehow gotten even paler. Her hands shook as she finished talking to Blanche. Blanche had her head in her hands.

"That you, August?" she asked without looking.

"It is," said August. "How's it going?"

"In circles." Blanche slammed her hands onto the table and stood. "Nathalie insists that she didn't steal the items and didn't realize where they were coming from, but she refuses to share who she bought them from."

"Not out of loyalty, though, is it?" asked August, and Nathalie flinched.

Blanche shook her head and asked, "Is their finding out you talked really worse than selling things that were stolen from the memorial?"

Her head shot up, and she opened her mouth. She lost her nerve before she could speak, however.

"Nathalie, what's the code to open this box?" asked August.

Nathalie's gaze dropped to her feet.

Blanche moved Nathalie to the small room that served as Fresne's only cell, and August picked up the lockbox again. He saw Ella's teary stare stuck on the lockbox and knew exactly what she was thinking— was her father's pocket watch in there? In pieces dotted throughout the town? Scattered across the cemetery by nature, returned to the earth as she had intended?

August didn't feel victorious. "We'll take the box with us when we return to court tomorrow. Some of the best locksmiths live in the city. We'll send word once we find what's inside," said August, ignoring Ella startling in the corner of his sight.

"I'll continue to gather the items from folks who have purchased from Nathalie and return them to the memorial," said Blanche. "That way, I can compile a list of everything missing and hopefully make a dent in what we have to return."

August nodded. "In case that doesn't work, I'll continue my research. Since we don't know why the objects make people forget who they love, I'm not entirely sure we fully understand what is happening."

He took the lockbox and accounts back with him to the inn. Martin and Ella followed.

"I forgot you're leaving tomorrow," Ella said as they walked outside. Somehow it sounded like a question.

The disappointment in her voice cut him to his very soul. He didn't know what to do with her sudden look of sadness.

"I am," he said. "My father wants to celebrate since I haven't actually been home in a while, and if I'm not home, he'll send out a search party. He only let me take this assignment because it was Fresne and I promised I wouldn't be gone long."

"You have to come see me tonight before you leave." She grabbed his hand. "Oh, and bring the lockbox. Maybe we can figure out how to open it, and we won't need your fancy locksmiths. Please?"

He couldn't deny her something as simple as that

when the very idea of it made her look so beautifully hopeful. It was a stark contrast to how she had first looked at him just a few days ago.

"Of course," he said. "I'll come by after supper."

She smiled and nodded, and August felt something catch in his chest. A few days earlier, he had been afraid she might not even want to speak with him. Now, anything seemed possible.

Martin slowly turned to August.

"Don't say it," said August, tucking the accounting book under his arm. "We leave tomorrow. What was I supposed to do?"

"I was going to say 'be careful,' but I can feel your defensiveness." Martin laughed. "I was there the last time she stopped talking to you. You're going back to the city and traveling and your *responsibilities*. I don't want to see you hurt again."

Right—marriage.

"It will be fine," said August, thinking of the weight of Ella as she had leaned against him the night before. The way the stars had glittered in her eyes. How she had smiled. "She's worth the risk, anyway."

~ 13 ~

In Their Own Little World

*M*ARTIN'S WORDS haunted August all the way to Ella's estate. He hadn't thought about the years after she stopped responding for such a long time, preferring instead to let them lie neglected in the back of his mind. He knew now that Ella had been a child who was in no state to communicate, but he had been a child, too. It *had* hurt.

It had hurt beyond words when she hadn't written and when Lady Tremaine had told him she never spoke of him. Their friendship had wilted like flowers forgotten in a vase, rotting as the weeks went by until it was finally little more than dust. It had taken years to be clean of the feelings of betrayal and failure.

August groaned. When had he become this fatalistic?

"Martin's rubbing off on me," he muttered to the lockbox. "I can't show up to Ella's with a head full of thoughts like bad poetry."

"Why not? I love bad poetry. It's much more interesting than good poetry, because someone somewhere thought it was good enough to be written down."

August spun around. Ella stood on a little path leading off the main road to her estate, holding a candle aloft. The flickering light made her smile look like laughter.

"I wanted to catch you before you arrived so that Lady Tremaine or my stepsisters didn't see you," she said, and nodded for him to join her. "You know, Stepmother says poetry is literature for people too dramatic to read."

He joined her on the little footpath. "What does she say about literature?"

"A hobby for people too indolent to attempt something that will actually make them look smart," she said. "She's very opinionated."

"That's one way to put it," he said, and snorted. "Does she think well of anything?"

"She's quite fond of cats, and that's about it. She likes how independent they are." Ella looped her right arm through his left, the warmth of her body stifling in the summer night. A drifting leaf caught in her hair, and he plucked it away, fingers itching to tangle in the strands.

The windows of the château, glowing a pale gold, came into view, and two small figures paced before one of them. August could only assume the dramatically gesturing one was Drizella. She would probably make a good actress. Pity that wasn't an acceptable pursuit for her.

"You know, I cannot wait until all three of us are away from Lady Tremaine," said Ella, staring up at the window. "Drizella will always see me as the stepsister she ordered around, I think, but that means she'll try to rub her achievements into my face."

"Why are you saying that like it's a good thing?" asked August.

"Because the only way she knows how to do that is to show off, and that will mean she'll invite me to a fancy luncheon every few months." She sighed and leaned against him. "Fruits taste so much better when they're shaped like flowers."

"Speaking of," said August, shifting so that he could reach into his coat and pull out a slim box. "A gift. Consider it an apology for showing up without warning and vanishing so quickly."

"Thank you!" She peeked into the small box and grinned. "Figs! Thank you!"

He had stopped by the market to buy them on

his way here, knowing Ella would never buy them for herself. He knew how much she loved them.

"This is perfect! I have some cheese pastries for us to nibble on," she said, and walked faster.

The little kitchen came into view, and Bruno ambled out of it, yawning. He woofed when he caught sight of Ella and loped over to her. She ruffled his fur and kissed the top of his head.

"Have you kept Lucifer out of the kitchen?" she asked.

He huffed and licked her hand.

"Good boy," said Ella.

The pair settled down on the kitchen steps, the tray of cheese pastries, chunks of cold bread, and the figs between them. Bruno lay back down at Ella's feet and sniffed about August until he slipped the old dog some cheese while Ella wasn't looking. She relayed how Madame Bardin and Blaise were doing after their eventful day.

"It's good that it probably won't affect anyone else," she said, studying the lockbox. "I don't think Fresne could handle anyone else forgetting."

August tilted the lockbox on its side and tested the strength of the hinges. Breaking them probably wouldn't help.

"Have you tried her birthday?" Ella asked, and prodded it.

He nodded, suddenly aware of how foolish he must look struggling to open a box. He ran a hand through his hair and shrugged. "And the day she came back to Fresne, along with a whole host of other six-digit numbers."

"The lock mechanism is behind the dials?" Ella asked, pulling the lockbox into her lap. She pressed her nose to the front and stared at the slim space between the dials. "I bet I could fit one of my smaller needles through here."

"Any needle thin enough probably wouldn't be strong enough to move the pins," said August. The way wisps of her hair curled against the nape of her neck made his fingers itch to touch them. "I don't want you to break all your needles for this."

She turned her head, cheek resting on the lock. "It's only a needle."

"But it's yours, and I can have a locksmith look at it tomorrow evening," said August. Her expression faltered, and he tried to quickly change the topic, offering Bruno a fig. "Do you—"

She smacked his hand. "He can't have that!"

"Really?" August asked, and hid it in his fist. Bruno nosed his hand. "Sorry, old friend."

"Figs make dogs sick," she said, and set the lock-box aside. "Not something they taught you at school?"

"No, they decided calculus was more useful than how not to accidentally poison beloved pets."

She snorted. "My father and I were surprised you were sent away for schooling. We thought your father would want to keep you close."

The world dropped out from under him.

"He did," said August slowly. "I couldn't stay, though. It was expected of me to study at university with the other noble children."

Despite their heart-to-heart the night before, August hadn't revealed who he was. There couldn't be any secrets between them now, though, with him knowing so much about her life.

"Ella, before I leave, I need to tell you something," he said. "I understand that you will be angry, but it wasn't up to me for a very long time, and by the time it was, we weren't really speaking anymore."

Ella's face fell. "What do you mean?"

"Well, given my station, certain things are not my choice."

"Are you betrothed?" she asked, and leaned back, almost as if she were recoiling at the very words.

"What? No," August said, shaking his head. He couldn't help laughing softly. "Why would I be betrothed?"

She sighed and smiled. "Oh, well, then I promise I don't mind whatever it is."

August ducked, sure that his blush would show even in the dark. She didn't want him to be betrothed?

She didn't want him to be betrothed!

"I hope you feel that way after I say this," he said, but he couldn't stop smiling. "It started with my mother, and when I was born, they decided it was best to keep it a secret still. We—"

The servants' door connecting the kitchen to the house creaked open. August nearly missed such a soft sound, but Ella startled. She spun, tense as a string about to snap. Lady Tremaine stood in the doorway, her fine gown at odds with the half-cleaned kitchen, and Ella rose to her feet and stepped in front of August. Lady Tremaine didn't step down into the kitchen.

"Ella, I wasn't aware we had a guest, and quite so late at night," she said, raising one brow in a look of practiced confusion. "My dear, I worry for your reputation. This is completely inappropriate. Your . . . guest . . . understands that, yes?"

"Stepmother, this isn't—"

"What it looks like?" She took the final step into the kitchen, looked around, and gasped. "This pot is scoured?" She picked up the pot Ella had set aside to soak and dumped its contents to the floor. "This bowl, washed?" She upended the leftover soup across the table. "These linens, clean?" She swept the freshly folded napkins into the mess. "Surely they are, since that is what I instructed you to do, and I am simply unable to recognize what a clean kitchen looks like." She stopped before August and let her gaze slide over him as if he weren't even there. "And there is not a strange boy in my kitchen at this tasteless hour?"

"How da—" August started, but Ella shot him a pleading look.

Lady Tremaine glanced at him, hellebore eyes little more than slits, and her nostrils flared.

"You are obviously either not working hard enough or lacking enough work to keep busy if you have time to loiter, so let me remedy that for you," said Lady Tremaine. "I want this kitchen spotless by the morning. I want tea and breakfast delivered on time and not a moment later. I want the laundry done on time for once, and I want the house fit for actual guests."

"Yes, Stepmother," Ella said, subdued.

"If I see a single speck of dust or you're a moment late tomorrow, you'll sleep down here until the new year, not only tonight." Lady Tremaine swept over the mess she had created and paused in the doorway. "And you, boy, won't darken my doorstep again, or I'll have the guards drag you from Fresne."

The door slammed shut behind Lady Tremaine with a clunk. In the quiet, with Lady Tremaine's footsteps fading and the soup dripping down the table legs, August watched Ella swallow, straighten, and brace herself.

"Please do not say anything," she said, voice steel. "This is humiliating enough without you telling me that I am wrong to stay."

August did want to tell her that. He wanted to say that there was no need for him to imagine Lady Tremaine a villain, because she was villainous enough without his imagination. He wanted to say that there was no need for Ella to prostrate herself at the altars of familial obligation and love, because she loved her family far more than they deserved and had single-handedly kept them from destitution by working herself to death. He wanted to say that this wasn't humiliating for her, because it was her stepmother who was an unbelievable embarrassment. The woman hid barbs and insults behind fake concern.

Ella loved her family and had gotten nothing but scorn in return.

Lady Tremaine could speak in backhanded compliments all she wanted, but it was clear now what she was doing.

"She's the one who should be embarrassed," he said softly. "Wasted perfectly good soup."

Ella laughed, and he knew it was forced, but she shrugged. "I did make it, so perhaps it tastes terrible."

"Or perhaps she has terrible taste," said August.

Ella toed one of the linen napkins and pressed it into the mess. "We might as well use these to clean some of this up."

She didn't look like she wanted him to say anything, so he didn't. He simply nodded and touched her hand. Ella sniffed.

They set to cleaning up the kitchen in silence. August worried that Lady Tremaine would have him escorted from the estate, but Ella assured him there was no one who could do that. It would be fine so long as he was gone by morning, and Ella slowly lost the stiffness that Lady Tremaine's scorn had caused in her. The kitchen was shining—as much as stone and brick could shine, at least—by the time they were done, and Ella collapsed on the kitchen steps. August sat down next to her.

"Will she really make you sleep down here?" he asked.

Ella's gaze darted to the large fire smoldering behind them. "She's all talk."

"Ella, I know I said I wouldn't say it, but she can't lock you out of where you live. Charmant has rules. Even if you were a scullery maid, she's not allowed to," he said, furious at the very idea.

"I'm not her maid. Those rules don't apply." She sighed and shifted, a nervousness he hadn't ever seen in her emerging. "You said I could get a job anywhere, but I do all of their clothes, you know, and they're not good enough for them. I don't think I could impress royals and courtiers."

"You've impressed two courtiers over the span of four days," said August. "You have created some of the most beautiful things I've ever seen—the ribbon embroidery you've done would delight any number of people—and of course they will not tell you that. They know that you could get a better job and family elsewhere so easily. They need you to think you're not worth more than they're giving you. They need you. You do not need them."

"But I want them!" Ella said, and her voice cracked. "I want them to love me and need me and be nice to me. I know they don't have to love me, but I thought we would at least be more than this."

Ella dropped her forehead to his shoulder, nose to his chest, and sobbed.

She turned slightly until she rested against his chest, and August leaned back against the doorframe. Her breath ruffled his shirt, warm and steady, and one of her hands slipped from his to rest against his other shoulder. He wrapped his free arm around her. After a long, silent while, she spoke.

"I've never left Fresne, and I think a part of you didn't, either," she whispered, and hugged him tightly. "I'll think about it. I promise. I'll meet you at the memorial in the morning."

"All right," he said, and returned the embrace.

As selfish as it was, he did want to see her face the first time she saw the royal city. He wanted to be there when she was commissioned as a seamstress and witness her joy. He wanted an eternity of memories with her, the good and the bad, because what did it matter if they parted again years from now so long as he got to be a part of her happier memories, and he was sure he could stand to face the statue now so long as she was with him and the future of them together was so promising. He—

Oh. So this was ruination. Or how it started, at least.

He understood perfectly now what everyone had been saying—what was the point of suffering a lifetime without love when he could live and breathe and love for decades and decades with her? This night with her was already better than all his years spent wondering how she was.

This was love.

He moved to leave, but Ella caught his hand.

"Wait. What were you going to tell me before Lady Tremaine interrupted?" she asked.

Here and now, it would be too much for either of them to deal with.

"It can wait," he said, and squeezed her hand. "I'll see you in the morning, and no matter what you decide, you will always have a home with me."

~ 14 ~

Agony

*A*UGUST SLEPT well for the first time in a week. His final morning in Fresne felt brighter—the chirping crickets less annoying, the sun less unbearably hot, and the weight of the memory loss mystery less crushing.

"I need to say goodbye to Ella before we head out," he told Martin as they finished packing up their things. They had traveled light, but August had a single clean shirt he could change into. He took great pains to ensure his traveling coat and trousers were clean and unwrinkled after his night of chores. "Do you have any of that orange leaf cologne?"

"You're going to be even more unbearably chipper today, aren't you?" asked Martin, tossing August a small vial.

"No more than usual." August flashed a dazzling smile. "Promise."

There was a part of him that wasn't chipper—he

would visit his mother today. She wouldn't want him to still be sad or afraid to face her resting place. She would be happy that he was happy.

And she would be overjoyed that he was talking to Ella again.

"Meet you at the crossroads?" Martin asked.

August nodded and turned toward the memorial. "Deal."

The path to the cemetery had been marked sometime in the last decade. Little stones lined the trail, initials and dates carved into their sides. The dread August usually felt at the thought of his mother's death was still present, a roiling unease in the pit of his stomach. He still hesitated the moment the statue appeared on the horizon.

A few days couldn't cure a decade of avoiding grief.

He lingered on the path, not quite at the memorial, and watched for Ella. He paced for half an hour, circled the cemetery without actually going inside, and finally, his anxiety drove him back to the memorial. This was where Ella had said to meet.

Yet she wasn't there.

Ella would never skip their meeting. She was honest to a fault.

August glanced back at the memorial. The helm was more weathered, but it looked the same as he remembered. He didn't look at the soldier's empty wrists or the bare spot at their feet. He nodded to them, though. Mother would understand a delay.

August half sprinted back to town. The market was bustling, people perusing the produce and wares with practiced ease. He didn't see Ella, but Martin was eating an apple with Oliver at the other side of the stalls. August made his way to them.

"Sorry," he said as he reached them. "Have you seen Ella?"

Martin frowned. "She didn't show up for your meeting?"

"No. I waited, but Ella was punctual even when we were children," said August, a new worry spreading through him. "Maybe Lady Tremaine kept her home?"

Oliver finished off his apple and pocketed the seeds. "I see her over there."

He pointed toward the entrance of the market at Ella, her hair tied back and her expression the same one of harried nervousness she wore when Lady Tremaine was around. She didn't have the look of someone thinking about leaving Fresne.

She looked as if she was too busy for the thought
to even cross her mind.

"Ella!" He ran to her and caught her as she
was leaving a stall selling venison. "What are you
doing?"

She spun, staring up at him with wide eyes.
"I'm sorry?"

"You were late," he said.

"I'm sorry, monsieur," she said again. "I think
you have me confused with someone else." She turned
and walked away without a backward glance.

Ruination.

August steeled himself from the horror gripping
him as his world began to spin. "My mistake," he
whispered as he bowed his head.

She had forgotten him. Like the others, she . . .

She forgot him.

"She loves me," he whispered, and stumbled into
the side of a building.

Joy and agony tangled in his throat, choking him
until he collapsed to his knees. Could it be possible?

"What was that?"

August startled and looked up. Martin and Oliver
were standing over him, concerned looks on both their
faces. Martin held out his hand.

August took it. "She has absolutely no memories of me."

This was bad. Ella had perused all the items in the shop. She had gone to the memorial. She had been exposed over and over again.

Just like Martin. Just like him.

"Not again," hissed Oliver.

Martin groaned and pulled August to his feet.

"Returning the items to the memorial will return the memories, right?" August asked, desperate.

Martin dropped a hat on August's head. "If it doesn't, then something else will."

"The world is ending," muttered August. "You're being hopeful."

"Would you prefer my usual countenance?" Martin asked, and snorted. "No, you wouldn't, so listen up—your relationship with her isn't dead and gone. She'll remember again. Figuring out how to make that happen is your job, remember?"

"As someone who's been around this longer than you and been forgotten, I know what you're thinking, and it's useless," Oliver said. "Everything you've shared with her still happened. It *feels* like everything is gone. Ella isn't gone."

"You're right," said August. "Even if we can't

return the memories, we can be friends again. We've rebuilt our friendship once before already."

It had only taken four days. He could do this. Martin and Oliver were right.

"Yes, you're very smart," said Martin, glancing at Oliver. "However, this development is helpful. It means that simply handling the items or that lockbox briefly is enough to trigger memory loss, so you're in danger. We need to get that lockbox to someone who can open it."

"Doesn't seem very helpful from my perspective," said August, though it was helping him focus. He could rebuild his relationship and solve this.

Martin checked the time. "I'm the grim one. That frown doesn't suit you."

"Why bother with looks that suit me when the only person I wish to look won't?" August said without really meaning it. He did feel better now that the shock of being forgotten was behind him. "You're right, though. It's time I leave. We need to get this open, collect all the items, and return them, and we can do that faster if we split up."

"Absolutely not," said Martin. "Your father will kill me."

"He won't, and he won't feed you to any bears,

either. You should stay here and help with the collection of the stolen items," August said. "The faster they're collected, the better. I'll get home tonight, give the lockbox to a locksmith, and speak with my father. He would much rather have me home sooner even if it means you stay here."

"Are you sure that's fine?" Martin asked, but his gaze was already drifting to Oliver.

Nothing was fine, except he had fallen in love and the world hadn't ended. She had forgotten him, yes, but she loved him in return. Memories could be remade. Returned.

He would find a way to return the memories and restore the memorial and would let nothing stand in his way. It was so odd, this new feeling that knowledge awoke. They had been apart for so long, and he had always been afraid that they would never speak again. There was something so comforting in knowing he had grown into someone Ella could love. She was kind and funny, charming beyond measure. Her loving him didn't make him feel ruined.

He felt powerful.

He could fix this.

They could come back from this.

"Keep an eye on Ella," he said. "Make sure Lady

Tremaine treats her all right and she's not over-worked."

Martin nodded, and Oliver agreed to do the same.

"Thank you," August said.

But it all felt different from the last time he had left Fresne. He knew, without a doubt or fear, he would come back. Determined to return and explain everything to Ella—who he was really, and all her lost memories of their time together—August glanced back at Fresne once, wondering if the silhouette vanishing far, far away over the hills was her.

He would find her again.

～ 15 ～

Only You, Lonely You

*T*HERE WAS nothing quite like waking up in a comfortable, familiar bed after traveling. August stretched, ignoring the sunlight creeping through his curtains, and yawned into his arm. He had arrived too late to bother the king, but August knew his father would come bustling in soon to see him. He rose and opened the shutters of his window, taking a deep breath of the early afternoon air, and studied the bright blue sky. It was such a vivid, burning color, like water spilling across a stone floor or the iridescent shift of a sheet of pearl in delicate hands. Fresne had skies like that.

"No reason to think about that," he muttered, and started to get dressed. "Nothing in Fresne for me but an unfinished job."

With any luck, he would get some more quiet time to himself before his father realized he was awake. August had given his valet the morning off.

Visiting Fresne had dredged up a lot of memories he didn't care to think about around others, and he definitely didn't want to think about them around his father. The man still got misty-eyed when he was even reminded of his late wife. August couldn't talk to him about Fresne.

"Best I finish dealing with this case before he shows up," August mumbled.

As an only child, sometimes the only person to talk to was himself. He hadn't really had a good friend until he went to school and found Martin. His early years in Fresne had been so lonely.

He penned a quick letter to his mother's fairy godmother, thanking her for responding to his father and asking if she could identify magical items. Confirmation that the items were the culprits would be helpful and put minds at ease. Once that was handed off to a courier, he moved everything off his desk and set the lockbox in the middle. He hadn't been able to find a locksmith last night—he planned on attempting some more combinations today before heading into town to seek one out.

"August!" Father bustled into the room, the gold fringe of his epaulets swinging wildly, and launched himself at his son. He caught August around the middle in a crushing hug. "About time, my boy!"

Father was a smotherer, but his love was a comfortable warmth, like sitting in the sun for a touch too long on a summer day.

"You saw me less than a week ago," August said, and laughed, hugging Father back.

"You were only home for a day," Father said. "You've got responsibilities you've been avoiding."

He let go of August with one arm so that he could waggle a finger at him, and August laughed again.

"I was working," said August. "Both times."

"Yes, yes. Bandits up north and loose magic in Fresne. You've been very busy away from home." Father huffed and looked him over. "Forgive me for wanting my only child safe and sound at home. Did you figure it all out?"

"Not entirely," August said, frowning. "Martin stayed to tie up some loose ends. All that's left to do is determine how to return the memories, but we have a running theory that the mayor is overseeing. There's also this lockbox that I need opened. We think it's holding some crucial information as to who is behind this."

"Very good," said Father. "Excellent work for five days."

"Well, don't congratulate me too soon," said August, thinking of the nine people who had lost their memories and the items stolen from the memorial by Nathalie's secret partner. "I'll need to return in a few days to finish the job. The memories haven't been returned yet, and there's a culprit still loose."

Father shrugged. "Still sounds to me as if there's plenty to celebrate! It's good for morale to get a win, even if it's small! Bureaucracy and all that court nonsense makes it hard to celebrate them, but you should! Tonight, even!"

"I'm rather tired," August lied, ignoring the sinking feeling in his chest. He had expected Father to protest more to his return to Fresne, but his bubbling excitement seemed to be overshadowing his usual temperament. August should have known Father would have something planned. Still, his own plans were to explore the city and find a locksmith. "Any court functions can wait until tomorrow."

"Court?" Father let out a bark of a laugh. "They wouldn't be able to plan something so quickly if I gave them the whole vault."

"And you did?" August asked. "What is it?"

Father tilted his head back and forth, mustache wobbling.

"I can honestly say that I haven't planned a single thing," he said. "You can blame the Grand Duke for it all."

The Grand Duke had been the king's adviser for longer than August had been alive and was unable to refuse Father anything.

It was why he had two other advisers.

"And how many potential brides will be in attendance?" August mocked. He knew Father, and he knew a scheme was underway.

"Look here." Father yanked August's shirt collar and pulled him down to eye level. "I've been patient and understanding, but you need to get married."

August groaned. "What exactly is happening tonight?"

"We're having a ball to welcome you home, and every eligible lady will be there." Father smacked his arm and let him go. "All of them! So, none of this 'I can't meet anyone I like' nonsense. You'll be meeting everyone."

One night was decidedly not enough time to determine if someone was fit to rule or fall in love.

"It's going to be a long ball," muttered August.

"You've only got yourself to blame for that."

August laughed and shook his head. "I know you want me to find someone and have a family, but I would love to do that on my own time."

"The rest of us don't function on your time, boy!" Father nearly shouted. "There's nothing to be scared of!"

"Sure there is," said August. "Ask anyone in Fresne."

"Memory loss like in Fresne isn't common," Father said. "So, they weren't just forgetting people, but loved ones, were they?"

"Even if the love was new," said August.

"'Tis a shame." Father quieted, mustache rustling with a sigh.

August shuddered. "It must be hard to not remember someone who loves you, learn to love them again, and then find out they've forgotten you. Thinking about it feels like someone walking over my grave."

And, oddly, so weirdly that he couldn't shake the feeling, made him feel empty, as if he had missed two steps while going down the stairs.

"One of the people who lost his memories said something about how forgetting was worse, and I don't understand," said August. "You can't be sad about something you've forgotten."

"Can't you?" Father mused. "Feels more like fear, then. Fear that there's something just around that road you didn't take, something great and wonderful that you'll never have the joy of knowing. You don't understand fear of missing out on love?"

"Losing Mother nearly killed you," said August, hands twisting in his lap. He tugged at the hem of his shirt, his collar, his hair. Did no one else remember how bad it had been? "I remember you. You were in pain. I've seen you get tossed by boars during hunts, but this was *pain*."

His father had returned to court one week before the mourning period was up to show that he was well, but he hadn't been. He had grieved for years.

"Oh, August," Father said gently, and pulled him into a one-armed hug. "Why would I want to live in a world in which I never knew her? Never saw her happy? Never got to take a small part in the journey of her life? Why would I not want the many wonderful memories I have of her? Knowing her changed me, and losing her changed me as well. That's life, boy. To not have known her, to lose my memories of her, would be to lose her all over again *and* to lose myself. Grief and pain aren't gone once a wound scars over, are they?"

August shook his head against his father's shoulder. The coat scratched his cheek, and the overwhelming scents of ink and tea cleared the teary burn in the back of his throat. "People were glad I was so young when Mother died because it meant I wouldn't remember much."

"People who've never lost anyone will say anything to avoid thinking about mortality," Father said, huffing and patting his shoulder. "I am sorry if I made you think love was dangerous, but it's not, and I want grandchildren. So do whatever it is you need, bathe, get dressed, and be on time tonight to meet your wife."

"What if, instead, I stay in my room and figure out how to open this lockbox?" asked August. "You know, do my job?"

"Terrible idea," said Father, and let him go. He laughed at August's eye roll. "I always say that the answer to any problem is going home or getting a hammer, and you've done both of them."

"How did you know about the hammer?" August asked, trying to laugh it off. Could home be the answer? He hadn't asked where Nathalie was from, but it wasn't terrible advice. He had thought it would be numbers, but what if it was a word represented by numbers? That was worth trying.

"Now," said Father, "I've got to make sure the Grand Duke's up to snuff. Need to make a good impression on my daughter-in-law."

He scurried out of the room, and August stared at the open door.

"He can't have invited everyone," August said, and chuckled as he shook his head. "Six letters. If they're not within the first nine letters of the alphabet . . . maybe they loop."

With a scrap of paper, he counted out *bauble* to 213235 and *trifle* to 299635. Neither worked. *Tinker* and *repair*—295259 and 957199—didn't work, either, but those were just what she did. What did she love?

It would have helped to know where she was from and had traveled before settling in Fresne.

August groaned. "It can't be that easy."

Six letters.

Fresne. 695155.

The lock flicked open. August laughed. So, Nathalie did love Fresne, but why was she hiding her supplier?

He opened the box with his heart in his throat.

Silver glinted as the light hit something inside, but it wasn't glass. A silver pocket watch, several rings, and various bits and pieces of things he couldn't identify rested on top of a pile of papers. The watch had a date inscribed, but he didn't know what it was for. Only two of the rings were intact; three were missing jewels, and he found two stones that had been removed from their settings in the corner. He had no idea what the small screws, metal scraps, and leather pieces could be from. He suspected they were all that was left of the stolen items sold to Nathalie.

The papers, though, he recognized. They were the pages cut from her accounts. Like he thought, the four-line notation was next to every single transaction connected to the memory loss.

Including the sales of the brooches given to Lord Moreau.

Except they hadn't been sales at all. These two entries clearly referred to the two marked sales that hadn't included prices, but Nathalie gifting the brooches to Lady Tremaine didn't make sense.

There were other pages as well, records of rent payments for her building, made out to the Tremaine estate. He knew very little about Lady Tremaine. He had glimpsed her tax records and seen the few properties she owned. Her estate accounts had indicated she possessed multiple types of income, including a few that hadn't been labeled—seven, if he remembered correctly. And she had steadily raised rents, but Nathalie's records indicated that she'd been paying the same rate for five years.

Had the brooches from Nathalie been free as thanks for not raising the rent, or was it something more?

No one had claimed the note and purse Nathalie had placed in the cart before Martin had left to find August. There had been quite a bit of money in that purse—more than August had paid for the pins.

About as much as the cost of the pins plus half of Nathalie's rent, now that he thought about it.

August tried to recall why the Tremaine estate's accounts would have been in the tax records he had reviewed, but the numbers kept interrupting his thoughts.

He looked through the other papers. Nathalie had seven transactions—excluding the two brooches that she hadn't charged Lady Tremaine for—marked with the odd four-line notation in total, and each of them was related to the memory loss. Nathalie, if his math was right, had not profited from those sales at all.

Nathalie risked impossible debt and eviction if she moved against Lady Tremaine, and if she had already been tangled up with the law before because of her mentor, she might go along with a plot to avoid arrest again.

It was more than enough to confront Nathalie with, and perhaps she would give away who had done the actual stealing during the conversation if she didn't confess it outright. He picked up the pocket watch, disliking how light it felt despite knowing Nathalie had probably used its working parts to repair other, less weathered watches. With the right replacements and care, it could probably be repaired.

"I guess finding your owner is my next mystery to solve," he said, and put it back into the box.

This was such a good step forward, and he should have been celebrating or at least been in the mood for it.

But he still felt, deep in the pit of his chest, that he was missing something crucial.

～ 16 ～

On the Steps of the Palace

*A*UGUST HAD thought Father was exaggerating. Everyone, he had thought, meant every noble from Charmant and nearby kingdoms, every courtier, or every eligible young woman who was already in the royal city. He had thought he had a handle on Father's hyperbolic practices.

He was wrong.

"Gran," August muttered to the Grand Duke. "When he said everyone, did you not say, 'No, we can't possibly fit them all in the building,' and if you didn't, why not?"

"You know how he gets, Your Highness." The Grand Duke brought his hands before his chest and tapped his fingers together. "He's lonely, and you're rarely home. I did suggest letting you get married at your own pace, but he was insistent."

"He's always insistent," said August.

They were both safely hidden from the near

thousand crowded into the hall by a large curtain. August had been introduced to people before. He had spoken to crowds he didn't know and groups he did. He had addressed the court at least once a month on topics he sometimes got only a ten-minute brief on. He was used to being in front of people.

"Don't tell me I'm to be introduced to all these people?"

"The visiting nobles, of course, and then any of the Charmant nobility and gentry," said the Grand Duke.

"I'm to fall in love with only the use of the phrase 'nice to meet you,' am I?" asked August, narrowing his eyes at the man.

The Grand Duke dropped the curtain back into place, monocle glinting as he laughed. "That would be most convenient for us all, Your Highness."

August groaned. At least everyone who wouldn't usually have been invited would have a good night. Father had followed through on the all-encompassing invitation and ensured there was enough food on the tables for anyone who might wander in.

"Someone deserves to have fun," he muttered.

The Grand Duke took off his monocle. "Did you say something, Your Highness?"

"I dare not," he said flatly, "when I'll be introducing myself for the next ten hours."

"Don't worry. We shall let you sit once it's the gentry's turn."

August smoothed down his coat and forced his smile a few times until it didn't feel fake. The Grand Duke scurried off to hopefully temper Father's fury at August's lack of interest in the ball. From the sounds of it, most of the people present were there for the spectacle of witnessing the prince pick a bride. He shuddered. There was a particular horror to knowing your every move was being noted.

Soon enough, a herald bustled out through the curtains and began announcing him. The curtain rose, he emerged and bowed, and the ball began.

"Princess Frederica Eugenie de la Fontaine," cried the herald.

A lovely young woman whom August had met many times approached, her aquamarine gown pooling as she curtsied, and retreated. They didn't need to be introduced; they had already rejected their parents' attempts at setting them up twice.

Not even a minute later, the herald announced, "Mademoiselle Augustina DuBois, the daughter of General Pierre DuBois."

It was going to be a long night.

August hated how the young women became a blur. This was absurd—he remembered half of them only because they had met before. He bowed and smiled, making a face at the few of them he knew well enough to laugh with over the situation, and glanced toward the far balcony. One of his great-great-grandfathers had been in love with opera, and this hall had been meant for showcasing Charmant's rising talents. Now, though, his father sat in the box watching him. His pale gold suit with shiny buttons made him resemble a stout pearl in a cracked-open oyster, the red banner of Charmant a lolling tongue.

"Mademoiselle Leonora Mercedes de la Tour, daughter of Colonel and Madame de la Tour."

The ball was getting to him. Oysters didn't have tongues.

August bowed. She had a kind smile, but they had never spoken. There was no connection, no shared intimacy. He didn't know her history or what she wanted to make of her future and Charmant's future, but they could learn that about each other. Not in the ten seconds they had, though.

August winked at Leonora—not entirely

appropriate, but she looked as exasperated as he felt— and glanced up at his father, yawning.

His father turned as red as the nearby banner, and August made out his epaulets bouncing as he raged. Served him right.

The next young lady approached him, and then the next. He knew far fewer of the ones in line after them. He wanted to be in love, but it felt as if something in him were already missing, as if a physician with careful hands had cracked open his chest and cut out his heart before stitching him up. His heart was beating, but it felt hollow and distant.

Like his chance at love had already run away with it.

He straightened up from what must have been his fiftieth bow and glared up at Father. The ball was making him melancholy when he should have been questioning Nathalie.

"The mademoiselles Drizella and Anastasia Tremaine," announced the herald. "Daughters of Lady Tremaine."

August groaned. That meant they were only partway through the gentry.

Lady Tremaine's daughters were pretty, but the

colors they wore didn't suit them. Drizella's complexion would have been better served by an emerald, not chartreuse, gown, and Anastasia's less embellished magenta dress—clearly less expensive than her sister's—washed out her paler looks and red hair.

Anastasia bent down to adjust her skirts and caught her sister's dress beneath her heel, and Drizella pouted. He had briefly met the redheaded one, Anastasia, before. She had at least been somewhat kind to Oliver and told August and Martin about her mother's meeting with the baron.

They did not appear to be from a family experiencing financial troubles, but one with money to spare.

The girls dashed forward. There was a lack of care and regard in the way they acted toward him and everyone else. Even if their introduction had gone perfectly tonight, he wasn't sure he would be able to get over how they and their mother had treated Oliver. He had no desire to be related to Lady Tremaine, either.

Especially since he'd learned that her position as Nathalie's landlord gave Nathalie a reason to protect her. Lady Tremaine could be more wrapped up in this memory loss scheme than he had originally thought. Perhaps he could speak with her before confronting Nathalie.

He looked up at Father as he bowed, and the old man frowned.

Good. At least they agreed upon this.

Now, if only this procession of pointlessness could be over. He watched the Grand Duke make the mistake of riling Father up, probably with an "I told you so" to accompany the monocle flicking, and Father buried his head in his hands.

A glint like glass caught his eyes.

At the back of the ballroom glided a young woman. She was alone, eyes so wide that he could tell how sky blue they were from across the room. She spun to take in the palace, pale blue dress swirling around her legs like waves, and he caught a glimpse of her wide, pleased smile. Her joy lit the room like a star. He couldn't recall the last time he had been that happy.

August broke protocol, stepped down from his place, and quickly made his way to her.

Maybe he could find what he was missing.

~ 17 ~

So This Is Love

AUGUST DIDN'T care how much attention he was drawing to himself by approaching her directly. He had no idea who she was, but her smile . . .

There was something terribly familiar about the crook of her lips.

"Excuse me," he said as he neared, but she was too entranced by the sights of the palace to hear him. He gently touched her gloved hand. "Mademoiselle?"

She startled and spun, hand slipping from his grip. The sudden loss racked him with a sorrow he didn't understand. August bowed to hide the sudden emotion.

"Apologies for surprising you," he said, flexing his hand. Her long gloves were a thin, shimmering lace, and yet the warmth of her touch lingered.

She curtsied—not quite as deeply as politeness demanded—and couldn't quite keep her gaze on him.

"It's my first time here, and I never realized how lovely it was!"

"Its loveliness pales in comparison to you," he said, and rose from his bow. "I'm August."

"August," she repeated slowly, and the sound of his name from her lips made him smile. Then, she seemed to remember that she needed to offer him her hand. "I'm Ella."

August had always abided by the rules of propriety even if he didn't care for them. They were essentially a secret language among nobles that revealed instantly one's station, and her movements, though graceful, were stiff. He took her hand in his and pressed a chaste kiss to the back of it. She blushed a rosy pink.

"It's a pleasure to meet you, Ella," he said, and pulled away.

Perhaps she was a governess or a seamstress taking advantage of the opportunity to attend a ball. She had to be, with such an exquisite outfit. From afar, her gown had appeared blue. The material was thin and opalescent, shifting from silvery gray to icy blue with every movement, like moonlight caught in rippling water. She moved with an unassuming grace and held herself as if she was savoring everything around her, from the dress to the palace, as a dream about to dissolve. The baubles in her ears weren't jewels but glass blown in perfectly smooth circles.

"Would you like to know a secret?" she whispered.

He leaned in close and whispered back, "I would like nothing else more."

"I'm not entirely sure what we're supposed to do at balls," she said. "Especially when everyone is standing around."

"There's supposed to be dancing, but since there are so many people here, the rules are out the window."

"Pity. They're lovely windows."

"Don't worry. We open them before we throw the rules out." He offered her his other hand and turned toward the dance floor. "Would you like to dance?"

She curled her fingers around his palm. "I would love to, but it has been a while since my last dance."

The music shifted from a lively minuet to a waltz, and August chuckled. For once, he was grateful for his father's meddling. Unfortunately, he and Ella drew nearly every pair of eyes as they approached the dance floor.

August risked one glance at his father. He was gesturing wildly while the Grand Duke tried to corral him, and the light in the hall dimmed as several curtains closed.

The crowds around the floor rippled, people whispering to each other. Ella's eyes widened, and she looked around at everyone watching them. She stiffened, and August squeezed her hand, trying to distract her. She smiled at him.

"You're sure?" she asked.

"Trust me," said August, and despite having just met him, she nodded.

His chest tightened. Maybe his father was on to something with all this romantic setup nonsense.

They slipped into position with a quiet understanding, and she raised her chin with a confidence he hadn't possessed at his first-ever ball. There was something familiar about the tilt of her head and blue of her eyes.

"Do you live in the city?" he asked.

"No, the countryside," said Ella. "I haven't ever left until now, to be honest."

That was it—the blue of Fresne's spring skies.

"Have you managed to see any of the city?" He spun them, turning so her back was to the prying eyes of the Tremaine family.

She laughed gently. "No, only what I could see from the steps of the palace."

"The castle has some of the best views in the city, especially at night," he said. "Do you like stargazing?"

"Does anyone not?" she asked, cheeks dimpling when she smiled. "At night, if I'm still working, I like to sit outside whenever I can. It's much more peaceful."

"And beautiful, I imagine," said August, trying to picture how her eyes would glitter under the night sky. "What do you do for work?"

"Nothing this interesting." She peered over his shoulder and then tilted her head back slightly. "Are there usually this many people here?"

August smiled, ignoring her deflection. "No, this is fairly unusual."

"I thought other people would join in the dancing," said Ella, her fingers tightening around his hand.

She had clearly expected some eyes to watch them, but she still looked nervous—very, very nervous—and seemed to be trying her best to follow etiquette. He didn't want to subject her to more scrutiny. It wasn't her fault that the nobility of Charmant was so nosy. She was doing well for her first meeting with the prince.

"Then let's leave and hope they get the message,"

he said. "Courtiers are required to gossip at least once per day." He loved the way it felt when she laughed, his palm flush against her ribs and privy to every shuddering breath. "Since it's so late, they're desperate to hit their quota." He gently pressed his hand into her side and directed them toward the balcony. With any luck, Gran would keep them away from prying eyes.

The curtains fell, separating them from the ballroom and leaving them alone on the balcony. August steered her farther from the windows.

"There are guards out here, of course, but no gossips," he said, and spun them so that she could take in the view.

And so that he could take in her joy at it.

August couldn't shake the feeling that they had met before, but he had met so many people on his travels. He wasn't so foolish as to think he could remember all of them. Surely he would have remembered her, though.

He was sure she wouldn't reveal her family name if she wouldn't even share what she did for work, and he didn't want to pry too hard. By the end of the night, he hoped she would have grown comfortable enough to open up to him.

Beneath the indigo swathe of evening, the stars glittered like pale fire in her eyes. She tilted her head back and closed them, mouth slightly open. His gaze slid from the bow of her lips to the bared arch of her throat. She exhaled slowly.

"The air's different here," she said softly. "It smells like oranges and roses."

He brushed a loose curl from her neck.

"The gardens are magnificent, if I do say so myself," said August. He wanted nothing more than to watch her eat an orange and didn't have the faintest clue why. It was as if the reason was on the tip of his tongue. This wasn't quite love, but it felt as potent. "Would you like to see them?"

She nodded and beamed at him.

He would've given her a greenhouse, the royal gardens, or any number of state secrets if she asked right then.

August twirled her toward a set of low stairs that led from the balcony and into the gardens proper. A fountain rippled in the quiet night, and they walked hand in hand to it. He was so taken by the weight of her hand in his and the rustle of her breath against his collar that he barely noticed them slip into a dance. They didn't stumble or step on the other's toes, as if they were flying. As if they had danced together before.

But that was impossible.

She knelt over the water and dipped her hand through the night's reflection.

"The stars feel closer," she whispered, staring not at the sky or the water but at him.

They had abandoned the waltz long ago, but he kept her hand in his. With a gentle tug, he spun her away from the fountain.

"An odd thing for a star to say," he said. "Here one is, glittering in the garden next to me, and you haven't even noticed."

She let out a soft laugh and glanced at him through her lashes. "Don't stars burn? If I were a star, I'm afraid the garden would be nothing but ash."

"Perhaps I prefer cinder to roses." He pulled her closer as they walked across a short bridge.

The pale stones clacked under their shoes, the sounds oddly loud in the calm night. Ella tucked herself against his side, her arm securely through his, and August led her up a set of wide stairs. The palace loomed over them, and shadows flickered across the high windows of the ballroom, where everyone else had finally started dancing. Ella sighed and gripped his hand tighter. He stopped at the top of the stairs.

"We don't have to go back inside yet," he said, and he helped her sit on the low banister. "Honestly, I prefer this. Talking to you is like talking to an old friend."

His father was going to be insufferable the next day.

"I feel like that, too," she said, pulling him to sit next to her.

Was this quiet vulnerability and inexplicable draw, this comfort and desire he couldn't extinguish with thoughts or reason, truly love? He slid his hands up her arms, brushing a thumb across the bare skin there.

She leaned in as if to kiss him, and August bowed his head to do the same. Her breath whispered against his lips.

Then, the clock struck midnight. Ella pulled away and gasped.

"Oh!" She stared at the distant clock tower in horror. "Oh, my goodness!"

"What's the matter?" he asked, disappointment coursing through him.

She rose and said, "It's midnight."

"Yes, so it is," said August, confused by her sudden change. It hadn't been that far from midnight when she arrived. He reached for her. "But why . . ."

"Goodbye," she said, and turned away.

"No, no, wait." He caught her wrist and stopped her at the top of the stairs. "You can't go now."

He had never met anyone and instantly felt at home with them, and she had, by all accounts, appeared to feel the same. What did it matter if it was midnight? The ball would carry on until dawn, like most did.

"Oh, I must. Please," she said, and pulled away again. "Please, I must."

"But why?" he asked, taking both of her hands in his.

"Well, I . . . I . . ." Her expression faltered, and she carefully took a few steps away. "Oh, the prince. I haven't met the prince."

"The prince?" He nearly laughed. "But didn't you know—"

The bells tolled again, and she gathered up her skirts to run.

"Goodbye!"

August sprinted after her. "No, wait. Come back. Please come back."

August's mind reeled. Chasing her, when she was

so insistent to leave, felt wrong, but he didn't want to lose her. He didn't even know her full name.

Oh, no.

"I don't even know your name. How will I find you?" he cried out, sprinting after her. "Wait! Please, wait!"

She ducked beneath the curtains and into the ballroom, and he barreled through them after her.

"Wait!" he called out again.

But Ella was already a quarter of the way across the room.

"The prince!" The crowd at the edge of the dance floor swarmed him.

August groaned. The Grand Duke huffed after Ella, chasing her in his stead. August tried to slip away from the crowd, refusing dance requests and turning down invitations to take a turn about the gardens, but there were far too many. Slowly, he made his way out of the crowd toward the Grand Duke.

He caught the older man at the top of the steps. "Did you let her go?"

"Your Highness," said Gran, cradling something in his hands. "I am so sorry, but I've failed you."

August eyed his hands. "Did you push her down the stairs?"

"August!" He harrumphed and held out the shoe. "I'm afraid she got away. I've sent out the guards who were on duty tonight, and I am sure they will chase down her coach. They will certainly catch her."

"She wanted to leave. Needed to, if her panic was anything to go by. You didn't need to send guards to hunt her down," August said, turning the shoe over and over in his hands. It couldn't be real. A glass slipper? "She's neither a criminal nor required to marry me because I liked her."

"His Majesty was very clear that tonight must be successful," said the Grand Duke.

His father had to stop threatening to behead Gran. It was making them both far too jumpy.

"My father may be as clear as he likes, but the final say is mine." August held the shoe up to the light. It *was* pure glass. The craftsmanship was exquisite, and the fit must have been perfect for it not to be painful to walk on. There couldn't be that many people in Charmant—or anywhere else—who could make something so delicate and functional. He had never heard of such a thing. "Tracking the person who made this will help us find her, but she knows where to find me. I don't want to hunt her. She isn't a deer."

Really, how many Ellas could there be in Charmant?

"Your father—"

"Will give you alternative orders, I'm sure. Don't let anything happen to this shoe. I'll try to find out who made it," said August, and he handed the Grand Duke the glass slipper. "It's odd, though."

Like her, the sparkling but sturdy glass felt familiar. It was cool to the touch when it should have been warm, and each clack of his nails against the glass rang out like a small bell. What did this remind him—

"What is, Your Highness?" the Grand Duke asked.

"Sorry," said August, shaken from his thoughts. "What?"

The Grand Duke smiled consolingly. "What's odd?"

All of it. The shoe, her flight, and all the moments they spent together that felt as if they had already happened. The whole time he had been with her, the hollow hole in his chest hadn't ached once.

"Nothing," he muttered, shuddering. "I feel like I knew her."

In the back of his mind, a voice that sounded suspiciously like Martin dredged up all his fears. People in Fresne had been forgetting those they had loved for years, and he had messed with the lockbox that morning. But no, only the pocket watch had been inside of it, and he had no proof it was from the memorial. He was being dramatic. If he had known Ella and forgotten her, someone would have noticed.

So why did he feel so uneasy?

Every Star in the Sky

*T*HE MYSTERIOUS Ella, who had escaped the guards the Grand Duke had sent out after her, haunted August for the rest of the night. No one had known her, not the guards or guests or servants, and no one had ever heard of glass shoes. August was certain they would be popular come the next party, but that didn't help him at all.

It was as if the Ella he had met had come into existence for a few hours only and then vanished without a trace.

And the longer August went without being able to find any hint of her, the more he feared he might never find her.

His father, furious that a potential daughter-in-law had slipped through his fingers, was rallying people to search for the shoe's owner, and August snuck from the city in the chaos. He needed to speak to Nathalie about his suspicions regarding Lady Tremaine. With any luck, the Tremaine family would be too exhausted from the ball to lie once he confronted them later.

And, seeing as Nathalie had traveled extensively and dealt in peculiar finds, perhaps she knew of someone capable of making glass slippers.

What was the other option? Making every young woman in the kingdom try on that shoe?

August groaned. Desperate to find her. Desperate to remember her.

"Maybe love is continual desperation," he muttered to himself, and squinted up at the sky. The road to Fresne was thick with people traveling home after the ball, and not a single one was Ella. His horse huffed.

Another rider pulled up beside him and whispered, "Riddle me this, Your Highness: Why was the prince pretending to be a footman only a few days ago, and why is he traveling alone now?"

"I fear the answer isn't as exciting as most riddles are," said August, and he turned to the speaker. "Lord Moreau, I didn't realize you were aware of my deception."

"I would be a poor baron if I were incapable of recognizing my kingdom's royalty," said Lord Moreau. The older man was in a toned-down riding suit, the only embellishment a brooch sparkling on his chest. He narrowed his eyes at August. "Also, my butler told me."

August laughed and nodded. "That makes sense."

"And that is the look of a young man pining after lost love," said the baron. "If you will permit me a bit of familiarity, which I think will do us good since you trespassed on my estate, it was bold to hold a ball to meet every eligible woman in the kingdom and then only speak with one."

"The ball wasn't my idea." August held back a snort. "Were you in attendance?"

"Ah, the plight of youth." Lord Moreau sat up in his saddle and tilted his head back. Fresne was only just becoming visible down the road. "I'm not one to turn down a night of good food and better gossip. Now, I imagine you wanted something from me?"

"Do you have the first brooch Lady Tremaine gifted you?" August asked.

"Oh, yes. Beautiful piece. Some of Nathalie's best work, I think," he said. "Mayor Fauconnier told me about what happened with her, and I find it difficult to believe."

Lord Moreau unpinned the brooch from his chest and handed it to August. It was a small and unassuming lily, the petals made from interlocking glass scales. Gold wire had been used to hold them together, the color running through the glass like veins, and a horrible, sinking certainty settled in August's stomach. He held the brooch up to the sky, and the grief gripped his throat. The light caught the glass as if it were full of stars.

This glass. These scales. That gleam.

August closed his eyes, a thousand different feelings burning through him. He couldn't breathe. He couldn't move. He knew the chill brush of these glass scales as well as he knew himself, despite not holding them since he was a child. He cleared his throat.

Lord Moreau sighed. "It's another one of the stolen items, isn't it?"

August opened his eyes and nodded. "Yes. The glass pieces are, at least."

"A pity," said Lord Moreau.

"May I keep this?" August asked, the glass scales cool in his grip. Everything felt cold despite the day's heat. "I was on my way to speak to Nathalie and then Lady Tremaine."

"Of course. Return it to whomever it was stolen from. I suspect I shall hear an earful from Madame Fauconnier about it soon," said the baron. "While you are visiting Lady Tremaine, tell that stepdaughter of hers that I have a job for her if she wants it. Heaven knows that Lady Tremaine is wasting her talents."

August nearly fell off his horse. "Lady Tremaine has a stepdaughter?"

How could he not have uncovered that fact?

"She inherited the estate and the girl nearly a decade ago," he said. "It was her second husband that granted her the title, and I am ever so happy to not be the third now. Though I hear the estate will return to the girl when she comes of age. She was playing the part of her stepmother's lady's maid that night you were pretending to be her footman." The baron laughed. "I suppose the two of you have quite a bit in common, then."

August had absolutely no memories of Lady Tremaine's lady's maid that night. He had been to the estate and spoken to Lady Tremaine's family, and yet he could not recall a single mention of a stepdaughter.

August shivered, the back of his neck prickling with cold, and gripped the brooch more tightly.

"I'll tell her," said August, the words bitter. "Why offer her a job?"

"Well, the girl's got skill with a needle and

thread. Talent should always be nurtured regardless of standing," Lord Moreau said, and nudged his horse forward. "Safe travels, Your Highness."

He clicked his tongue against his teeth and took off down one of the side roads leading toward his land. August hesitated at the crossroads.

How had he gotten into Lady Tremaine's study to see her accounts? He couldn't recall anyone being with him, but how would he have known where the study was?

August went straight to Blanche to request a meeting with Nathalie. Not much had changed in the days he had been gone. Blanche took him to Nathalie without a fuss, and the merchant didn't so much as look at him when he entered the small room where she was being held. She was paler than she had been the last time and had worried the corner of her thumb bloody. August held the brooch out to her.

"You made this, didn't you?" he asked.

She glanced at it, flinched, and nodded.

"You know, I wondered what the thief could possibly have on you that would demand such silence, and it's not that she's blackmailing you, is it?" August asked, and a muscle twitched beneath Nathalie's eye. "Do you really want to protect Lady Tremaine?"

"Of course not!" she cried, more animated than he had ever seen her. "Why would I want to be like her! She stole from the memorial! I'm not a monster. I know what that means to people."

"She sold you items stolen from the memorial, told you to rework them, and took the payments when you sold the remade items?" he asked.

Slowly, she nodded. "I didn't know they were stolen at first. She had brought me other things before, and I thought this was more of that arrangement. Then she told me to make them unrecognizable. I didn't know why, but I didn't want to refuse a lady."

August ground his teeth together and tightened his grip on what had once been his mother's bracelet.

"She owns my building. I can't lose my shop. It's all I have. Was all I had," whispered Nathalie, shaking her head. "I did what she said, and didn't ask where they were from. I paid too much for what she sold me, gifted her two things made from it, and turned over the money I earned selling the rest. In return, she never raised my rent. She brought that up quite a lot. If I refused her, she would put me out."

August's silence settled over the room.

Nathalie groaned. "I didn't ask questions, either, I know, but when you came in asking only about them, I put it together. I don't know how they hurt anyone. I wouldn't have done it if . . ."

"Of course not," said August, wanting to keep her talking. "Do you have proof Lady Tremaine sold the items to you?"

Nathalie nodded. "I used a special mark to signify it was her, a symbol for her cat. But she's gentry. She knows people would believe her on principle. She would blame me for the theft and then call in her debts."

August swallowed down the shame he felt at her insistence that people would believe a member of the gentry first. That was one of the things he had to change in Charmant.

"I shall deal with Lady Tremaine," he said, and stared at the brooch in his hands. "You will tell Blanche everything when I send her in. Detail every moment, meeting, and conversation you had with Lady Tremaine. Do you understand?"

Nathalie nodded but sadly muttered, "She'll never admit it, though."

"Probably not, but the thing about greed is that people are rarely greedy only once," he said, thinking back over all his investigations for the court over the years. "Lady Tremaine kept your rent low, yes?"

Nathalie nodded again.

He didn't have access to Lady Tremaine's personal records—yet—but Martin already had the tax records. Lady Tremaine had raised the rents of her other tenants, and August would bet she had underreported her earnings. If she had, it would be easy enough to find out. That would support Nathalie's story against her.

"If she hadn't kept it low for you, do you know what you would have paid?" he asked.

Nathalie told him what she paid, what she would have been paying without the deal, and who else Lady Tremaine collected rent from. It would be easy enough to determine if Lady Tremaine was lying about her income to the kingdom. Leverage was always useful.

August stormed from the building. There was a crowd forming in the market square. Rumors of a mysterious girl with clothes made of glass who had bewitched the prince had spread, and everyone knew that the palace was on the hunt for her. August left a note for Martin about the tax records at the inn and set out to confront Lady Tremaine. He could speak with her and settle this all quickly. Then, he could find Ella.

Except he didn't even have to think about how to get to the Tremaine estate. There was something off about that. Even the house wasn't right, as if he were staring at it through a slightly off-kilter window. He remembered its exterior, well manicured if a touch plain, and that the entry hall was a lovely slate blue that reminded him of winter. He also remembered that if he turned off the road to his right, there was a foot-beaten path to the kitchen. He remembered how narrow the servants' stairs were. He remembered which room was the music room.

But none of those memories felt right. If Lady Tremaine had a stepdaughter, shouldn't he have met her that day or at least have seen her? If that was his first time in the building, why did he remember thinking the interior had looked better before Lady Tremaine moved in? August shuddered.

Given the current happenings in Fresne, he couldn't shake the uneasy sense of wrongness that washed over him.

However, August ignored it as best he could and walked toward the front door. Lady Tremaine had to provide answers today no matter what.

A giant black cat slunk around the side of the

building, a struggling mouse in its jaws, and startled when it saw August. Its mouth fell open, and the mouse darted away. August froze.

The cat, too, was familiar, but in a different way. It was frozen, watching August with narrowed green eyes. Four whiskers quivered as its fur fluffed up.

Like an X with the center gone.

"Lucifer?" muttered August. He couldn't remember who had told him its name.

The frantic pounding of hooves on the road sounded behind him. August turned, the cat fleeing back around the house. A coach, wreathed in a cloud of dust, appeared far down the road, and August stepped off the stairs to the side of the path. Sunlight glinted off the gold decorating the carriage, and August winced when he recognized it as the Grand Duke's. Fortunately, the old man was snoring beyond the fluttering window curtain, and August darted to the side of the building and out of sight. The Grand Duke and his father had probably made a list of every noble and genteel family nearby and decided to visit them first. August had no desire to get berated for not looking for Ella yet. Surely the Grand Duke would leave the moment he realized this was the wrong family. August could have waited outside until then.

But instinct or suspicion or fate drove him onward.

August didn't know how he knew that this path led to the kitchens. There was a newly built goat pen and chickens pecking along the path, which ended at a step up into a large kitchen. An old hound dog was asleep in the open doorway, and August, nervous about waking it, hesitated. Before he could move, the dog cracked one eye and loped over to him. August knelt to pet it.

The dog's name came to him from a memory he couldn't place. Perhaps Oliver had mentioned it.

"Hello there, Bruno," he said, and ruffled his fur. "Can you be very good for me and not bark?"

Bruno huffed, licked his face, and made his way outside, settling down in a sunbeam. August laughed under his breath.

August made his way up the servants' stairs in the back of the kitchen. Muffled by the walls, he heard the herald announce the Grand Duke's arrival. The hallway he emerged into was blessedly empty, and the trumpet echoed clearer and louder through the halls. The Grand Duke read the royal proclamation, August nodding at the predictable words. The study was down the hall, if he remembered correctly.

Why did he remember that at all?

A cry, stifled by the walls of the house, barely reached his ears, and August turned, trying to pinpoint where it had come from. The hallway he was in would lead to the main stairs, and there he would be able to overlook the proceedings with the shoe. Curious about Lady Tremaine's disposition, he headed that way.

Then he heard it again—a muffled cry drowned out by the clatter of piano keys. What was the Grand Duke doing downstairs?

August made his way to the landing overlooking the first floor. Drizella was arguing with the footman attempting to help her try on the shoe, and Anastasia was looking on with vague envy. The person crying had to be Lady Tremaine's stepdaughter, but she was an eligible maiden. She should have, by law, been down there trying on the shoe.

Drizella had managed to squeeze her foot into the shoe, her arch at the most uncomfortable angle he had ever seen. At this rate, Lady Tremaine would start cutting off toes.

The faint yowl of a cat got his attention, and August's first thought was *Lucifer's at it again.* There was a loud crash high above. Beneath him, the shoe popped off Drizella's foot.

It went flying. Gran and the footman dove for it, Gran barely catching it on a finger. August couldn't make out the words he exchanged with Lady Tremaine as the footman replaced the slipper on his cushion, and a rattle of paws against stairs drew his attention away. The sounds were definitely coming from the door at the end of the hall.

"You are the only ladies in the household, I hope," the Grand Duke said, and then caught himself. "I presume."

"There's no one else, Your Grace," said Lady Tremaine.

Except a stepdaughter no one had ever mentioned and whom August couldn't remember despite his time here. He darted for the door.

"Quite so," said the Grand Duke, turning to leave.

August reached for the tower door, but before he could grasp the handle, footsteps came from behind it. It flew open, narrowly missing his face, and he tucked himself between the wood and the wall. A young woman in the clothes of a scullery maid, soot stains at her knees and tears streaking her cheeks, stumbled onto the landing. Her eyes were red-rimmed, and her hair was loose, but there was no mistaking her.

This was Ella, his Ella.

He had found her.

~ 19 ~

Sing, Sweet Nightingale

"*Y*OUR GRACE?" Ella addressed Gran.

She sounded like August remembered, and she moved with the same poise as she had last night. August stepped forward before recalling where he was and hiding again. He wanted more than anything to clutch her hand and ask her why he hadn't remembered her as Lady Tremaine's stepdaughter. Though, he had a terrifying, wonderful suspicion.

"Your Grace, please, wait," she cried, and hurried down the stairs. "May I try it on?"

But mostly, painfully, August needed to let her see this through, because there was a dark suspicion unfurling in his mind that Lady Tremaine was about to be exposed, and he wanted to watch.

Lady Tremaine huffed. "Pay no attention to her."

"It's only Cinderella," said Drizella.

*Cinder*ella? August pressed his lips together to keep from shouting.

"From the kitchens!" said Anastasia or Drizella, and they couldn't help speaking over each other. "She's out of her mind."

"A scullery maid," continued Lady Tremaine, ignoring that Ella was her stepdaughter. She tried to block the Grand Duke from reaching Ella. "Yes, yes, just an imaginative child."

That made the Grand Duke square his shoulders and pull himself up to his full height.

"Madame, my orders were 'every maiden,'" he said, and swept past her to offer Ella his hand. "Come, my child."

He escorted her to a chair and gestured for the footman to bring the glass slipper. August leaned over the railing, eager to see Ella thwart the Tremaine family, and gasped. Lady Tremaine slid her cane out and tripped the footman. The shoe tumbled from the pillow.

It shattered before Ella with a heartbreaking clatter.

"Oh, no!" The Grand Duke fell to his knees and covered his face with his hands. "No, no, no. Oh, no!" He tried to gather up the pieces. "Oh, this is terrible. The king! What will he say? What will he do?"

Lady Tremaine sneered down at the entire

scene. The smugness radiating from her stance made August's blood boil.

"Perhaps, if it would help," Ella said gently.

The Grand Duke waved her off. "No, no. Nothing can help now. Nothing."

"But you see," said Ella, pulling out the second glass shoe from her pocket, "I have the other slipper."

Lady Tremaine's face distorted in horror. August laughed into his arm to prevent being discovered and ducked back slightly. He would have to reveal himself soon, but he so wanted to know how Lady Tremaine would try to get out of this one. She had been digging her grave for a while, and it was more than deep enough. She was petty enough to keep shoveling, though.

The Grand Duke placed the slipper easily on Ella's foot. August grinned. Now that he had found her, they needed to get their memories back. Since she hadn't recognized him at the ball, she must have forgotten him, too. He had thought it so unlikely, but working together to investigate the memory loss would explain how they had gotten close. He had seen the same bond form between Martin and Oliver.

But five days to fall in love? August couldn't believe *he* would fall in love that quickly. Though, he still felt as if he were missing something.

"You little thief!" Lady Tremaine shoved past the Grand Duke and pinned Ella to the chair with the cane tip in her shoulder. "Who did you steal that shoe from?"

"Madame!" The Grand Duke leapt to his feet. "Unhand her this instant."

"Forgive me, Your Grace, but you're not familiar with her deceptions. I took her in after her father died as a kindness, and she has repaid me with robbery and willfulness," said Lady Tremaine.

She didn't dig the cane into Ella's shoulder or raise her hand, but Ella flinched as if hit. Then she braced herself. August gripped the railing.

Ella grabbed the cane. "I am not a thief, I didn't steal anything, and I have never stolen from you."

Five days must have been more than enough, because he was falling in love with her all over again right now.

"Do you see what I have put up with? This girl cannot be the lady from last night, because she is not fit for public. If she was at the ball, then she stole the dress and shoes from some unfortunate soul after I banned her from attending for trying to sabotage my daughters' dresses," said Lady Tremaine, and she glanced at the Grand Duke. "His Majesty will appreciate our saving his son from such a horrible criminal."

"I'm not a criminal!" Ella snapped, and pushed the cane aside. "I didn't steal anything! You're the ones who destroyed my dress!"

"Hush," Lady Tremaine said. "You've committed a terrible crime, Cinderella. I'm trying to help you."

Cinderella—August shook his head. This was too much, and Ella shouldn't have to deal with it alone.

"I doubt that, Lady Tremaine," August said as he descended the stairs, and everyone turned to stare at him. "The Grand Duke and my father might not recognize the girl I met last night, but did you really think I wouldn't? Did you think that I would only look at the slipper, see that it fit, and not look at the face of the person wearing it? That I wouldn't speak with her?"

He would have been insulted if he weren't so angry.

"Your Highness." Lady Tremaine dipped into a low curtsy. "I wasn't aware you were here."

"That was by design," he said, and glanced back up the stairs. "Imagine my surprise when I came to speak with you and heard sobbing from the tower room."

Ella stiffened in the chair. Lady Tremaine opened

her mouth to speak, and August held up his hand. Making her first smart decision, she stayed silent.

"Ella?" he asked softly. August knelt before the chair and laid a hand over hers. "Do you mind explaining what happened last night?"

"It's going to be very difficult to believe," she said, staring at him as if she would never be able to look away again.

August squeezed her hand and studied her just as desperately. "I have quite the imagination."

"I was going to wear my mother's dress to the ball, but it was damaged," she said, and August knew she meant by Lady Tremaine. "I was outside wishing I could go because I wanted one night to have fun, a night when I didn't have to worry about anything at all. I didn't wish it aloud, but she came to me."

"A fairy granted you a wish," he said, and smiled.

That only happened when someone good was in great need.

"Preposterous!" Lady Tremaine said. "No fairy would grant her a wish to attend a ball."

"That's exactly the sort of thing one would do if the wish was for happiness," August said.

Ella smiled at him and squared her shoulders.

"She said I had to return home by midnight. That was when the magic would wear off, and I almost made it. Everything she had transformed with magic returned to what it had been before. Everything except the slippers."

"It's a gift to remember the wish by. They always leave one." August swallowed. Ella must have been kind beyond measure to earn a wish, and it made him want to know her all the more. "Ella, I believe you. I remember you from the ball. Last night was perfect."

She grabbed his hand with both of hers and said in a breathy whisper, "I didn't realize that you . . . I thought . . . You're the prince."

She said it with a disbelief and reverence he didn't like, but her smile didn't falter.

"I thought you were another guest," she said, blushing.

"I didn't realize you thought that until you were leaving, or I would have mentioned it," he said.

"I'm not the Ella you met last night," she said. "She was a dream."

"She seemed very real to me, and I quite like this Ella before me now," August said, leaning in so that only she could hear him. "I'm not always how I was last night."

She laughed. "I'll keep that in mind, but I like this version of you, too."

From behind him, Lady Tremaine made a disgusted noise in the back of her throat.

"And between you and me," whispered August, "I think we've met before."

Ella's mouth opened slightly, and he nodded as realization widened her eyes.

"Do not think I have forgotten you, madame," August said, rising and pivoting so that he was between Lady Tremaine and Ella. "Do you know what's curious?"

"That such a well-educated prince has been taken in by a scullery maid?" she asked.

"That you haven't asked me why I was on my way to speak with you but wasn't part of this procession," said August.

Lady Tremaine arched a brow at that. The Grand Duke had taken a few steps back and watched him with interest. Anastasia and Drizella were glaring at Ella, then her feet, and then her again. August pulled out the glass lily brooch.

"You gifted this to Lord Moreau, the Baron of Ghent," he said.

"Yes," she said. "Forgive me, Your Highness, but I don't understand why this matters. Is generosity a crime?"

"It matters because this is stolen," said August.

"Oh, how terrible," she said with all the appropriate affectations of shock and horror. But given the conversation, she was far too nonchalant. "However, I'm afraid I still don't understand."

"Nathalie identified you as the person she purchased stolen items from, and she said you had her remake them so that they wouldn't be recognizable when sold," said August. "You will say, of course, that she's lying. That's fine. Given her account books—and I'm sure yours, once we see them—there is more than enough evidence to detain and question you for the theft of items off the Fresne memorial alone. Nathalie even used a special notation to mark the money she paid you when she sold the remade items."

The Grand Duke looked as if he had swallowed every lemon in the kingdom, and August wished that Martin were here.

"How dare you!" Lady Tremaine shrieked. "Your

Highness, I have always respected the royal family, but to sneak into my home, accuse me of lying about my maid, and then this? It's nothing more than speculation and slander! It's unheard of."

The Grand Duke cleared his throat. "It is quite unheard of, Your Highness."

"So was memory loss and someone stealing from a cemetery, and yet here we are," August said. "You stole the items from the memorial and sold them to Nathalie, and in exchange for her silence, you didn't raise her rent."

"If there is evidence of such theft here, it's surely because of her," said Lady Tremaine, gesturing at Ella. "You cannot believe this nonsense about a fairy. She's my maid, and a poor—"

"Stop saying that," Ella said, and swallowed. Then, more loudly, "Stop calling me that. Stop acting like I'm nothing to you."

Lady Tremaine's eye twitched, but she turned to August instead of addressing Ella. "This girl is clearly unable to discern real life from dreams, and you think a girl who would not hesitate to steal to attend the ball and then lie about it wouldn't steal from the memorial?"

"Stop it!" Ella launched herself out of the chair.

She planted herself next to August, her arm pressed against his. She trembled with each word. "I am not your maid. I am your stepdaughter, and we are standing in my father's house. You have always dismissed me and used me, but no more! I won't have you leave a stain on his legacy by doing something so foul as stealing from a cemetery and blaming it on me. The estate may be falling to pieces, but you will not ruin his memory!"

"You ungrateful clod," spat Lady Tremaine. "You dare question me? Deprive my daughters of their birthrights? Your father cost me everything!"

August raised an arm to step between Ella and Lady Tremaine again, but Ella pushed him aside. She laced their fingers together and squared her shoulders.

"What I find curious," said August, "is that you don't even need the money, so far as I can tell. You could afford to keep this estate up and running like normal quite easily if you wanted to." He had seen as much from her estate's books. "So why bother with all of this?"

"You could?" Ella asked softly. "You said I was helping. You said the family needed help."

"I did," snapped Lady Tremaine. "He left

everything to you, and the moment you come of age, I shall have nothing."

Ella reared back and whispered, "You thought I would give you nothing?"

"So you stole to prepare for the encroaching loss of funds," said August. "You overcharged Nathalie and robbed a cemetery."

The woman glanced between him and Ella and whispered, "Prove it. I shall take my chances at court. I do not believe for a moment she didn't steal those shoes. Good things come to those who work for them."

"Our mother would never!" Drizella lunged forward to stand before her mother, voice pitched with disbelief. "It's Cinderella. It's always Cinderella!"

The Grand Duke stared at her. "Always her doing what?"

"You know, everything wrong," said Drizella, deflating a bit under his gaze. "But on purpose. She dropped the breakfast trays this morning."

"Be that as it may, it's not a crime," said August. "I am sure all of this can be solved easily, Lady Tremaine. Show us the books for the estate so that we may compare what Nathalie paid for the pieces with your income." August squeezed Ella's hand. "And we can compare the handwriting to determine who documented the income, of course."

Lady Tremaine tensed. "I will do no such thing."

"Mother, tell them!" Drizella cried. "She ruins everything. Show them!"

"She's never stolen," muttered Anastasia, but Drizella shouted over her. "Mother!"

August inclined his head toward Anastasia, and Lady Tremaine sniffed.

"I will not stoop so low as to be forced to reveal my financials in such company," said Lady Tremaine.

"But you will trip a man and break the glass slipper?" August asked. "You will cast aside your stepdaughter and use her as a lady's maid so that you can hoard money? Lady Tremaine, I did not come here to investigate you. The evidence will speak for itself. Now, about your daughters—"

"They had nothing to do with it," she said quickly. "You shall not speak with them. They are children."

Drizella's eyes widened. "Mother?"

Even Ella looked shocked by the words. It was basically a confession.

A loud rapping at the front door cut off anything else she might say. Everyone glanced at the door, and then Anastasia and Drizella glanced at Ella. August nearly laughed.

They expected her to answer the door *now*?

A bit uncertain, the footman the Grand Duke had brought with him opened the door. Martin and Oliver stood in the doorway, the former holding a small journal. Oliver stayed a step behind him, and Martin bowed to the Grand Duke and August. He smiled at Ella, too.

"You got my message?" August asked.

"And came as soon as possible." Martin nodded. "I went back over the records for the estate as you asked. You were right—the income reported doesn't match up with what it should be based on what Lady Tremaine collected in rent from her tenants."

Lady Tremaine paled, and August smiled, giving in to pettiness for once.

"Excellent," he said, and cocked one brow at her in an attempt to match her constant look of disdain. "Lady Tremaine, care to explain that?"

She opened and shut her mouth, but the only sound she could make was a croak.

"I think we have heard enough, madame," said the Grand Duke. "Sir Tremblay, if you could assist me . . ."

"No! No, Cinderella," Lady Tremaine cried, and turned to her stepdaughter. "This is a family matter. It should stay in the family. Please, your father would hate for you to do this to me."

Ella's expression hardened, her eyes becoming ice. "I don't think it's me who my father would hate right now. You are lucky that I shall work toward forgiving you, but I shall not lie to the court for you. I shall not forget what you did to me despite the fact that we are family." She glanced at her stepsisters and frowned. "Or what you've done to them."

"To them?" Lady Tremaine reared back. "I have done everything for them! Leave them out of this."

Drizella nodded, but Anastasia bowed her head, hands clasped behind her.

"Anastasia," Oliver said, voice soft and slow. "You should go upstairs and pack for yourself and your sister so that you can travel to the city with your mother. Can you do that?"

She looked at him blankly, and Ella quietly said, "Your traveling bags are under your beds."

Anastasia scurried up the stairs and dragged a stunned Drizella with her. Oliver sighed.

"I'll go get the accounts," he said, and gently

touched Ella's shoulder as he passed. "The study, *step-daughter?*"

"Thank you." She nodded and flushed. "I'm sorry I never told you."

"Don't worry about it," said Oliver. "But we're friends, Ella, so don't hesitate to ask if you need help."

He raced up the stairs after Anastasia and Drizella, and Ella seemed to take in what had happened. She blinked and swayed, and August wrapped one arm around her waist.

"I'm glad you came back to talk to her," Martin whispered to August as he went to help the Grand Duke escort Lady Tremaine outside. "I know it will be tough with her having forgotten you, but you'll both get through it."

It was the confirmation he had been waiting for. And all his old fears—of loving someone and losing them—felt so dull and insignificant now that he knew he had survived it with Ella. They had forgotten each other completely.

And loved each other the very moment they met again.

"Ella," he said, holding her close. "Are you well?"

She was pale and drawn but smiling.

"This is impossible," Ella said. She collapsed on

the steps of the house, her house, and watched the
Grand Duke and Martin help her stepmother into
the carriage. "I've had dreams like this, but I always
woke up before she was taken away or I kissed the
prince."

"Well, if it will make you feel better, we don't
have to kiss and can take in her departure fully."
August sat down next to her. "You're not alone. You
don't have to be alone ever again if you don't want. If
you need my help, you have it."

She laughed then. There was no questioning the
affection burning through his veins, and it flourished
when she laughed. He would forget her every day of
his life and fall in love over and over again if it meant
he got to hear her laugh like that.

She sighed and leaned against him, hair tickling
his nose. Then she whispered, "What did Martin mean
about me forgetting you? Did he mean like the rest of
Fresne forgetting people? Because my memories of the
last week are a little fuzzy in places, and I don't know
why I spent so much of it investigating with Martin."

"See, I remember investigating with him alone,"
said August, and he pulled a handkerchief from his
pocket. He dabbed at the tear streaks still shining on
Ella's cheeks, letting his fingers linger along her jaw.

Her cheeks warmed beneath his hands. "I don't have any memories of meeting you until last night, and I trust Martin with my life. If he says we met, then I believe him."

"I don't have any memories of you, either, and if you were here to investigate, I would have met you." Ella reached up and touched his face. "Hard to think I could forget you."

"That's my line," he muttered, and she laughed. "It does imply that we were taken with each other."

"In love, Your Highness," she said. "It means I loved you and you loved me, and even if that weren't true, I love you now."

She tilted her head back, smiling up at him. There were no glass drops glittering in her ears and her hair was tangled from her time in the tower, but it was *her*.

Slowly, August leaned down and pressed his mouth to hers. She responded as if it was the most natural thing in the world and curled a hand around the back of his neck. The kiss was sweet and soft, chasing away all his thoughts like a warm summer breeze.

He pulled away, kissed her lips lightly again, and said, "I love you."

And then, like the morning sun burning away a fog in his mind, he remembered everything.

~ 20 ~

The Dream That You Wish

*E*LLA THREW her arms around his neck and deepened the kiss, nearly knocking them both down the front steps. August laughed against her lips and threaded his fingers through her hair. Her nose bumped his.

"I can't believe I forgot you," he said softly.

Ella kissed him again and pulled away enough to say, "I love you, too."

"I can't believe I twisted myself into knots over loving you twice," he said, and pressed his forehead to hers.

"I can't believe I made the prince do laundry." She threw her head back and laughed. Then her mouth went slack with horror. "Oh no—I put beetles in your bed once!"

"To be fair, I volunteered to help with the laundry," he said. "The rest, though, will definitely have to be addressed, possibly with beetles."

August reached up and curled a strand of her hair around his finger, tugging it lightly. That had been so long ago, before their childhoods were lost in the fog of grief.

"I'm sorry for never finding the right time to tell you who I really was," he said.

Ella laughed. "You're the prince, and I'm free."

August wrapped her in a hug, turned his face to kiss her temple, and exhaled against her crown. He had never fully understood her hesitancy to leave or to push back against Lady Tremaine's treatment of her, but he was more than happy to help Ella find her way forward now that her stepmother was gone.

"August!" Martin's shout made them both jump. He was sprinting full speed back to the house from the departing carriage, one hand waving in the air, and he stopped before them with a huff. "Our memories are back!"

Joy and confusion rolled over him. It wasn't just his and Ella's memories. Everyone's had returned.

"Why would our kiss bring everyone's memories back?" asked Ella.

"Well, it was a very good kiss," he said.

She rolled her eyes and kissed him again. "The memory loss didn't start with us. Why would it end with us? Things like this—being granted a wish by a fairy, secretly meeting the prince, forgetting true love, the wicked stepmother being caught in her schemes— only happen in fairy tales."

"Well, yes, my darling. We're why they're called that."

August and Ella whipped around to stare at who had spoken. A fairy, wreathed in twinkling lights and clutching her hands to her chest, stared up at them from the road with a warm smile. She was cloaked in a pale periwinkle, and her black eyes reminded August of the warm, solid dark of a summer night. Everything about her exuded care.

"Oh, you're back!" Ella untangled herself from August and threw her arms around the short woman. "Thank you! Thank you! Thank you! I can never repay you enough!"

"Your not giving up on your dreams is repayment enough, Ella," said the fairy, returning the hug so tightly that she nearly lifted Ella off the ground. "Oh, it is so good to see you happy. Sit, sit. I imagine you have questions, and I don't want to pull you away from your prince."

She shooed Ella back to the front steps and stood before the two of them with a smile August usually saw people direct at especially cute puppies. She sighed.

"I adore happy endings," she said.

Ella laughed. "Did you return only to witness your handiwork?"

"No, my dear. This time, I am not here for you," said the fairy godmother, turning to August. "I am here for your prince."

"Me?" August asked, surprise sobering him instantly. "Why?"

She smiled, sadly, instantly making August feel like a child, and gestured toward his coat. "You wrote to me asking if I could identify magical items that might be causing the memory loss in Fresne. I am here to do so."

"Oh." His mother's fairy godmother was the one who had helped Ella. He never thought he'd meet her in person, but he had imagined what he would say to her if he ever got the chance. He wanted to ask about his mother as a child, the memory loss in Fresne, and why kissing Ella had returned what they had forgotten. All that he managed, though, was a second, weaker, "Oh."

"My dear boy," she said, and wiggled her fingers

in his direction. "Please show me what you're carrying in your pocket."

Slowly, August reached into his coat and pulled out the brooch that had once been his mother's bracelet. He hated how beautifully it still caught the sunlight.

"It is very lovely work," said the fairy, "though I think my original design was a touch better, don't you?"

August nodded, confused.

"Do you remember what it once was?"

"My mother's bracelet," said August.

"Which she received as a gift after I granted her wish," the fairy said. "I placed the bracelet on her wrist myself. Her wish was quite vague, but she was a child, so it was understandable."

From the corner of his sight, August saw Ella staring at him, and he cleared his throat. "My mother wished for everyone to be happy."

Dread settled deep in the pit of August's stomach, and he closed his eyes, his grip on the brooch cutting into his palm.

"All fairy gifts have a drop of magic in them. The magic from the bracelet had years and years to spread to the rest of the items left on the memorial."

That made sense, as infuriating as it was.

"But why did the magic do this?" asked Ella. "Why would the magic make people forget who they're in love with?"

"Well, that was August's wish, of course!" The fairy godmother shook her head. "A sad wish but a wish nonetheless."

"But I didn't make a wish," said August. "I've never been offered a wish, and if I had been, I certainly wouldn't have wished for people to forget their loved ones!"

"Of course you would never have done any of this on purpose," she said, and reached out to pat his shoulder. "But do you remember the day of your mother's funeral?"

August dropped his face into his hands. His elbows dug into his knees. What had they talked about that day? His father had been so sad, and Ella understood since she had gone through it with hers after her mother's death. He had wanted to avoid love so that he wouldn't end up like his father or Ella's.

"It wasn't a wish. Not really," he muttered. "I was talking. Lamenting."

"It's not your fault, August. What person—what child—expects their words to come true?" The fairy godmother made a soft sound in the back of her throat. "You wished to forget love, and what little magic was left in your mother's bracelet tried to fulfill that wish. To make you happy."

"But then you left the bracelet at the memorial and didn't return," said Ella, still staring at August.

"So the magic started to leach over time," August continued. "And when Lady Tremaine started taking items from the memorial that had absorbed the magic, the wish spread around town."

"Quite unusual indeed," the fairy mused.

"But we wrote you, asking about a wish," said August. "You said a fairy hadn't granted one in Fresne."

"Yes, but a *fairy* hadn't granted one, since the wish was crafted with residual magic."

August groaned. "I hate semantics."

"Unfortunately, the rules of magic do not," the fairy said. "It was not a wish we granted, so we could not discuss it."

"And only I could fix it all," said August.

"That I sort of understand, but why did the town's memories return when we kissed?" asked Ella, looping one of her arms through August's. She squeezed.

Despite her reassurances, he still felt terrible.

"Yes, the kiss," said the fairy, lips twisting into a wry grin. "Was it only a kiss?"

"You!" Ella's eyes lit up, and she prodded August in the chest with her free hand. Her smile was infectious. "You said you loved me!"

August laughed, caught her hand, and kissed it. "And? How does the truth return memories?"

"Because it was the first time you had said it." The fairy smiled. "Since August created the wish, only his finding and accepting true love could break it."

"How am I going to explain this to Fresne?" asked August.

Ella kissed his cheek. "They'll understand it was an accident. It wouldn't have even happened if Stepmother hadn't stolen everything from the memorial and sold it."

"And, most importantly, you've solved it!" The fairy godmother applauded. "Now, let me assure you again that everything is fixed," she said. "All the memories have returned and all the items are distinctly unmagical now. The important thing about being a prince is not always being right or fixing things perfectly on your first attempt. When you do make a mistake or do not fully understand what you're working with, you must deal with the consequences, which you have done admirably. Face your fears instead of avoiding them, August," she added, as if hearing that you had stolen people's memories and found your true love was a normal, everyday occurrence. She turned to Ella. "And you, my darling, are free! Your hope is restored."

Ella nodded, smiling, and said, "It is. Thank you."

"One last thing. If I'm not mistaken, you're missing a shoe, and your prince is missing a bracelet." She waved her empty hand and nothing happened.

Ella chuckled, and August managed a weak smile.

"Oh, not again! Where did I put that thing?" she asked, patting down her cloak and spinning around. Ella cleared her throat and pretended to snatch something from the air. The fairy gasped and copied the motion. A wand appeared between her fingers. "There we go! Thank you, my darling."

She muttered a series of words August didn't understand and waved the wand over Ella's feet. The shards of glass from the broken slipper marched out the front door like mice on parade and re-formed into a shoe. It slipped itself onto Ella's bare foot.

"They're perfect," Ella said, wiggling her toes.

Her fairy godmother beamed down at her. "When you wear them, remember to never give up hope. Sometimes all you need is to accept another's help."

Then, she turned to August. He laid the brooch on the step and braced himself. He had dreamed of his mother and her bracelet often those first few years, and he wasn't sure what seeing it returned to its former state would do to him. He felt the change before he saw it, and the glitter of the glass scales danced across his eyes. There was a pinch, his eyes burned, and then he blinked. Then, the feeling faded.

"It's odd to see it now," he said, and picked the bracelet up. He remembered how heavy it had felt when he was a child, but now there was a lightness to it, and the scales let out an almost musical trill when they clinked together. He slipped it over his hand. "Thank you."

It was as if he had never left it on the soldier. No weathering. No cracks. No evidence of a wish gone wrong.

"You're very welcome," said the fairy. "Wear it and remember that you shouldn't give up love to avoid loss."

She waved her wand again, and little stars of magic shot up into the sky and fell toward the town. The fairy godmother smiled, and a breeze scattered her into a thousand glittering stars.

"Did she do that last time?" he asked, blinking at where she had been.

"I don't think she's realized it can be disconcerting," said Ella with a laugh. "She helped more than she let on. If I hadn't attended the ball, we wouldn't have found each other again, and the memory loss would have been left unresolved."

They had fallen in love all over again in the course of a night, and it wasn't because some supernatural power had entangled them or had intended for them to always be in love.

They fit—and even though they had grown up and grown apart and become their own people, they were still the kind of person the other appreciated and needed. Ella wasn't the same girl from his childhood, and he was glad. She was who she needed to be.

And he loved her, each and every her that she would ever need to be.

"Neither of us is allowed to hypothetically wish or use figures of speech in the presence of the shoes, though. Just to be safe," August said with a chuckle.

"I'm thinking I only wear them for special occasions, like operas, when it would be rude for me to speak, much less wish," she said, and leaned against him, head on his shoulder.

He wrapped an arm around her waist, bolstering her. "Loving and forgetting and loving you again has been one of my best adventures. I would do it all over if you accidentally made a wish."

"I'll be sure to save it for a boring week," she said, and kissed him.

Epilogue

CHARMANT, SUMMER

Ella,

It has barely been two days since you left for Fresne, and I miss you terribly already. Father is rejoicing in the fact that we're going to get married (despite my reminding him that it has only been two weeks since we remembered each other).

Enclosed, you'll find your father's pocket watch. I've wrapped it, so you don't have to look at it until you are ready. Father knows a good watchmaker and we set about repairing it. The original inscription is still intact.

How is running the estate going? I'm sure it's easier without any interference. Are Drizella and Anastasia behaving?

Martin is disgustingly adorable for the

first time in his life, by which I mean he's
pouting that he's in the city and Oliver is in
Fresne. I didn't think he could frown more
than he already did. He does love proving me
wrong.

That is really about all that's happened
here. It's terribly boring without you.

In love,
August

◊——→

FRESNE, SUMMER

August,
I had no idea your father wanted us to get married.
Why didn't he say anything when I was in the city with
you?
All joking aside, it's rather nice how excited
he is. I know he wanted you to marry anyone and
that was the point of the ball, but he seems genuinely
happy that it's me. Tell him to be patient. I need to get
a handle on the estate and my stepsisters. Then, we
can discuss marriage.
Lord Moreau has loaned me his estate steward to

help get everything in order. There was quite a lot that wasn't being done.

I asked the court that Lady Tremaine not be formally arrested and jailed and that she instead work to pay back what she stole from Fresne. Blanche and nearly everyone else agreed. I hear that she is less than thrilled at her job in a large estate's laundry.

Anastasia, though, has taken to working better than I thought she would. Lord Moreau offered to employ her for a time. She's been working there— washing up, making bread, and running all sorts of errands—and doesn't hate it. She's quite good at cooking, apparently. She's been visiting the bakery to learn more, as well.

Drizella is not adjusting as well. I do not wish to speak ill of her, so I won't speak of her at all.

You'll be very happy to know that I have finally had time to make costumes for all of the mice (I was practicing making sweaters and didn't want to waste too much yarn), and they have successfully defeated Lord Lucifer. Honestly, it wasn't hard. Lucifer misses Lady Tremaine even more than her daughters do, I think.

I miss you. It's odd. We were apart for so long, but I already dislike being apart. Writing to you is a balm. I'm counting down the days until you visit next, though. Please tell me it's soon? I'll have the mice prepare something new.

With love,
Ella

$\wp\!\!\longrightarrow$

CHARMANT, WINTER

Ella,

I have only been gone from Fresne for a day, and—like last time—miss you already. It's terribly unfair that Martin got to stay for an extra week. How did that dress you designed turn out? I wish I could have stayed to see the finished project, but I suppose I shall see Mademoiselle Leonora in it soon enough. I'll tell you what the rest of the city thinks of her new dress once she wears it.

Did you send me an unlabeled box of terrible honey cakes? They showed up the day after your last letter with no note. The Grand Duke thought it was a poisoning attempt, but they weren't deadly.

I've convinced the fairies to keep an ambassador in Charmant (and possibly the other

Epilogue

kingdoms) to offer help with magical issues. I enjoyed negotiating that more than I thought I would.

I know the mark of a bad ruler is someone who thinks they will be good at it, but I think I might enjoy it at least. Talking to people, resolving issues, helping communities, and keeping everyone happy and hale—I like doing that. I know they're not real ambitions, but I don't want to do the sort of great things that legends talk about. There are no witches or dragons in Charmant, and I'm pleased by that. Existence comes with enough complications.

I've already convinced my father to let me research education reforms. I remember enjoying being sent to school with children from other kingdoms, but most children are tutored at home. If I convince the court, I think Charmant could do better than that—for everyone.

So, that's next on the agenda. I'll visit as soon as the initial research is done and you're not swamped with dress orders.

I love you.

In love,
August

Prince of Glass & Midnight

➲——→

FRESNE, SUMMER

August,

 I'm no less excited to open your letters than when I received that first one. I know writing every few days is an expensive habit, but I can't bring myself to care. If it's my worst vice, so be it. I miss you.

 After you left, Martin received a letter from your father asking him to find out why we weren't married yet, and you'll never guess what happened!

 Martin was complaining that it wasn't that simple. Oliver turned to Martin and asked if he would like to get married, and he said, "See? It's easy."

 And Martin said, "Not if the answer is no."

 I don't think either of them realized what he had asked until then. So those two might get married before us, and perhaps that will take some of the focus off us.

 (I know it won't, but let me hope.)

 Blaise and Joan are married now, by the way.

Epilogue

Blaise keeps referring to her as "you know, my wife, Madame Joan Jullien" when all of us have met her before. Picard thinks they're insufferable, but I think it's sweet.

  The next crate of Blaise's baked goods is labeled. I still wouldn't eat them. Madame Jullien's been trying to get rid of the extra cakes all day.

  Did I tell you that my sisters have started talking about their father since you were here? They never, ever mentioned him before, and that was fine, but I think it was their mother's doing. Regardless, I'm glad they're more comfortable now.

  Anastasia is "not being courted, but how mad do you think Mother will be" by Picard's apprentice, Robert. Lady Tremaine is going to be furious, and I wish I could be there when she finds out. I think she would have preferred prison to hard labor and a common son-in-law.

  I know you will be in Fresne soon, but it feels like ages. I can't wait to see you. Travel safely.

With love,
Ella

Prince of Glass & Midnight

FRESNE, SPRING

Mother,

Fresne is about the same as you would remember it.

They put up a sign at the memorial: "No wishes allowed, especially by princes." Don't laugh.

Fine, laugh a little bit.

A lot has happened since you've been gone, but I don't want to bore you with a hundred-page letter. Most of what's happened is due to Ella. I never knew how nice it could be to simply exist with someone who knows me so well that no words are needed. We write to each other and visit, of course, but sometimes I know what her letter will say before it arrives. I ask her anyway.

I thought it would be terrible to be known and to know someone so well that our lives became inseparable, but there's something so unspeakably comfortable about being completely and utterly seen. Ella knows me, every feeling and flaw, and she loves me despite them. I'm not terrible, but still.